A VALLEY TOO FAR

A JAZZ NOVEL

BASED ON A TRUE STORY

BY

OLIVER LYLE

Back cover painting by Oliver Lyle is titled "Jazz Trio".

This book was printed in the United States of America.

ISBN: 9798744053109
Imprint: Independently published

TABLE OF CONTENTS

FROM DENMARK WITH REGRET

Time flies. It had been thirty-some years since expatriate African American Myles Andrews left his beleaguered homeland for the sanctuary of peace and love and acceptance in Copenhagen. He was once a young man who exuded happiness since setting foot on foreign soil. It wasn't exactly like being electrocuted, but there was a little culture shock upon his arrival, which was one thing he would never forget. That culture shock started upon checking in at his first Danish hotel. It featured a thing called *spontaneous collaborations*. He never thought about what that meant until an attractive, ivory-skinned woman entered his room, saw him, and smiled. Myles remembered smiling back in amazement as she set her bags down and started to unpack, taking half of the closet space for herself.

"Excuse me," Myles had said politely, "but this room is already taken . . . by me."

"Yes," she said cheerfully and kept unpacking.

Myles recalled putting his newspaper aside and slowly rising from his easy chair. "I'll just go down to the front desk and get this whole thing straightened out," he recalled, and reached for the doorknob. And then, for whatever reason, he realized that racism was more of an American thing than a Danish thing. It was a vibration that gripped him from the moment he stepped off the plane and into a new brand of humanity.

"Yes," she said again with a smile. Unpacked, she removed her shoes and lay discreetly across her half of the bed for a rest.

Myles remembered reading her sincerity for a long moment and then reclosing the door. It was like *When in Denmark, do what the Danes do*. There must have been some sociological reason for the way things are done over here, but he didn't care, all he could remember was being too tired to question it. Besides, this was a long way from land of lynch mobs where they would lynch a Black man on the spot for even *looking* at a white woman and then ask questions later. At least that was the epitome of the southern USA at the time he decided to leave. But he wanted to rise up out of the ashes of America's mess and think selfishly. He wanted to think that playing his music could help heal him, and he thought that it did. The USA, he said was a place which all those decades earlier produced the kind of vile racial hatred that brutally murdered a kid named Emmitt Till for wolf-whistling at a white girl and that malicious and cowardly bombing of a church in Birmingham which killed four innocent Sunday school girls, and a coward who shot Medgar Evers in the back with a distant deer rifle, and another cowardly mentality which murdered three *northern meddling* voter registration workers, as well as racist conspiracy which assassinated Martin Luther King. Just as Black people as a whole were getting their shit together, the Ku Klux Klan was getting its sheets together trying in vain to put a resistant Black genie back in the bottle.

Myles never forgot the instantaneous decision he made about leaving the United States of America. He was sitting on the steps of his house listening to his boom box. Jimi Hendrix was playing his famous rendition of The Star Spangle Banner. Between the recognizable phrases, Jimi was making a statement with the screeching strings and deliberately induced loud feedback out of his enormous amp system. It was about the social discord and anti-war rebellion. As a young army bandsman, he accompanied that stupid war stateside from ten thousand miles away from where the so-called enemy was a four-foot-tall figment of the administration's imagination. It got so bad on the street that *brothers* in the hood didn't know the difference between a redneck honkey and a real nice White guy.

It was time to leave, and he popped out of the bottle like the aroma of a fine wine and made it across the Atlantic Ocean before it was too late and before now, in spite of his family back there, staying away from America had become his own obsession. But that was all back then. Myles heard through the grapevine that things had changed for the better, and in all these years, horizons had expanded considerably. He knew that besides family, he matured to know that there were some things to love about America, but only if you weren't planning to be a jazz musician. He made his choices. His first love was jazz, and his second love was a place to play jazz for a decent living. From across the ocean, Europe called, and Myles answered YES! Now all these years later, he was doing a middle C passage back to America.

Just a couple of hours ago when the plane lifted off from Schipohl Airport, Miles thought it was ironic that the song running through his head was the same one he'd heard before arriving all those years ago. As a kid, he picked it up from watching too many musicals, that thing in three-quarter time about "*Wonderful, Wonderful Copenhagen*". Until he got there, it was always just a song. But it was a song that grew legs when he landed in Wonderland. Myles savored the indelible memory of a paying gig he stumbled across on a stopover in Amsterdam. The sheer thrill of just jamming with some great cats at the renown Scheherazade Nightclub, affectionately known as ZADA. It was a great session in front of a great crowd. At the end of the evening, the owner stuffed wads of real money in the shirt pockets of the players. The attitude about jazz was off the decency chart. It was a sweet belly for the rebirth of jazz in his soul. He learned quickly that the Scheherazade was frequented by fans from Moscow a thousand miles away. Those Russian enthusiasts were nuts about American jazz and wanted to learn more about it. Certainly, by now, they knew all our jazz secrets. It was like *"Look out, the Russians are coming!*

The Russians are coming!" What a wonderful problem to have!

Myles was a few decades removed from his army return, but once again, his destination was Minneapolis. He heard the comparison many times that Copenhagen and Minneapolis, being almost the same latitude and ethnicity, could get away with being sister cities. Myles would always agree that it was true in all ways except one: Copenhagen liked American jazz much more than Minneapolis. He already had chance to check out the differences in their respective moral and political mindsets. Denmark used Jazz as the protest music of choice against the Nazis. It freaked out Hitler and the Third Reich that Danish radio stations played this *devil* music. After the war, the Danes stopped playing this music because it only reminded the country of history's darkest hour. Now jazz was back because they had time to heal wounds and listen to a type of music they loved all along. In Copenhagen, jazz was nothing but liberated and successful. In Minneapolis, Jazz was a hot potato demonized by city regulations. Musically, he knew it was going to be like leaving heaven and going straight to hell. But he would take solace in the fact that his family would be there to take the sting out of the flames. He would pray that he could just say, "Hello", and everything would be cool. He would connect with them. They would still be able to see the kid in him through a graying middle-age façade, something he trusted would be mutual.

Myles was all dressed up with someplace to go. Over his olive shirt, he wore a coco linen jacket with the fashionable wrinkles across the back along with pleated gray cotton slacks and a brand-new pair of Danish ankle boots. Make no mistake, Myles was leaving Scandinavia well-bootied, sitting on traveler's checks, plenty of cash, and credit cards. He owned a bag in the overhead carrier, and somewhere in the belly of the 747 jumbo jet was his bass fiddle, clearly labeled with special handling instructions.

Once again, he pondered it, then removed a few items from is breast pocket. There was his Danish-stamped passport and return ticket. Then there was the photograph, a mugging-the-camera act at Tivoli Gardens with he and his long-time girlfriend, singer Yvonne Christiansen and her best friend Anita Anderson, an executive in the offices of Tivoli Gardens. There was his pocket calendar full of upcoming gigs in neighboring countries: Oslo, Stockholm, Paris, Vienna, Geneva, and London. This annual jazz tour was sponsored by the Danish National Jazz High Society. He traveled to all these cities with great musicians for many lucrative and enjoyable years, musicians from the outer limits of genius to the more-abundant down-to-earth jazzers. They were the ones who were the living pulse of the culture. They were a crowd. And everybody knows a crowd of jazz musicians is a gig waiting to happen. *So, you'd better have the bread ready because the jam is waitin' on you!*

As he thumbed through the notes of some past gigs, it was the Far East trips that intrigued him the most of all. The land of the magic miracle of Asian jazz artists knowing Cole Porter tunes without charts was a myth-busting answer to that nagging obnoxious speculation that *jazz standards don't migrate well.* But Myles saw it with his own ears that some poor souls on the other side of the Pacific Ocean were dead wrong with their North American nonsense. He pondered many times why the hell should there be more jazz clubs in Shanghai than in the entire United States! It made him relish being in the network of an international brotherhood where there was less than a ghost of a chance ever having to wait for a gig. He came ready to play.

It took him back to his early days. Copenhagen had a way of encouraging serious jazz players by providing a place to practice. Good ol' Fielmaub Halls Rehearsal Haven, sponsored by the city. Myles often went there for lessons and practice. He would walk in the door and pause to listen to the conglomeration of muffled notes coming from almost soundproof doors along the hallways. Vocal arpeggios, drum rudiments, advanced piano concertos, horn chromatics in a variety of keys. It was enough to make him check out a bass fiddle and reserve his own practice room for a little noise of his own. He was very thankful for that because a home could stand only so much bass playing.

He was back to that photograph. He was looking at a place that had become his home for a long enough to be able to legitimately call it home. He clutched the photo to his chest as something to cherish until he got back. He remembered those words of hers just before he left. "I suppose it's more admirable to admit you're jealous before being told you're jealous," she had said, "but, I am jealous. Jealous of the USA because you are going there without me." She bit her trembling lip.

He remembered saying, "I'll be back soon, but until I do, I'll have my picture of you. And I'll have my memories of you. I'll have everything but your ninety-eight point-six degrees."

She was fighting a losing battle with the tears. "Well, don't forget the ninety-eight-point-six degrees," he recalled her saying.

When all was said and done, it was what it was, and he was where he was, seated in one of the deuce seats in a crowded first-class section. For another six hours, the number on his boarding pass required him to be paired up with Joe from New York. Schenectady to be exact. Shortly after introductions, the plane took off and Schenectady Joe happened to be a salesman of more styles of shower curtain rings than anyone could ever shake a stick at in a lifetime. Trying to tune him out by getting lost in his dreams was becoming a colossal exercise in futility.

"Mind if I ask what your do?" Joe asked.

"I'm a jazz musician," Myles said almost bursting with pride.

"Any Money in *that*?"

"Of course, Saw it with my own eyes," Myles said of Europe. Jazz was too big of a product to sell on a plane, but after a while, enough was enough. The asinine duel for professional superiority was just human nature acting up.

Another idea caused Schenectady Joe to hold up an index finger as he stood up to retrieve something else from the overhead compartment. Down he came with several more photo sample books of more shower curtain rings. Myles was craning his neck to look left and right over his shoulders with intensely searching eyes. There simply were no empty seats in first class, and it was probably the same in coach. Joe was very much aware of this fact, too. Like a deep-sea sports fisherman with guile and cunning, he was confident that a musician marlin would bite on one of his rings.

Myles searched the pouch in front of him for something to read. He came up with a yellow vomit bag with directions printed on it. He read those directions very slowly several times, but the next round of rings was upon him. Schenectady Joe opened the next book, turned on both seat lights and restarted his descriptions from the top left page, pointing things out with his pinkie. Myles was nodding with mock approval, but he was already tuning out. His eyes glazed over. His thoughts and mind were back in Copenhagen for a few pages, and then he was back again.

"So, what do you really do for a living?" Myles countered. "Do you work?"

"No, not really," said Joe. "But these little babies get me ten grand a month."

Miles was doing the math in his head as he wondered exactly how many years of training went into selling some goddamn shower curtains rings. "Interesting," he said trying not to gnash his teeth. He couldn't help thinking of all those countless hours of lessons, practices, rehearsals, and long-ago gigs he went through to play the bass fiddle. Then there was the very thought of having to leave the country in order for the money to start getting serious.

But Schenectady Joe wasn't quite finished yet. "I've got a buddy who sells nothing but screws," he said. "He's a millionaire."

If Myles had a tie, he would be adjusting it like Rodney Dangerfield. "Sounds kind of screwy," he said knowing full well that his bass playing wasn't on anybody's thin ice. He looked longingly out the window at the moonlighted blanket of clouds drifting below. New York was out there somewhere.

But Joe had been holding out. The smirky look on his face telegraphed an impending thousand dollar finale to a rather dull fireworks display. He held the last catalogue book in his hands not withstanding perhaps five hundred unseen books in the overhead. This *had* to be the all-time heavy hitter of shower curtain ring — the real fake book of his product. Now he was transposing things up a step with a tickle of ivory rings, chords of wood from bonsai all the way up to sequoia, the harmony and audacity of brass rings, the be-bop of gold, platinum and silver-plated rings, the clunkers of pewter rings, and for the very careful, the tinkle of it crystal rings — and for the whole kit and caboodle, variations on the theme.

"Yeah, man," said Myles trying his best to inject some hambone rings into the act, "Now you're improvising! Yeah, man, you're playin' by ear!"

The plane bounced moderately on a stretch of clear-air turbulence, but the ride soon settled back to smooth. "Oh, you're gonna love this," Joe said as he licked his thumb and flipped through a seemingly memorized number of pages. He deserved some credit for knowing his charts. "This one." He pointed it out again with the pinkie. "It's going over big with our hamburger loving crowd. *Imitation onion rings*!"

Physically, Myles was nodding slowly, but mentally he was regurgitating every single fucking hamburger he'd eaten in his entire life. "Come to think of it," he said with a fiendish gleam in his eyes. "There *is* a style I've been trying to get my hands on for a long time."

"Well, you got on the right flight," Schenectady Joe said victoriously, his high-test nylon line acutely bending his fishing pole with a huge marlin bite. He hooked up his harness and let the whirring reel unwind freely, trying to set the hook. "What would you like?" he said with the gentle confidence of King Kong. Joe was going to reel this one in for sure. It was just a matter of a mahogany or walnut mounting board.

"Smoke rings."

"How . . . many . . . would you like?" Joe felt the marlin making a run. The screaming reel was starting to smoke and needed a splash of sea water.

"Oh, I couldn't possibly order anything without seeing a sample," Myles said, thankful for the permanent no smoking signs.

The high-test line snapped. The marlin got away. A sport, Joe said good-bye to the hook and reeled in a catch of emptiness.

Myles was sweating bullets that there were still hours left before landing. He had to get his mind right. With all due respect to the damn shower curtain rings, his attention again escaped back to the past twenty-four hours. He had shower curtains rings around his eyes, but he could still see out the window. Whisps of clouds zipped past with a highlight of airspeed. A break in the blanket below allowed him to see dots of light on the black waters of the Atlantic Ocean. Those were ships which may have been doing thirty knots, but they appeared to be standing still. Such was the case with time. As each passing mile brought him closer to America, he could feel in his gut the insidious devaluation of his profession from that lofty European esteem.

"What's it like to be a jazz musician in America?" Joe asked earnestly.

Myles thought for a moment. "I *could* say it's about knowing all the wonderful tunes, or I could say it's about walking into a club or turning on a radio station where standards are played and knowing right away what the tune is during improvising solos. Aren't you sorry you asked?"

"Not at all," Joe said.

"Well, in that case," Myles continued, "I could also say it's about a man calling a fellow player *baby* and doing stiff-arm handshakes which almost pull you off balance. But no, I wouldn't say that. Instead, I would say it's about the love of being a member of an artistic fellowship of jazz musicians who are actively resisting the threatened death of an American invention."

"How long did it take you to memorize *that*?"

Myles shook his head. "I don't know," he said, "ask my soul."

"Sounds like a rough life to live," Joe said. "Ever thought about doing something else?"

"Not after I landed in Europe. Never gave it a thought. I'm an artist. I'm not going to just up and quit doing something just because I'm an artist, you know."

"But you're going back," Joe said. "What about all of America's problems with your music compared to where you're coming from? Is it worth it?"

"Well, it sure beats the hell out of selling shower curtain rings."

Schenectady Joe threw back his head and laughed. "Tell me," he said, "is this . . . jazz . . . thing any good if it's played by White players?"

"Hell yeah," Myles said emphatically. "Some of the best jazz players in the world are White. With this music, it's not about race when it comes to performing. The jazz ear is colorblind. Discrimination against this kind of music is as American as apple pie when it comes down to hiring practices and payment attitudes. All jazz needs to thrive, besides getting paid, is freedom and individual style."

"Nice to know," said Joe.

Myles saw a slight chance to do a little marlin fishing of his own, *without* pictures. "Just take a look at all the White American Jazz superstars. Many have come and gone" he said. "Artists like Stan Getz, Chet Baker, Paul Desmond, Bill Evans, Phil Woods, Gerry Mulligan, Gary Burton . . . the list is endless." It was truly a hook-line-and-sinker which on any given Sunday should bring in the honcho of marlin territory.

"Never heard of 'em," Joe said.

Fishing for a hidden jazz fan was over before it began. The only marlin Myles was going to catch was waiting for him in a can on a grocery store shelf. "That's okay," he said, "tens of millions of other jazz ears will forgive you. But just remember," Myles said with a last-ditch effort to convert, "jazz is the pearl, baby, the currency of romance! What better way is there to romance a tune than with jazz?"

"Country western romances a tune all the time," Joe defended.

"That's not romance, that's rustlin'," Myles said, his hopeless gaze aimed back out the window.

"So, do you need to read music a lot?"

Myles exhaled a deep breath and let a few miles go by. "Sometimes," he said, "but when it comes to jazz, you're better off just jammin' because at the end of the day, a good jam is what you ought to be able to spread on crackers."

Just then, the hostess rolled the beverage wagon into view. It was great timing as throats were getting a little dry. Myles ordered a gin and tonic, and Schenectady Joe ordered a half-pint of milk. They were quickly served.

"You a family man?" Myles asked after taking a sip to clear his raspy throat.

"My family? Oh yeah, they're in on it too! Wait'll I show you the one that I sold my brother-in-law." Joe grabbed the book and found it in an instant. He must've been getting serious. He pointed the thing out with an index finger. "Isn't it a beaut?"

"I don't know how your brother-in-law can stand it," Myles deadpanned.

"Oh, that's nothing," Joe said as he licked his thumb for more page turning. But it was the wrong book. He again stood to retrieve a different sample series. "Lemme show you the one I sold my wife." The serious index finger found it. "That'll make her love me forever," he said proudly.

Myles took a hard swallow of his beverage and started scanning the walls of the first-class compartment for an emergency parachute. There was none. It was a good thing anyway, because his ocean swimming was a little rusty. He was resigned to the cold fact that he was just going to have to tough out the shower curtain rings. Myles took another sip and looked out the window as if looking at a black television screen. Then her image lighted up that screen. It was Yvonne, his soulmate. He thought of her shower curtain rings. They were never used because she was too *au naturel* for shower curtains. She thought they were too confining. Gift curtains were neatly folded and stacked in the closet. After refreshing, she shut off the large, neat gentle rain shower and strode lithely through the house singing. Self-consciousness didn't exist with her. There wasn't a shy bone in her body, which made her totally unabashed about being nude in mixed company. He smiled while remembering how easy it was for him to forget a cover-up piece of plastic hanging from shower curtain rings. But it was something he would never try in a smaller, splashier shower. She was drying only her face like there wasn't enough towel to dry or cover the rest of her gorgeousness. It was generally understood that nudity wasn't lewd or immoral. It was just an excepted Danish tradition; it was Yvonne. She loved to show off her enormous stash of goose pimples as she sang with a girlish trill, with that phrase-ending vibrato in her lovely voice.

He could never forget just before they met, Yvonne recently returned from fulfilling her father's wish of having his body returned to Got Hop, where he was born. "Where the hell is Got Hop?" he remembered asking. It was the capital city on the southwest corner of Greenland she had told him. That was a place where people really bundled up against the cold. She dressed for the weather, and she dressed for her gigs, something he really appreciated. On a dreamy window image, he was transported back to the first time he saw her. It was on the corner of Vesterbrogade and H. C. Anderson Boulevard, inside the Chock-Full-Of-Nuts café. He took the last available lunch counter stool. It was next to her, and it was the middle of the afternoon. He ordered a sundae and turned to look at her. It was the same moment that she turned to look at him. And all of it was the exact same moment some inexplicable connection was made. It was somewhere in their eyes.

"Will you make me some ham and eggs in the morning?" he remembered joking.

She looked at him warily for a long moment. "What kind of hen should lay your eggs?" is what she said. And whatever kind they were, those eggs were cracked fifteen years ago. They became inseparable as he allowed her to settle him down, at least as much as a touring musician could be settled. He also recalled how she continued to call him "*Papa*" immediately after each climax of their many affairs of passion. The curtains in the house should have had many climbers by now, but there were none. Whether that was luck or tragedy, he couldn't say.

He took another sip. The airplane window was a memory screen which faded to black. But it came back clearly enough for him to recall a recent Thursday afternoon. They were on a pedestrian walk street. Myles veered and headed into the door of Andersen's Musikhandel. Yvonne tagged along trustingly.

"I need new fiddle strings," he had said.

"You just got some the other day," Yvonne said.

"I wasn't satisfied," he said.

"You're *never* satisfied," Yvonne needled.

I agree," he recalled saying. "We've been all over Europe, and I've bought strings everywhere we've gone. Amsterdam, London, Munich, Hamburg, Geneva, Stockholm, Paris, and I'm *still* not satisfied with the strings."

"But you always make any of them sound great," she stroked.

"No," he recalled. "I just always think there's some better strings over the horizon. It's an obsession."

"No, it's a sickness," she said. "You're sick."

At the time, he threw his head back and laughed, but in real life he merely smiled at the memory that he went ahead and bought another brand of strings before they headed for the fruit stand on the corner. It was the thought that pulled his strings.

Like the day they were sitting in the coziness of their comfortable home, and they were discussing the theatre of improvisation over lunch. There was a meow, and that strange cat hopped on the table and casually strode the length. Without missing a step, he managed to get two paws in his cream of oyster soup that they were letting cool.

"Look," said Yvonne like he didn't see it. "We've got a new cat. What should we name it?"

Back then, Myles recalled looking at her with a playful sneer, and then the brazen critter with a critical eye. "How about *bass fiddle strings*," he remembered saying.

Yvonne tried to hide a laugh, but the single pig-like snort from her throat betrayed her tickle. She slowly went into a convulsing chuckle and slapped him on the shoulder. "That's mean," she said with the tears of a full-blown belly laugh. "Never mind," she continued, "it already has a name."

"Well, what is it?" Myles remembered asking with sarcasm.

"Her name is *Encyclopedia*."

"What? *Encyclopedia*? Now why would anybody name a cat *Encyclopedia*?"

"Because she gnaws everything," Her attempted deadpan exploded.

Myles recalled when they finished laughing, he turned dead serious. "I guess this means I'll have to go out and find an ironclad bass case," he said keeping an eye on that cat's every next move. She was still laughing but trying her best to stop.

Together at home, they had more fun than people should. He learned long ago that Copenhagen really knows how to unpack a man's suitcase, but it was Yvonne who he gave credit to for knowing how to unpack his soul. But now he was in the air, and it was like leaving in the middle of a good movie. He was leaving paradise with every memory flashing before his eyes and through his entranced brain. It was just enough for him to know that he would be back, and that coming back wasn't an *if thing*, it was a *when thing*.

Thoughts of those earlier times must have been on a leash because they were never far away. Like the evening of running through the rain from his car to the Montmartre Jazz Hus on Gothersagade at Store Regnegade 19, the joint on the corner. The Montmartre Jazz Hus was hot. The featured artist was a foreigner, a great American pianist named Herbie Hancock and his group. They found scarce seats and ordered French fried mussels with lemon, bread, and beer. It was a grand time. Buoyed by excellence, they emerged from the earthly confines of the Montmartre after the last Hancock tune and round of rousing appreciative applause.

"He's from another planet," Yvonne said at the time.

"No, he's from Earth. Our ears are from another planet. So why don't we fix that by going for a nightcap?"

"Ya," she said, and they drove some sharp-angled boulevard turns a medium distance to *The Casanova Bar*.

As they navigated into the crowded disco, the vintage jukebox was playing, "Mister bigshot, who do you think you are". They shimmied a few dance steps on the way to a little libation. Arabs in the corner fighting over a crap game couldn't dampen the mostly interracial party atmosphere. It was an after-hours place. They were happy. They had their fill. It became the night they called it a day. He remembered when they got back home and walked in the door, there were some wonderful chords coming from the piano keys. They looked at each other with smiles. It was only, Thelonious Yvonne's pet marmoset who just happened to love jazz. Thelonious was a ham, a showoff who never ceased to amaze everyone with his compositions.

The plane was once again experiencing clear air bumpiness. A tone sounded as the *fasten seatbelt* signs came on. His window picture momentarily went black. As he glanced at Schenectady Joe, he could only surmise if it was the memories or the milk which had him sleeping like a baby beneath his blanket of shower curtain ring books. It was a good thing, because when the aircraft settled down, the window screen lighted up again. This time, through his eyes he could only imagine Yvonne's Greenland-born father and her Denmark-born mother to whom she was very close and whom he had unfortunately never met. She swore up and down they would have loved him. But when they died on their vacation in Switzerland, she felt like she hadn't been close enough to them. When that damn cable carrying the mountain tram broke, her beloved parent went down a mountain to their deaths along with all the other passengers, leaving her holding all the love she had left to give them. That decade after they died was really rough on her. She was glad he was there to help heal her. Up until then, nobody could, so she said. But he got her back into singing and believing in herself. They played many good gigs together, and that was because there was only one sly, Cupid-hearted agent in town who saw to it that they did. They concluded years ago that those gigs were a mutual thrill. It was healing. It was also healing for her when he accompanied her to Bern, Switzerland to visit her aging aunt. And the settlement was a big help too. The next of kin of all the accident victims were awarded millions of wrongful death francs from the tram company. She was set. Over the years, it was Yvonne who stayed on his case to keep his American citizenship renewed, which he did, although now he was in his final months of being a legal American. Myles remembered the countless times she urged him not to forget the blood bond of his siblings across the ocean. She was an only child, but she could nevertheless empathize with them.

The clouds out the window which carried his nostalgic visions suddenly disappeared leaving the reality of a tenuous view of the black ocean below. But those indelible memories returned visually the instant the window went cloudy again. And he would forever cherish those memories of many trips to the Grand Rue of Montreux for the Montreux Jazz Festival off Lake Geneva, Switzerland, all under a backdrop of snow-capped Alps, and above the beautiful, very deep and very blue Lake Geneva, a wonderful forty-five-mile-long splendor of the world.

He rubbed his eyes but continued to see that image somewhere in the clouds of his window screen. Myles truly wanted to shake the fearless hands of those who dared to mix the beauty of American-born jazz with such a gorgeous geographic venue. But he would just be obligated to remember the other side of the coin. It was that jazz, the music itself, had to leave the desert sands for a more fertile soil to grow and thrive and survive on. He knew for sure that jazz has more brains than some people think. The memories were so good that Myles crossed his fingers tightly hoping and praying that the plane didn't hit anymore turbulence to awaken Schenectady Joe. The window screen changed channels, and he was back to several days ago finishing up a bass and flute duo gig at the Lanelinie Pavillion on the Yderhavnen waterfront. A remarkably large gathering of humanity was dispersing peacefully. The flautist and his girl hugged them as they excused themselves on their way to the Friheds Museum. As the sound technicians disassembled the hook-up, Myles carefully laid his fiddle on the cobblestone plaza and unzipped the back pocket. He pulled out the wheel and stuck it on the end of the peg. Myles and Yvonne strolled and rolled over to *The Little Mermaid* for a little fun photo shoot. The green, finned girl on a rock would again serve as a backdrop for a serious shutterbug.

"Take off the cover and put your hands on the strings," she directed while adjusting the lens setting on her Hasselblad. He remembered being a good sport with a smile. After all their time together, they were still clicking as much as the camera.

"Haven't we done these shots a few million times before?" he recalled saying as he clowned and mugged.

"Not from this angle," she always said.

But his inward chuckle was about the same old location, and his need to keep close watch on her for any outgrowths of little green fins. Those were some foolish things that reminded him of Yvonne. On their way home that night, he remembered that he and Yvonne were walking toward the commuter train station with his rolling bass when he had to stop and put the instrument down. He wasn't tired but leaned his elbows on the waist-high stone-built wall overlooking a water channel. He reassured her that he wasn't having a heart attack. It was a premonition that gripped him for several minutes before they could move on. Their train was pulling out, and they would catch it, bass fiddle and all.

The next day, he was just as busy making the living he relished. He remembered that it was an hour after the gig and all the way to the end of Ostergrogade that he dragged himself and his bass into the comfort of their elegant home.

Her voice greeted him from the kitchen. He set his gear down and went to peck her on the cheek.

"What are you making?" he recalled asking.

"Andesteg," she said, crying over her chopped onions.

"Aw, gee. We have roast duck all the time," he remembered teasing. He ducked the potholder she threw at him, and they made up with a kiss.

It was that kind of a schedule, and it was wonderfully manageable. Life was good. But it was that premonition of days earlier that hung in the back of his mind as he kept up with his busy bookings.

Through the airplane's window screen, he vividly recalled grabbing his bass and taking off for a train and ferry ride to the Rembrandt Jazz Festival at that fabulous Amsterdam park, one of the finest in Holland. He could never forget how the backstage of Rembrandt park was teeming with all the familiar great European players. They were his respected colleagues. He would be taking stage with a group that formed spontaneously — a drummer from Helsinki, a Black piano player from Stockholm, a sax player from Vienna, and a trumpet player from Rotterdam. It was nice to see those guys and others again. It didn't matter which group was playing, the overflow throng of hip fans were always going to be in for some good listening at the three-day event. And along with it, there was food and beverage, there were occasional phantom puffs of marijuana smoke rising here and there, and there was peace, love, and order without laws.

Myles stroked his chin as he recalled that it was his sweetheart, Yvonne, who was kind enough to travel from Copenhagen, across the Baltic Sea and Germany to Amsterdam. She sought him out to hand-deliver an unopened telegram from America. But who could ever find anyone at Rembrandt Park? On a smaller scale, it would be like looking for somebody at Woodstock. Myles was pleased to remember that Yvonne was a musician who was savvy enough to know where the bodies were buried. She went backstage and spotted him just about ready to go up and play. Through the window screen, Myles saw the image of her running towards him holding up that puzzling yellow envelope. Their eye connection transmitted and received something urgent. He took the envelope, and they stepped around a corner where he could open and read it. A weight of sadness descended upon him as he slowly handed it for Yvonne to read. Apologetically, Myles had to bail out of playing in that wonderful festival before he even started. He needed to pack up and leave immediately. They felt for him with deep understanding. Someone would cover for him. They were indeed colleagues; they were brothers who had the same thing in common. They all knew the tunes.

Myles took a long, nostalgic breath as the image on the window screen momentarily faded. From his opposite breast pocket, he pulled out the yellow envelope and re-read the telegram. It was the bad news which wasn't going to get any better no matter how many times he opened it. His mother just passed away, and his family members needed him badly. In his gut, he felt the urgency of their pleas through the brevity of a telegram, and he was responding to his blood.

But his memory couldn't escape the many discussions he had with Yvonne about staying in touch with his family members thousands of miles away, and for the most part he had, although less frequently as the years passed. There was a tear in his eye as he remembered that he didn't really want to forget his family at the time. It was just time for a change in his life, and he welcomed the change with open arms.

The plane was once again experiencing a bumpy ride. A tone sounded as the *fasten seat belt* signs came on. It reminded him of the damn doorbell he once gave Yvonne for her birthday, and now regrets that he did. It didn't chime

Swing Low Sweet Chariot, instead, it chimed *Comin' for to Carry me Home*. He glanced back out the window and saw her face on the screen at Schipol Airport those hours ago. They were doing emotional tug-of-war with each other. They exchange long and silent, knowing gazes. "Jeg synes sä godt om Dem," she said.

"I like you very much too," he said, "and I loves you."

"I loves you too," she said with one quick high-pitched sob. The big tears in her eyes did the boogie instead of rolling down her cheeks. "Vil De kalde pä mig?"

As they walked slowly towards the gate, Myles memorized putting an arm around her shoulders and pulling her close. "Yes," he promised. "I will call you." Their goody-for-a-while hug was as embraceable as a ewe. And nobody cared but them. The window screen returned then back to now.

The drink wagon came along again, but Myles was still nursing. He asked for more ice. From close behind, the aroma of dinner was in the air. Thoughts of Copenhagen almost made him forget he wasn't alone in the row of seats.

"It actually *is* a nice flight," he answered the question of an awakening Schenectady Joe. Passengers in first class were served and dined heartily on filet mignon or walleye with asparagus and mashed potatoes, courtesy of KLM Royal Dutch Airlines. Myles and Joe drank and ate and small-talked each other's light out, until the oblivion of sleep slowly crept in and rescued them both from a death of mundane.

After a while, Myles woke up and immediately put on the sanitary headphones for his personal television screen, the real deal. Out of the corner of his eye he could see Schenectady Joe's mouth moving, ring books in hand, trying to strike up a conversation and a sale. But Myles was fixated on a colorful television performance by Ray Charles who rocked from side to side with the music he played so soulfully. A three-tiered, red-robed chorus of Black female gospel singers glided in unison from side to side. As Joe tried to talk, Ray and the singers were doing their great hit, *America the Beautiful*, and they were right at that part, "from sea to shhhhhhhining sea". Not yet wearing his headphones, Joe couldn't hear the shush but he soon got the message and buttoned up his rings.

The airliner banked gently into a turn, and that's when the startling nighttime skyline of Manhattan gleamed majestically through the port windows. The reality of being back in America overwhelmed him for a moment. But then Myles was over it already. He wasn't going to get real foolish about it. The signs came on telling passengers to fasten their seat belts. The cabin speakers clicked, then it was the extremely calm voice of the pilot stating the obvious, that indeed was the city of New York on our left, and he thanked everyone for flying KLM Royal Dutch Airlines. Frank Sinatra's "*Come Fly with Me*" belatedly welcomed a pack of tired fliers.

The 757 jumbo jet listed sharply as it lined up for the landing on a strobe-lined runway. And while it maneuvered on its ear-popping, gliding descent, Myles gripped his arm rests hard enough to show the whites of his knuckles. He wasn't worried about the landing hurting his bones, he was worried about the landing dropping the sound post in his bass below. But he needn't have worried. The pilot landed the plane on a velvet carpet. This was America, and for the home of the brave, he steeled himself for that first fork to be stuck in him.

His airplane weariness was being rejuvenated by the electricity of the city. He paid and tipped the driver and unloaded his bag and fiddle from the airport shuttle taxi van inside the Port Authority bus terminal. Myles had no doubt New York was still the same after so many years. Summer, spring, winter, and fall, still big and cold until you get to know it again. The streets were far too un-kissable. He stopped for a moment to reattach the roller wheel to the bottom of his bass. Then he gripped his suitcase and steered his instrument out the door and down 42nd Street. The sidewalk suddenly rumbled beneath his feet. It was so unlike the sound of a passing subway train. A glance over his shoulder barely gave him enough time to get himself and his luggage out of the way of a dozen pairs of spike heels peppering the pavement. It was a stampede of fleshy and voluptuous, scantily clad ladies-of-the-evening which passed him with the perfumed draft of a freight train. They were sprinting away from pursuing vice cops and trying their best to avoid the annoying inconvenience of being in jail for two hours.

"Only in America," Myles said aloud. He was heard only by the lingering musk in the air. Foghorns on three harbor tugboats unwittingly played *Love for Sale*. Cole Porter would've loved it. But this was the land where tugboat companies could be assessed heavy city fines for playing standards without a cabaret license, and where the police had the license to bust a girl about socializing for money. But Myles Andrews had bragging rights. He saw the other side of the coin with his own eyes. In Copenhagen, the police don't chase prostitutes to *arrest them*. It's legal. They chase prostitutes to *hire* them! It was an odd dichotomy of intentions by mutual law enforcement. Myles could only shake his head as he resumed walking his bag and his roller bass down ever busy and wild and crazy Broadway. It was duck soup for an in-shape road musician.

After two New York blocks, he found a small Hilton and checked in. Stretched out on the couch, Myles tried to convince himself that he was sleepy, but his mother and Minneapolis had his mind filled to the rafters. Sleep was prohibited. Out the window was Manhattan, beckoning. He looked at his watch and there was time to catch some nightlife and time to catch a plane to Minneapolis tomorrow afternoon.

Sans luggage, he was back out on the street fifty pounds lighter, but a heartache heavier. Finding some good jazz could give his soul a lift. Along the way, he stopped at a newsstand and picked up a Downbeat magazine. Myles opened the magazine like a kid opening presents Christmas morning. He shuffled pages from front to back, then from back to front. Then he looked up and moved closer to enough streetlight. He tightly blinked his eyes for more moisture. Now he used thumbnail to slowly go through the pages one-by-one, making sure he didn't miss anything. It was all there in abundance! Everything but the jazz section. It used to be ten pages long, couldn't miss it. Once more, he went through the pages, but this time he went even slower the other direction with his left thumbnail. There it is! Almost one-half of a lower column near the back! The jazz section! He tore out what there was of the jazz whereabouts and put it in his watch pocket. Myles was used to playing it by ear — ears that were wide open for the sound of jazz above the honking of car horns and subways.

He strode into his walk, trusting his legs to properly unwind from the cramps of an airplane seat. It was a warm evening. The air of New York City was filled with the smell of Chicago sausage. The world's greatest cross-section of humanity from all walks of life graced the streets with him, but without him. It was New York! Tonight, Myles could take a bite out of the big apple. As he walked a little farther, his keen eardrums picked up a sound resembling jazz. He got there. It was an alley entrance. Two trumpet players were swinging with tightly woven and melancholy harmony. The tune was the *Whiffenpoof* song with three little lambs who had lost their way, baa, baa, baa. The players were standing in front of their homes, large cardboard boxes in close proximity to garbage dumpsters. A stab of pain for them shot through his gut. This is America.

He took out two twenty-dollar bills and placed one in each open instrument case at their feet. They nodded in appreciation without missing a note. They had the sound of somebody good enough to make it. Maybe their only mistake was coming to New York, a cold and unforgiving place for the unproven, a city which has chewed up millions of aspirations and spat out the seeds. Or perhaps those two fine horn men simply showed up at a time when lady luck was on vacation. But it was definitely kudos to his comrades for resisting the pawn shops. Myles walked on until the tune and the pain faded into the sounds of car horns, sirens, and indigenous loudmouths.

There were plenty of street corner vendors, but none roasting chestnuts on open fires. It was too early in the year to buy that little warm bag of nostalgia, but he was certain he would be back in Copenhagen before that time rolled around. He settled for a bratwurst on a bun smothered with sauerkraut. So far, it was still New York. And New York was no stranger to him. He made it to the city many times back in the day, especially while stationed at a historic Virginia army base.

In a while, he was coming out of *The Blue Note* on West Third Street. The music was fair, but at least it was still there. Later, a swift cab ride saved him some time getting over to Seventh Avenue at Eleventh Street, where he hoped *The Village Vanguard* would be. It was, thankfully though, because he heard long ago through the intercontinental jazz grapevine that the famous *Village Gate* was defunct. No more lines of double-parked limousines from uptown, whose rich passengers were down slumming, stopping in to catch a set of Miles Davis live. That was the best that America could do in the heyday of great bop. It was anyone's guess which would be the next venue to fall.

Myles stayed at the *Vanguard* for a good solid set from a hot quartet playing standards to a house packed with predominately Asian fans who just may have thought they had died and gone to Shanghai! The appreciation level was sky high. It was all great, but he looked at his watch and ran out. Myles then hailed a cab and ordered a ride up to midtown West 44th Street. The grapevine also told him that *Birdland* was still there, but two blocks into the ride, he felt an urge to run up to Harlem. He stopped the cab, paid the driver, and hurried underground to catch a speedy subway. From Harlem of Amsterdam to Harlem of New York. It was all Dutch to him as to what happened to the abundance of jazz clubs where many of his European colleagues once upon a time did gigs. He wanted to see for himself to believe they were gone. Myles waded into humanity and managed to squeeze into a northbound train. Standing upright, he tightly held an overhead grip and swayed with the crowd as the motors hummed like the invasion of the giant hornets, the speeding wheels clacked a beat of calypso before the screeching around the type of curve which justifies overhead grips. The stop-and-go rodeo ride finally deposited him at 125th Street, muscle-bound from hanging on. As soon as he was back on the street, he recalled the place he only heard about.

Minton's playhouse was where musicians played for free and for fun. And it was where raw chops matured like fine wine. If only it was still there. It was just a ghost in the memory of the mind. As Myles breezed along the avenue, it was becoming abundantly clear that ghost venues were as common as the cold. He could see it, and he could feel it. Jazz was in jail and needed to get out on bail. Then he saw it and slowed to an appreciative stop. He was at the biggest thus far, the ghost of the *real* Cotton Club, a place where the back door was the only friend to working Black musicians, and where Black customers were routinely denied entrance in *any* door. He could feel rehabilitation in the air with people and places. He saw peace as he strolled carefully among the feathery carpets of land-lovin', bold and fearless night owl pigeons convening in the way of everything except human kindness. It was all good, but after a few memorable hours, Myles was within reach of hitting the wall. And before too many more hours, his flight to Minneapolis would land him in the first round of hometown healing. For now, he would find his way back downtown to a waiting hotel bed.

It was after five o'clock in the afternoon when the wheels of a 727 United Airlines plane touched down at Minneapolis/St. Paul International Airport. Lugging his bag from the overhead rack, Myles was restraining himself from pushing people aside as he hurried into Humphrey Terminal with a pro-active mindset. He hurried down some back stairs and through an *employees only door* which led outside to the tarmac. Then he saw it right away. His curvaceous bass case was about to be off-loaded from the plane's luggage hold onto the downward conveyer belt. With his heart pounding, he set his bag down in his tracks and took off on the dead run to intercept it. His eyes were popping out of his head as he saw a luggage handler bear-hug his axe in his waiting arms and was leaning back to heave it on top of the transport carts. Myles got there just in the nick of time to take it out of a careless handler's hands. It was like cutting in on a ballroom dance floor to rescue a well-wrapped, plus-size damsel in distress. He couldn't help it. Myles Andrews was a bit jealous. He had strings attached. When he walked back inside carrying his bass across the threshold like a new bride, a dozen men in uniforms and badges called off the security breach with a fair warning. With a little help, Myles made his way back to the proper intake channels and pulled out his passport and international drivers' license. But security was not interested in documentation at this time. They simply wanted him to step aside and strip off the bass cover for a little inspection, noting the unusual circumstance of his retrieval of the instrument. Myles not only complied but seemed to calm everybody down when he plucked that haunting bass line, the cool three-four blues feel which leads onto the classic *All Blues*. It was too funky. Security cited decency laws and requested the recovering of the fiddle. They were happy. Myles was in.

He found a phone booth and dialed the memorized number to his mother's house near Parker Lake in Minneapolis. His only sister, the schoolteacher, answered. The disbelief was a bird out of its cage. Then his only brother, the carwash owner, took over the phone.

"Yes, it's really me," Myles assured him. They *knew* where he'd been all this time, but they asked anyway. "To the moon," Myles answered with sincerity. "I'll be there soon," he said before hanging up.

He stood up his roller bass and grabbed his bag as he headed toward the door. But then he stopped and turned back to the booth to make another call. The phone card numbers were entered, and he waited for a hook-up. In less time than he expected, Yvonne was on the line from Copenhagen. He needed her to know that he just landed back in his hometown. She reiterated her condolences and promised to keep the light on for him. The brief, but sentimental, chat with her was a recharge from across the Atlantic.

Myles left the airport terminal feeling happy and refreshed, his bass and bag light as feathers. He had an extra bounce in his step, or something, *anything* that could help him deal with splashdown back in his family. Out on the sidewalk, he stopped again to brush off the soles of his shoes on the sidewalk. He wanted to feel at home. The scent of ten thousand lakes was in the air, disguised as auto and diesel exhaust. A red-capped airport greeter appeared, relieved him of his bag, and led him to the gaping open back hatch of an airport taxi van. The redcap probably had some experience with other bass players. He knew enough to keep his hands off the fiddle while admiring the impressive array of foreign stickers and tags on it.

"Welcome to Minneapolis, sir. Enjoy your stay," he said with a smile.

"Thank you," Myles said as he palmed him a fin within the handshake.

He took a seat in the driverless cab with the bass lounging beside him. Shortly, an older Black fellow with graying hair jumped in and started the engine. With the assistance of sideview mirrors and a traffic cop, he slowly pulled it away from the curb and into the outgoing flow of cars.

"Where to, sir?" he asked, so far not showing his face.

"Forty-four thirteen East Parker Lake Drive," Myles said.

"Very well, sir," the driver said as he flipped the meter on, concentrating on changing lanes. "You just visiting, Sir?"

"I'm comin' home for my mother's funeral," Myles said with a lump in his throat.

"Sorry for your loss."

"Thanks."

As they accelerated out of the airport vicinity and onto Interstate 494 West, Myles tilted his head trying to remember where he'd heard that unusual nasally voice before. Then a glance at the bulgy road-watching eyes in the rearview mirror caused something to click. "Lester Ride! Is that you? Is that you?"

"Yeah, man. Who dat?" asked Lester Ride, trying his best to keep from swerving as he searched the mirror for a face. "Well, what do you know," Lester said when he found one. "It's Myles Andrews, you old alligator. Last time I saw you, you said, 'see you later alligator'."

They both laughed long. For a moment they were too close to the car which blew its horn.

"Seriously, I thought they say you was dead," said Lester.

"Wel-l-l, I'm resurrected," Myles laughed, "but I'm not wholly ghost."

"Then why are you scaring me . . . a lot?"

They both laughed again.

"How have you been, Lester?"

"Fine, fine. Just doin' this every day and slowly going nuts," he laughed.

"Well, how nuts have you been long?" Myles kidded in Be-bop tongue.

"Since I haven't played my drums on a regular gig. Too long," Lester Ride confessed.

Myles displayed genuine jaw-dropping shock. "You? You're a top drummer! What's up with *that*?"

The cab was stabilized and steady at 70 miles an hour. "I'm afraid it's not just me," Lester said with a sigh. "It's a lot of people. The anti-jazz gremlins have been very busy."

"Unbelievable," Myles said. "Well, then where *is* everybody? How about ol' Bats? Is he still playin'?"

"Naw, not much," Lester said. "He used to drive a Yellow Cab, but right now he's working on the Great Northern Rail Line as a redcap."

"Sad. What a great hornman," Myles said. "So, what about Sleepy McGhee?"

"He's driving a Blue and White Cab."

"I say. And what about ol' Jack Sargent? I just *know* he's still playin' his great piano — the Steinway."

"Yeah," Lester said after a little knowing chuckle. "But just like everybody else, up and down the talent scale, not as much as before. Jack Sargent? He's driving a Red and White Cab."

Myles was silent for a moment. "Well," he finally said, "from the looks of things around here, I s'pect you better carry me back to the airport, or I'll wind up driving one of them Checkered Cabs."

They both laughed but it was to keep from crying.

"How about the strip clubs?" Myles continued. "At least that was a gig that put food on the table."

"Nothing," Les said. "Those places long ago went to canned music and accordion players. And some of the players left that scene here to go and do the same kind of gigs in Vegas for the show girls and more money. And after those gigs dried up in the desert heat, they all moved to St. Louis and Branson to play for the 'show-nuff' girls. That was all more than twenty-five years ago, and we've all gotta do what we gotta do. But personally, I'd rather drive a cab. It's less boring."

"I'm afraid you're preachin' to the choir, my friend," said Myles. "I did those gigs too. I've fallen asleep draped over the bass many times, but only in America."

On the sly, Lester was checking the eyes of his old friend in the rearview mirror, waiting for the right moment. A passing ambulance provided the perfect distraction. He turned off the meter with a quick hand. "It's been a long time," he said after the re-unioning died down. You missed us a *little,* didn't you?"

"Yeah," Myles said, "and it seems like a lifetime ago since my last gig in this country. Remember? Four nights a week on top of the Hilton in St. Paul?"

"How could I forget the Carousel Room," Ride said. "Get a three-sixty view of the city skyline and the sunset while you dine gourmet style."

"And then there was the music," Myles redirected. "Good ol' Wallace Billings and his quintet. That was a fun gig. And people didn't come there for the music," he said. "They came for the dining, but they *really* complimented us for the music . . . all the time."

"Do you think any of those kind of people are still around?" Lester asked, almost jokingly.

"Of course," Myles said. "They're not going to go away just because the music went away. They'll just go to their nearest used record store and load up on all the great jazz superstars and play them when the authorities ain't lookin'," he said.

"It may seem like the prohibition era compared to Europe," Les said, "but give us a little credit for being freer than that, my brother."

"Oh yeah, we's free," Myles mimicked, "but just don't, don't go around saying that too loud. We don't need a bunch of jazz club and swank restaurant owners to be thinking we're free."

"Good point," Les concurred.

"How have things been?"

"Well, you know already," said Lester. "The jazz club scene changes and shifts like sand drifts in the desert. Here today, gone tomorrow, you know."

"Yeah, I know," said Myles, "but be honest, Les. Just how *is* the jazz scene around here?"

"I can't make it up. Jazz is 'dismal' according to *Alberta Clipper*, the local jazz writer for the *Tribune,* but I'm a little more optimistic than that. I see it as a cauldron of soul that's still cookin' on low, waitin' for somebody to turn up the heat."

"How does this *Alberta Clipper* keep her job if things are so . . . dismal?"

"Ask her boss. He's the one who always has a smile on his face," Les said.

"Exactly what kind of gigs have you been doing?" was Myles's burning question.

"Nothin' since way back when I had that six-week sleazy hotel gig with the infamous Hawaiian singer Kay Maulapenme," Les confessed.

"Sounds exhausting," said Myles.

"Right, it was a lot of hula."

"So, what happened?"

"I don't know," Les said. "The show folded up its tents and left town in the middle of the night. We were left high and dry with a bag of empty promises. We're still waiting to be paid for the last two weeks of that gig. Bills, you know."

"Yeah, I know," Myles sympathized. "And I actually forgot that musicians could be treated like that, but you should feel good about it."

"What? How can you say that man?"

"Well, she must've really been in love with you guys because she came all the way from Hawaii to screw you."

Lester's shoulders shook for a moment with silent laughter. "I'm really glad to see you're still the same old Myles Andrews," he said as he worked the outside mirrors to change lanes in the swift flow of traffic.

"I almost am," Myles said rubbing a hand over his graying afro. "And I was leaving town just when they were starting to sterilize jazz out of Hennepin Avenue and the surrounding area," he said. "Places like *Freddie's, The Marquee Club, Big Al's, The Blue Note, The Downtowner,* just to name a few. "

"And don't forget the *Peacock Alley*," said Les, "and all the rest who were the victims of reckless wrecking balls."

"So, why didn't they all just relocate?" Myles asked.

"We'll never know," said Les. "The answer must be locked in a city hall vault. And one fine day, while they're researching the effects of jazz on American society, they're gonna find out that there used to be jazz on Mars."

"Careful," said Myles. "You're going to have me warming up my Theremin."

"You think that's weird? The weird thing is that this cab is my life," Les said, "but I still need whatever gigs I can get."

"Not ready to retire?"

"Naw, man," Les said with a laugh, "because when most fathers die, their children are remembered in their will. When my father died, I was remembered in his won't. Nope, no retirement for me. Not just yet. I mean, I've got a gig you understand. I just never thought my gig would wind up growing rubber tires."

"Only in America," Myles lamented.

"Yeah, and there are a hell of a lot of us jazz musician hacks roamin' around out here. Too many."

"What about that singer with the real high voice, ah . . . Miss Heckett," Myles remembered. "Is she driving cab too?"

"Kitten Heckett? Another sad story," Lester said. "A long time ago, long after she was an adult, her tonsils swelled up and she needed to have them removed."

"Sounds like a *good* thing," said Myles.

"It was a good thing until after more than a week of silence and ice cream eating, doctors were baffled about why she went from a high soprano to a bass singer," Les said. "Last I heard, a Los Angeles recording studio hired her to do voice-overs on some Barry White albums. Her sister Button also is a singer."

"Sounds like the ol' girl landed on her feet," Myles said.

"Basically, Kitten Heckett got lucky," said Les.

"Indeed," Myles was pumped with curiosity. "And what about that great guitarist, Gottlbee DesHyden?"

"He's in prison."

"What? What for?"

"They convicted him for racketeering in illegal fakebooks," said Les. "He's doin' life just because he made a fortune selling them to China without paying taxes."

"Sounds harsh," Myles shook his head. "Only in America."

"Yeah, said Les. "It's kind of a shame too because he had been working on trying to get a little snarl back into his playing. He started hanging out at the zoo to study the ways and sounds of a certain jungle beast."

"Oh? What beast is *that*?"

"The Burdzurf lion."

Myles tipped his head both was to make sure there was no water in his ears. "All you guys need are more gigs," he said, "because with this cab driving, you've got too much time on your hands and not enough tunes in your head."

The cab ride exited the freeway in south Minneapolis and headed east for about two miles. As Myles surveyed the sights along the way, some neighborhood familiarity started to come back to him as if he'd never left. But he was saddened to see that the tall, old-growth boulevard trees did leave, replaced by short pitiful-looking saplings which were doomed to grow old without him. The right turn onto Parker Lake Drive brought it all back. This after all was his hometown. Soon, they rolled to a slow stop in front of the house of his mother.

Les had been shutting up for a minute, letting him absorb his return in peace. "I *am* very sorry about your mother," he said. "God bless her. This is on me."

"'preciate it," Myles said, the lump in his throat somewhat restricting his thankfulness for the blessing, but he didn't want to argue about the turned-off meter. What's fair is fare. Outside the car they did the combo handshake and back-slapping embrace. Myles palmed a wadded fifty into the handshake, and he ducked and dodged it like the plague when Les tried to give it back. Then Lester suddenly was too tired to try again and closed his fist on it like a Venus's fly trap.

They exchanged cards, and Myles said goodbye to his buddy, and the cab drove off leaving him standing on the sidewalk with his bass and bag. Sounds in the neighborhood took him way back in a melancholy way. Now it was the sound of dogs barking in English, a long way across the pond from the lands where dogs barked in Danish and

French and Spanish and Swedish and Dutch and German. This back in the states thing was very real.

Again, he glanced down the street at the cab which was now a distant dot. If only he had asked for just one more spin around the lake, but it was time to stop stalling and go on in. He looked up at the house. The tree in the yard was old when he left, but now it was thirty-some years taller and fatter and more protective of the well-kept three-story brick and stucco home on parker lake Drive. He was so nervous his ankle boots were starting to sound like church bells. He lugged his stuff up the stairs to the front door and knocked. Waiting, he noticed cars jammed in the driveway as well as bumper to bumper street parking. The door opened, and it was his only two siblings, Al, the carwash owner and Althea, the daycare operator from the northside. They stared at him in disbelief. Then the tears started running with Myles leading the way. They did a long group hug, three siblings and a bass fiddle. It was a true-blue reunion.

"Is Momma comin' back?" said Myles, choking back a sob.

"Naw, she's gone to be with Daddy," said his older brother Al.

They entered the house crowded with mostly quiet mourners. Myles ditched his bass and bag in a corner, then looked around surrounded by a lot of faces which didn't ring a bell. Myles held paranoia on a short leash as the eyes of certain men and women seemed to be staring at him. He was a marked man. And then, almost as if on some unseen and unheard cue, they all approached him simultaneously. Who were they? He patted the pocket holding his return airline ticket. It was his escape in case things turned sour. His brother and sister had his back, stepping in and commencing with introductions of a long-lost brother. There were neighbors and friends of the family, and there were favorite customers of his mother's flower shop. They were well and good. But it was his uncles, aunts, and grown-up nieces and nephews which made him feel like shit for not knowing them. The sadness was pervasive, but for the next two hours, Myles worked the room. His citizenship and kinship were already earned, but like his well-traveled boots, they were in need of some polish.

It was a few days later, and the hour arrived. Myles turned off his alarm in a spare bedroom of his mother's house and arose with a yawn that was flavored with sadness. He pulled out his church clothes and touched them up with his international travel iron. His last few days had been blessed with finding out that there were no estrangement bridges to be rebuilt among smart and respectful siblings. He was loving their breakfast, lunch, dinner talks, but today, the bantering and teasing and reminiscing failed to come up with the sun.

At eight o'clock in the morning, Myles, Al, and Althea met in the kitchen all washed and dressed and ready for business, but first, another group hug was on.

Five family stretch limos were lined on the street with their flashers on. At the front of the line, two white motorcycle cops were doing penance by having to wait patiently for the family's go-ahead. At eight-thirty, the doorbell didn't need to ring before aunts, uncles, nieces, nephews, and close friends started coming in for the planned limo assembly. Reverend Elisha Robertson needed only to stand in the middle of the floor and clasp his hands together for everyone except the cat to bow their heads for a prayer. His amen came too soon. He must've been saving himself for the church, worn down by tireless run-throughs and rehearsals. He looked at his watch and let everyone hold a thought for a moment. Reverend Elisha then made a gentle gesture towards the door. They led his follow. And now, on a mild and overcast day, the sleep-deprived Andrews survivors loaded into the family carriages for the ride.

Even with some bonding under his belt, Myles felt awkward, but togetherness was the only necessary language of the moment. The house was locked, motorcycle engines boomed, and they were under way.

The ride and family seating went smoothly. Parker Lake A.M.E. Church was packed with mournful souls who came out to celebrate the life of Isabelle Andrews, her last day on the face of this earth before being transitioned to heaven. Many extra chairs were set up in the lobby and in the basement to accommodate the overflow. Lovely bouquets of flowers adorned her silver casket and the entire front of the church from wall to wall. The pianist did an appropriate four-bar introduction as the large, blue-robed choir stood to sing, richly accompanying a wholesome, caramel-skinned, mellow-voiced young lady who stepped forward to solo with, "*Were you there when they nailed him to the cross.*"

That did it for Myles. He intercepted a box of tissues being passed along family row, joining the others in wiping away tears. He'd come from afar to attend the ceremony of her death, and the fact that he wasn't around to see the last light of her eye would be a pain that would hang in his heart for the rest of his life. He endured the sadness of having to getting reacquainted with his mother through a procession of loving speakers who knew her, and the soothing a-bomb of a eulogy delivered by the Reverend Elisha Robertson, his eyes drooping with sincere condolences as they slowly panned family row. Myles nodded slowly, entranced with the feeling that his mother, Isabelle would soon be in the hands of heavenly ushers. His religion was a broken fixture in the basement, but he watched respectfully as Reverend Robertson lifted the congregation on the wings of glory for the mother of Andrews and brought them back down to earth with a better place for Isabelle. The pianist took over and got the feeling going, a funky gospel into in three-quarter time. The director brought the choir to their feet and guided them into a harmonious rendition of *Amazing Grace*. With impeccable precision, they swayed from side-to-side every three beats. Myles endured it with the excruciating wish that he had his bass with him as he rose with the family to join selected pallbearers. He held the front handle of the casket tightly and followed the lead of the reverend and trustees in slowly rolling it to the rear of the church and out the front door. As the pews and extra seats emptied, cars with little orange magnetized fender flags filled with lots of people who cared.

The silver stretch limo was filled from the front to the back where Myles caught the last available seat. He nursed his grief stoically after graciously acknowledging introductions of some of his mother's flower store employees, ladies who themselves were in no mood for extra chatter. The procession moved slowly and majestically through a red light, okayed by the presence of the motorcycle police escort which roared ahead to block crossing traffic at the next intersection. After a mile the lead car turned west and onto the great curve around the shores of Parker Lake. Myles looked out the window over his shoulder and saw the Impressive following, a head lighted caravan snaking as far as the eye could see. Like a slow-but-steady train, the motorcade dominated the right-of way along Edgewater Boulevard for three miles. And just as smoothly, the lead car started a protected and protracted left turn process, followed by more than a hundred cars through the golden gates of the vast, well-kept Laced Hill Cemetery. The destination inside was the waiting green tent with chairs and the elegant casket poised for internment. Time waited for cars to park and people to finish gathering at his mother's final resting place. Myles was on the front row with siblings Al and Althea while the Reverend Elisha Robertson delivered kind words of transition. He closed the brief and somber ceremony with an *amen.* As her friends placed single roses on her casket and slowly walked away, Myles paused, bowed his head and sent a silent prayer to his mother Isabelle, just like he had done many times before.

After the funeral, family members were at the post-service luncheon in the carpeted and soft-lighted dining hall downstairs from the church. Myles saw it coming and should have expected it. American soil was starting to fly, getting all over the chicken and waffles, barbeque ribs, brownies, and chilled punch.

"If you didn't like *this* country so much, why did you go so far away? Why didn't you just go to Canada and try to make 'em jealous from across the border?"

Myles held the juicy rib between his fingers like a harmonica, contemplating which key he should start chewing in. Otherwise, he didn't know if it was a Jeopardy question or a 60 Minute interview. "I didn't go to Canada because Canadians don't caribou about jazz," he said with a wink before taking a big bite in the key of see, I told you.

Everyone else simultaneously stopped chewing and rolled their eyes. It was all in fun. His aunt Sarah from Atlanta put her brownie down, planted her fists on her hips and squinted with a smirk. She got it too. "You haven't changed a bit since you was a boy," she said pointing at him.

"Oh, I've changed," Myles said with a friendly exaggeration of wiping his fingers and dabbing his mouth. "Because now I know what it's like to be *really* free."

"What do it feel like?" His aunt Sarah asked.

Myles did a distracted double-take and braced for the heavy-set elderly woman coming at him with deliberately squinted eyes and pointing her scythe-like red fingernails at him. He guessed she wanted a hug and stood up.

"Bawwwy, you've grown so much," she said with a smiling frown.

"Are you referring to me, Madam?" said middle-age Myles. It was too late. She hugged him like a catcher's mitt on a fastball. His freedom was momentarily shot.

"Excuse me," his sister Althea interjected. "In case you may have forgotten, this is your other aunt from North Carolina, our Auntie Carmen."

"Ooooh-yeaaaah," Myles was in the process of recalling. "Haven't seen you since grade school. That was way back when Dad died, and you were at his funeral."

"Bawwwwy, your memory is so good," she said. "Why haven't you called me?"

"I-I guess I must've lost your number Auntie," Myles managed to say from the depth of her bear hug and breath.

She finally let go of him, and he was free at last, but she didn't have the look of someone who was finished. "Why you go and leave the country?"

Myles was beginning to see that it was a question he was going to wear like the callouses on his fingertips. "As I just said to someone a little while ago, I left because of the injustice in the country. And I left because of the little issue of not getting paid for my chosen profession. They won't admit it, but they ever-so-dearly *want* jazz, but they don't want to *pay* for jazz, and we know who *they* are, don't we?"

"Well, couldn't you have just stayed here and fought it out?"

He gave her a long look and dropped his eyes to the floor. "Look, Auntie," he said as gently as possible. "I'm a musician. Musicians don't fight; they play."

But his Auntie Carmen wasn't buying it. "A musician can fight as well as a soldier can. Ain't you never heard of an army band?"

"It rings a bell," said Myles. "You could be right, but back at that time, there were too many things to start a fight over. It was easier to just leave for greener pastures."

"But what about your family?" she said softly, but with other conversations going on, nobody was listening anyway.

"I know, Auntie," he said. "I've got a lot of catching up to do, but I love them to death for respecting my personal decision."

Myles' sister snared him by the arm and dragged him to another introduction. She was sitting at the end of another table of his mother's friends – a little old bespectacled White lady with silver hair and a very pleasant, rosy face.

"Remember her?" sister Althea said with a smile.

Myles closed one eye, bit his lip, and tweaked his chin trying to remember. He just couldn't. "I . . .I . . ."

"This is Miss Lenore Graham," Althea said while maintaining her smile. "She used to be our babysitter."

Myles slapped his hands to his face and bent over backwards with embarrassment, but he was laughing as he leaned to hug her.

"You *ought* to remember me, young man," Miss Graham said as she wagged a playful finger at him. "You always called me *'Graham Cracker'*."

They all laughed. Myles couldn't quite spit out the words of sorrow, but forgiveness was in the air. And later they all cried and praised the life of Isabelle.

Myles and his surviving family members scheduled a meeting time at his mother's house to discuss the disposition of the estate, including the house and the flower shop. The time came and the meeting went well. They voted with a show of hands and the single raised tail of a cat. It was unanimous. Aunts, uncles, cousins, and siblings were all on the same page about maintaining everything, flowers and all. It was about keeping the free-and-clear house as a family monument to her memory, and the story as a tribute to her very loyal customers. They decided it was worth it, if just for the comfort of a period of mourning.

And now, with the funeral and meetings ten days in the past, Myles removed his elongated wallet from his back pocket and opened it to see if his return ticket to Copenhagen was still there. He knew it would be, but as he looked at it, his gut was telling him that he wasn't quite ready to go back yet. He didn't call Yvonne to tell her *that*, but instead, he called her to reaffirm their standing dinner date when that time came. For now, their language would have to serve as a poor surrogate for a hug.

His family's respect for his choices were still valid, but hypocritically, campaigning had already begun in earnest. Each sibling and extended blood were repeatedly buttonholing him to renounce his foreign adventure and once again, pledge allegiance to the United States of America. They were stroking him with restaurants as well as home cooking and picnic outings, and they promised to maintain a vigilance for some decent jazz. His brother Al and sister Althea threw another treat into the mix by taking him out to the suburbs where there was a little town completely built indoors – a place called *The Mall of America*. It was a crushing blow to his cherished image of Tivoli Gardens. He thanked them very much for the offer, but he didn't need to go up-side down on Snoopy's rollercoaster to prove anything. It was just enough to push him over the top about changing his schedule to hang around for a few days to give his hometown a little love. It was a fast relearning experience for him, that you can take the boy out of the hometown, but you can't take the hometown out of the boy.

Two days later Myles was having coffee in Isabelle's kitchen nook with his two divorced siblings. Their occupational success, he thought, could be contributing to their relative happiness, despite their fractured family situations. It was a happiness which reminded him of how they were in their youth, full of hope, full of ambition, and empty of fear. Those things were worth a million bucks of un-spendable currency, but all he could think was that seeing them again was a long overdue treat to his retinas.

"Do you think you've missed much?" sister Althea asked.

Myles had been glancing on and off at the weekly pulp automobile magazine. "Hell, yeah," he said. "I've totally missed out on watching you guys grow old in your own homes."

They all laughed, but it was a laughter which faded upon the realization of just how short life was. Myles had a feeling he could count on their reminding him of that fact. Around the table, they formed a ring of held hands and said a prayer for their mother Isabelle. They finished coffee and another round of fun while-you-were-gone stories. Myles took one last look at that automobile magazine and made up his mind.

"That's it!" he said, "a cheap old Chevy to buzz around in."

"You don't have to do that," Al said. "I've got two cars you could use."

"Not a problem," said Myles. "I'm going to buy this thing," he circled it, "and I'm going to use it to make it around for a while, then I'll just give it to charity, lock, stock, and insurance."

"Well, would you at least let me drive you to pick it up?"

"You're on, Brother."

"Are you guys going to be back by six o'clock?" Althea asked. "I'm doing southern fried chicken, spinach casserole, black-eyed beans, candied sweet potatoes, cornbread, and blueberry pie ala mode."

"What? No chitlins?" Myles kidded.

"Only if you really, really, really want them," Althea conceded.

Myles acted dumbfounded. "You . . . you guys don't just want me *back* home; you want me *down* home!"

Althea was smiling as she got up and started pulling out clean and ready pots and pans. "Like they say," she said, "you can take the boy out of the country, but you sure can put some country back in the boy."

"Is somebody betting that I won't show up for that?" Myles laughed. "Sounds fine. And oh . . . ah," he said with a wink, "hold the chitlins."

Myles and Al left the house on a vehicle hunt, and it was a whim, but two hours later Myles was driving the thing, satisfied that it had passed the pre-purchase test he'd conducted. It turned on and off three times in a row without a hitch. Good start! He popped the hood to eyeball and eardrum the running engine, which was much to his satisfaction. It didn't burn oil, the brakes were alive, and the front passenger seat could lay down flat. The bass would fit! He paid cash to the private owner, a friendly elderly lady who simply didn't want to drive anymore. He haggled her down three hundred dollars, paid her cash and took over the keys and title. It warmed his cold bargaining heart that she was pleased to be rid of it. Before peeling out, Myles thanked Al for the lift and promised a full report on the test drive at dinner.

It was all so sudden, and he was driving down the road once again in his hometown. Street names would come back to him like long-lost orphans. Before long, there was a ping from the dashboard. Myles smiled and almost broke out laughing when he noticed why a yellow light was flashing. The little old lady forgot to tell him that the tank was empty. It was fine, he thought, because this was America where there was a gas station around every corner.

Dinner, libation, and fun last night was a dream that Myles lived. He awoke with the sun high in the sky and the siblings long gone to work, and with a gratitude that they let him cop some catch-up snooze time. While he brushed his teeth and dressed, he glanced out the window several times at his all-blue Chevy on the street. It was comforting to know that hometown was going to get a lot smaller a lot faster. Down in the kitchen, smiley-face notes with arrows directed him to the fruit and milk in the fridge for the cereal box and bowl and spoon on the counter. He lighted up at the biggest note which said: *Don't get on any plane when we're not looking.* It was just a clowning carry-over from the past evening's shenanigans. Next to the note, they left him an additional spare front door key to Isabelle's house. He shook his head with an incredulous smile knowing that there was no way he was going to lose the first one. He almost made it to the door, but before he left, a certain hankering to play caused him to detour to a previously empty corner of the living room. For a quickie, he unzipped and removed the cover of his Hofner and started in with a brisk bass line which was accompanying a tune in his head. It was the fix his masochist fingertip callouses needed for a musical addiction. Between gigs, it was a fix he would steal whenever he could. When he was satisfied, Myles covered his ax and leaned it back in the corner before heading out the door and throwing the deadbolt.

HOMETOWN JAZZ SAFARI

Outside of family members, there was one thing that gave him a back home feeling, and it was the long-lost sight of the street signs. After Myles picked up a load of gas, he set out to re-acquaint himself with the Twin Cities. So many freeways was something which did not register with his memory. He turned a corner and got swept in by an east-bound entrance ramp. It wasn't the direction he wanted to go, but he was nevertheless headed across the Mississippi River and into St. Paul fast enough to keep the rear drivers off his tail. One memory did come back to him just before he took the Lexington Avenue exit and headed south. There was once a decent jazz club far down the summit to Randolph Avenue. He found the location and pulled over to the curb. Myles sat for a few moments and stared at all that remained. The sight of dirt and wild weeds on an empty lot saddened him. He compared this devasting scene to the many European clubs which to this day are being allowed to age gracefully. The noble art of jazz simply wouldn't stand for their demise. In Europe, the good ol' days of jazz was ageless. He ran the gamut of memories of what used to be on this lot back when, then restarted the engine. His curiosity drive continued for a loop-de-loop spin into and around good old downtown St. Paul before sitting in the freeway jam back to Minneapolis, the City of Lakes. He was eventually back to the sanity of residential streets, and it was the south-bound Hennepin Avenue rout which visually reminded him how different things are, and yet how much they are the same. It would all come back to him from moment to moment. Uptown arrived without protest. Long, tight veins of traffic were catching the mercy of consecutive green lights and arrows. He drove west with the flow, and there it was — a familiar body of inner-city water. Myles took it all in, how his journey had taken him from the decades near the seas of Scandinavia to a long, slow and relaxing orbit around beautiful Lake Calhoun.

It was the water which reminded him of her. He smiled as he thought of Yvonne on such a gorgeous day, lending her presence to one of these populace beaches and doing exactly what she wanted to do with her towel and goosepimples. What a culture clash that would be! He would be sure to tell her that when he went back to Copenhagen. He had enough time to grow old enough to know that if he just called her about a beach, she may not actually do it, but she might be inclined to hang up on him. Water was her thing. As he drove, he smiled again when he recalled the first of her hanging up abilities, seemingly a hundred years ago when he needed to call her back fifteen times in five minutes just to get a loving word in edgewise. It tickled him pink that she hung up on him that many times, but she also answered the phone that many times. He could only hope that her days of hanging up on him were truly behind her, and he remembered that their very few so-called fights unusually didn't amount to a row of pins anyway. Hell, he mused, he would be sure to mention the beach when he called her. He would make it music to her ears. It was the least a jazz musician could do. But right now, he didn't need radio music because as he drove, tunes were running through his head. His fingers itched to be accompanying them by pressing and plucking his fiddle strings.

When he ran out of lake and turned back east toward uptown, he eventually spotted something else which right away set his mind to working like the mechanics of an old clock. The rental sign was for an off-the-street mansion-like group of buildings. Myles drove around the block once, twice, three times as he mulled it over. A place of his own to practice for a few days or weeks would be ideal. He knew his own habits, such as coming home from a gig and winding down by gently playing his ax a stones' throw farther into the wee hours. Only another musician would be so tolerant of such behavior, and one of those was his roommate abroad. Myles decided to show some respect for the quiet walls of his mother's home. Some would call it brainless, he thought, but he would prefer to view it as a no-brainer to inquire within. After being re-directed to the proper person in the proper office, he was ushered to a small solid structure across the yard. The manager, a Mr. Peepers type, unlocked it for a look-see. It was a little island of basic accommodations and furnishings downstairs, and a half-loft upstairs. The manager hemmed and hawed as he struggled to be perfectly honest. He finally gathered himself enough to inform Myles that back in the day, the place was servant's quarters. Myles panned his eyes across the ceiling, because starting right now, it would take a hell of a lot more than that to scare him off. After a short waltz of terms, he signed in and came up with the first-and last down payment. He was impressed. An unattached brick shithouse? Visions of undisturbed peace danced in his head as he thought of all those upcoming jam sessions. The beauty of it all was that he could always leave the landlord holding a bag of unused rent. Thirty minutes later, the door opened, and he emerged from the office a proud man with a modest month-to-month pad to invite his siblings and some musician cats over.

Connecting up fast with the local scene would require some local conduits. It reminded him of the business card in his shirt pocket which he plucked out and saw Lester Ride's name. A jazz musician driving a cab is the world's greatest grapevine! Myles called Lester, and they would hook up at eleven o'clock tomorrow for coffee.

His next call was to Yvonne in Copenhagen. He missed her terribly and told her so. Their great understanding chat would be the dessert of the day. He would sleep well.

After a predictable sound sleep, Myles was up with the first light of day. He instinctively looked to see if his bass was still there. It was. At the sink, he yawned and stretched before splashing his face a few times with cold water. He was soon toweled and dressed and ready to go after a snack from his newly bought bag of groceries. He was doing some back in the Americas samba steps as he sashayed across the room to the kitchenet where he continued his time keeping by flipping on the grill and reaching in the abbreviated icebox for a fresh carton of batter mix. The tune running through his head must've been Dizzy Gillespie's *No More Blues.* The dance was over; it was time to pour. Two sizzling medium size splotches of mix froze in their tracks and began to brown. They weren't exactly like *Aebleskivers*, those cue ball-sized Danish pancakes that Yvonne taught him to make years ago, but they were the kind that were flattened when they landed on this side of the ocean centuries ago. He grabbed his new spatula and flipped them before setting the table with plates, forks, butter, and syrup. Almost forgetting where he was made him chuckle but he would just leave Yvonne's plate on the table as a symbolic gesture. When those flapjacks were done, he harvested them and slathered them with soft butter, followed by a drenching with the finest prize of a maple tree. It was mouth-watering, golden-brown simplicity teasing his tastebuds. He turned to the icebox for a waiting glass of chilled orange juice. He sat down with his eyes closed in great anticipation, feeling blindly for his fork.

As soon as his eyes opened, he recoiled with horror and disgust. That fast, a bold cockroach was doing the *hotfoot rhumba* on top of his pancakes while stuck unforgivingly to his syrup. Myles studied the rafters for the launching place of this trespassing Blattidae paratrooper which landed dead-center on his precious cooking. At least Danish cockroaches, if you can find them, have much better table manners than this! Deflated, he flipped the top one over, creating a roachcake sandwich, and then scraped the whole mess into the garbage. Myles gulped his orange juice down and went to his bass in the corner for a short session of anger management, running up and down a progression of scales until they no longer sounded fishy. His fingers had their fix, and he was out the door.

It was noon, and at least on this day, Myles arrived at the perfect place to meet. It was show biz to standing room only at a pancake factory. It was *Al's Breakfast* in Dinkytown. It soon became their turn to graduate from patient wallflowers to seated customers at the crowded counter. Myles was all smiles not only to see his buddy and colleague, but he relished the opportunity for a pancake make-good as their orders were promptly taken.

"All kidding aside," said Myles, "what's the reality of the gig scene around here?"

"Like I said before, there are a few gigs around if you want to just play and be happy and not worry about how little money you make, and put up with people asking, 'what do you *really* do for a living', well go for it. That's what a lot of cats are doing to fight starvation. The rest of us who haven't quit are driving cabs."

Myles could only shake his head incredulously. It was the wrong time to start drawing comparisons with overseas, but his mind was working overtime with the greenness of those pastures. He patted his back pocket and found that his return airline ticket was still there. "All I hope is that we don't forget about all the people in this country who truly love our music. They're out there."

"That's fine," Les said, "but don't they have any imagination of their own? Can't they envision rich jazz musicians? Why do they have to be so damn sure there's no money in being a jazz musician? I mean would I ask an ear doctor what he *really* does for a living?"

"Of course not," said Myles. "I wouldn't be that rude either."

"We do something good for the ears too, don't we?"

"I heard that," Myles said.

It was probably in record time, but after a seemingly long-enough wait, their twin stacks of hot buttered blueberry cakes and bacon arrived. They inadvertently talked with food in their mouths.

"Are there enough musicians left to cover whatever is out there?" Myles asked.

"Oh, you know, same old feeding frenzy," said Les, "jazz musicians have been known to stampede towards the first hint of a gig. Everybody wants that one gig because everybody has waited long enough to get it."

"I used to know the feeling," Myles said.

"Well, if you stick around long enough, you'll see why a lot of axes are winding up at the *Pickle Hock* pawn shop. That place has helped many players eat for a week between gigs."

"What a shame," Myles mumbled.

"It's the nature of things," Les joked, "and as you know, you can't mess with Mother Nature, 'cause Mother Nature knows what he's doing at all times."

Myles' eyes smiled at the comment as he jaws gyrated.

"I beg your pardon, couldn't help but over-hearing you, but as the governor of the great state of Minnesota, I must agree with you about doing something good for the ears," said the gentleman to their immediate right, wearing a brilliant white shirt with a donkey-blue tie. "You see, I have a pretty good collection of jazz records at home which I've cherished since I was in college here at the U." He extended a napkin-wiped hand for shakes. Myles and Les were stunned to speechless chewing. The pancakes were already delicious enough, but now they were going down easier. After a short chat, the governor rose from his stool and left them with an unnecessary explanation. He needed to get back to the state capitol at the other end of University

Avenue. Myles finished chewing with his fingers laced and his elbows on the counter as he watched the governor gladhand his way to and through the door.

"You know, that's just what jazz in America needs," he said. "Lip services in high places."

"I'll drink to that," Les said, toasting air with a raised coffee mug, "but the only problem with the governor is that he's going back to the *Big House* with his mouth plastered up about jazz being a national treasure."

"So why don't we just get out there and make our own noise?" Myles teased.

"We're already out there making our own noise," Les insisted. "What everybody is trying to figure out is how to make our noise turn green."

"Only if we live long enough," Myles said. "Didn't I hear someone say you went to New York?"

"Oh, yeah," Les confessed. "I went to New York way back when, to try to make it."

"So how did your New York debut turn out?"

"Fine. It was fine," Les deadpanned.

"Fine? Is that all you can say? *Fine?*"

"Well," Les shrugged, "to be honest, it didn't go well at all. I saved up to go out there thinking I could catch a gig right away, but before I knew it, I was broke. Didn't have a cent."

"So, what did you do?"

"Well, here I was, going to New York to seek my fortune where big-time jazz is supposed to be, right? I was a fish out of water, but the *Big Apple* gigging aquarium had thick glass and no doors."

"Too much good competition, I guess," Myles said.

"No kidding," Les agreed. "But whenever my stomach started growling for food, I went over to Seventh Avenue and pulled garment racks around for a few bucks, washed a few dishes here and there, you know."

"Not too fine," Myles said.

"No. That's why I decided thirteen months was enough, and that I better go back and get better prepared for the big stage of New York. So, me and my drumsticks came home."

"That's the finest thing I've heard," said Myles.

"I got so skinny that every time I put my left hand down, my wedding ring fell off. Finally, I had to hock it for bus money back home."

"That is *so* not fine."

"No, it ain't," Les said, "especially when I got home and found out my wife had run off out west to live. So, I thought, *fine*!"

Myles was through eating, but he swallowed anyway. His momentary thoughts were three thousand miles away, but he was trying his best to avoid the feeling of being on the clock. "These cab drivers, they're still good players, aren't they?" he asked.

"They're all excellent, competent and wonderful jazz musicians, truly representative of our unrecognized national treasure," Les said.

Myles was already through thinking about it. "There's always just a little blood left in the turnip," he guessed, "so, why don't we start up a group and try to squeeze out a gig or two?"

"Have you been drinking?"

"Not yet," said Myles, "but while I'm here, I'll bet it could be done."

"That's quite a crystal ball you're lookin' at, my friend," Les said with a knowing tone.

"Look, this is a country where there's no regulations on guns and all kinds of regulations on jazz. Go figure," Myles said. "So, that's why we need to sharpen our axes and start doing a little DE-regulating!"

"You're kidding."

"No, I'm serious," Myles insisted. "Let's do it, let's be like guns. We could call it *The Urban Cab Quartet*."

Les was pulling out his mental wallet to see if he could afford to buy it. "The Urban Cab Quartet," he repeated slowly as if only to hear himself say it.

"So, what do you think of it?"

"Dockta! Dockta!" Les answered slapping a hand to his forehead as he mimicked an ill patient. "Da pain is startin' ta go away awready!"

They laughed as they each cascaded their dollars and coins onto the counter and rose to relinquish their stools to some other extremely patient and hungry wallflowers standing behind them. They worked their way outside where the fresh air was the cherry on top of the pancakes.

"With your help, I'll scout around and see if there's a club owner who has the balls to hire and pay a decent jazz group," Myles said. "And if they don't have the balls, we'll settle for a little plain ol' fortitude."

"Sounds like a play," Les said. "Right now, I've got to get my almighty meter going again, but I'll call you with a short list of once-upon-a-time paying jazz venues so you can go and take your turn at twisting their arms for compensation. Maybe a new face will shake them out of their stubborn ways."

"Think so?"

"Yeah," said Les. "There are three or four clubs that will let players jam on Monday and Saturday afternoons. They won't pay you to play a straight-up gig, but you're welcome to go there and jam yourself into a stupor while their customers drink watered-down booze to the sounds of our music."

"Wow, those owners must get over like fat rats," Myles said.

"They do," said Les, "'cause it's *only* a session. They don't have to *pay*."

"Sounds like they could use some good old-fashion civilizing," Myles chuckled. "But you know, at one time they all knew what to do, and then all of a sudden they all dummied up at the same time. Maybe it was something in the water. I don't know."

"Wish I knew," Les said. "But I do know that between nightclubs and supper clubs, playing for diners is usually greener pastures than playing for drinkers, if you can find a dinner gig," he stressed.

"Simple case of scared management," Myles diagnosed, "and sadly, that's an American thing. Fear of American jazz is hard to find in Europe and Asia. So, I think it's about walking into their business, especially the supper clubs. But the trick for dinner musicians is that they need to be quiet, but *very good*," Myles said. "You don't need to blow the steaks off the plates."

Les shook his head a little. "A lot of players just can't play their axes quiet. They want to be heard. They want an identity over the next guy," he said.

"Nothing wrong with that," Myles clarified, "but for dinner gigs, though, we'll just hang with those very few players who have the soul to raise the roof by playing quiet."

"Oh, I get it," Les mimicked, "da show is da steak, an' we's just' da goin' down music, is that it?"

"Yeah," said Myles with lilt in his voice, "now what could be more appetizing than getting well paid for *that*, baby?"

"Go get 'em tiger!" Les rooted.

"Ti-gers, ti-gers," Myles corrected to encourage inclusiveness and mass participation. "But first I've got to go and get my hands dirty potting a few plants at my mother's flower shop."

With a departing fist bump, they were all-in with hooking up later.

Four hours later, Myles drove up to a place called *The Shepherd Hook.* It was one of the joints Lester suggested checking out for music, a storefront on the edge of downtown. When he walked in, the place reminded him of some of the scenes of decades back, except that it was all aardvarks. The lounge was too sterilizing for the likes of truly dedicated lizards. Management was seeking higher standards through visible cameras and brighter lights. The brightest lights were on the stage playing, and that was not a surprise to him. Old jazzers never die, he thought. Hell, they don't even have sense enough to fade away. He ordered a beer at the bar and laid in the weeds for a turn to light up somebody else's fiddle. His fingertips itched. His right heel rose and fell on two and four as he kept time with a fairly good tempo. The familiar tune gracing the room was the Victor Young – Ned Washington composition, *Stella by Starlight*.

Myles was watching the bass like a dog on his mark, ready for a bone to be tossed. That bassist up there was strong enough to carry a drummer on his back, and way too good for *pro bono*. If only the lizards knew what they were missing!

Solo improvising by all the musicians carried the tune's theme on a silver platter to a rousing conclusion of applause. Myles was a step too far away and could only watch as another regime of musicians quickly took over. He paid his tab and shook a few unfamiliar hands as he vowed to better position himself near the stage for a better chance to sit in on his next visit to *The Shepherd Hook*. In a few minutes, Myles was back in his car and headed to another venue on his list.

He arrived and parked in the unattended and half-filled lot next to the place. Before he got out of the car, he pulled out his electronic calendar to satisfy a burning curiosity. He pushed a few buttons to find out where he would be right now if her were back across the pond. There it was. He would be finishing up a gig at the *Montemartre Jazz Hus* in Copenhagen, and then off to a ten-day booking in Paris. As he got out of his car to go in, he could only hope without holding his breath that his replacement wasn't all that good. As Myles looked around the inside the door of *d'Urville French Restaurant*, he figured Les had to be kidding about American jazz in a posh French restaurant outside of France. Classical string quartet music played softly from overhead speakers. On a little dare with himself, Myles politely tipped the gracious hostess to summon the manager. The wait for the head man to respond was respectfully short. He arrived with an air of accommodation and sporting a dark tailored suit, slicked-back hair and a miniature handlebar moustache.

"Why yes, you most certainly may be of some assistance," was Myles' answer to the question. "I represent a group of musicians who could raise your establishment to an even higher level of class," he said.

"I see," said the manager whose nametag read *Pepe*. "Tell me, are your musicians baroque?"

"We are right now," Myles played along, "but we won't be broke if you'll give us a gig." He fought to hold a straight face.

"We had a management and format change several months ago, sir," he said. "But if you would be so kind as to leave your information with the hostess, we'll call you," said the manager slightly tilting his head with a bowing exit.

Myles knew there was something in his jacket pocket which needed attention. He reached in and pulled it out. It was his cherished transatlantic airline return ticket. He kissed it with an audible smooch. "Maybe later," he said as he walked out with a sardonic smile on his chops. He owned him some catbird seat.

As he headed down the road, his only amusement was feeling like an international fly on the wall, experiencing the sad contrasts of attitudes between two peoples, three thousand miles apart. After a short in-town drive, Myles pulled up in front of another place on the list, a club called *The Showcase Lounge*. Just ahead of him, a panel truck was coming to a stop. The lettering painted on the back jogged his memory. It read O. K. PIANOS. Les had mentioned more than once that this was *not* a musician-friendly vehicle. He said it was driven by the infamous Octavius Killjoy, purveyor of those dastardly player pianos which put real musicians out of work. Myles was in a perfect position to get a look at the elusive, sly, slick phantom gig bomber. There he was, getting out of the van and looking suspiciously over each shoulder through deep-set animal eyes under one eyebrow, two pointy ears, and long, mangy scraggly gray hair. He must be one hell of a salesman, but whoever sees him doing his dirt? Myles relished the opportunity. This he had to see with his own eyes. He spotted him a minute then sleuthed in the door that Killjoy entered. The lights were lower, and the smell of beer was higher. The only music for a few patrons was whistling bartender. Myles could only speculate as to whether or not the musician's union knew about him. If they did, he thought, they didn't need to collect dues from him. They needed to collect *don'ts*. The one he was serving at the bar appeared to be Killjoy, but because of the lighting, he couldn't be sure.

He sauntered over for a closer look. It was the same face, a holdover from Halloween party who was dressed in a dumpy brown suit and a designer tie of piano keys against a black shirt.

"Live around here?" Myles asked in a neighborly fashion.

"Yep, m' liver's right here where it belongs," he said pounding his midsection with the thumb side of his fist. "What's it to ya?"

"Oh, I was just wondering how much for one of your pianos," Myles said.

"Beg pardon?"

"Isn't that your truck out there?"

"'Fraid not," the man said and took a swig of beer.

"Sorry, my mistake," Myles said retreating. It was definitely the same person who got out of the van, but Myles saw no benefit in pushing it. He turned to the source of sudden piano music. The automatic player piano was working. He turned back to see that Killjoy had vanished.

The man who was standing next to Killjoy turned around and introduced himself as the owner of the bar. "Do you know him?" he said with only the piano to gesture to as it played *Out of Nowhere*.

"That a Green and Heyman thing," Myles said.

"No, I mean the fella who just left," said the owner.

"I don't believe so," Myles said in all honesty. "Just who is he? I mean, who does he *think* he is?"

"That's Octavius Killjoy," the owner said. "I just handed him a check for this instrument he delivered a few days ago."

Myles swallowed and showed restraint as the player-less piano mocked him with its look-ma-no-hands performance. He had love for the music but boiling contempt for the empty insult. "Wouldn't you rather have live musicians?"

"I can't afford live musicians. They take too many breaks."

"Really?" Myles said flatly. He could feel his temples throbbing. "Well how much does a piano like this cost?"

"Ten thousand dollars. Continuous music, no talking to the girls, no asking for raises, and for me, no hassles with the city about cabaret licenses."

"That's rich," Myles muttered. "It must be the deluxe model that can do Erroll Garner, Thelonious Monk, Oscar Peterson, and Bill Evans."

"I don't know names, but names don't matter to me as long as I can get music without ever having to write anymore checks," he said. "Yes, with this baby, it could be the beginning of a beautiful friendship."

Myles was beginning to see that this joker was going to require a lot more work than the time he had to spend on trying to convert him. They stood and watched as the keys finished the tune and immediately launched into *Bye Bye Blackbird.*

"I understand Octavius has a silent partner in this business," the owner tried to joke.

"Yeah? Well, his silent partner needs to learn how to shut up, doesn't he?" Myles said as he excused himself from the remainder of the tune's ghostly player. A cobweb tickled his face as he left a haunted barroom. Outside, the sound from a nearby street corner had the flavor of New Orleans' French Quarter. A Black man wearing a white t-shirt and a brimmed straw hat was stomping time with his foot as he ate a Cajun harmonica sandwich. Who couldn't love that tasty sass of jazz origins! It was an elixir for the past sour hour. As he moved on, the recall of his hometown was a work in progress. He could have bet an arm and a leg that among the many souls coursing the sidewalks, beautiful jazz standards were playing in the only indelible venue for those enthusiasts, the mind.

"*No, no, you can't take that away from me*," he sang.

A higher skyline rose above wider streets with the same old potholes. He passed a large digital clock on a building and remembered it was about the time that Les would be ending his shift. The plan was to hook up at the *Dreamland Café* in south Minneapolis to sharpen the fishhooks for landing some walleyed gigs.

Myles arrived early and relaxed behind his steering wheel as he waited outside the café and smiled as the approaching taxicab in his rearview mirror grew large enough to stop directly behind him. The engine of those wheels-for-hire died with a few lingering knocks, and if that taxi had a tongue, it would be hanging out. The vehicle appeared to be listing on the port side, undoubtedly under the weight of all those tips. It was indeed Les, the drummer. They got out and went into the Black-owned music café and sometimes after-hour joint whose transparent windows didn't always tell the whole story, according to Les. The picture became clearer when Myles saw Lester's eyes hone in on a bronze shining-bald and paunchy old fellow who had *owner* written all over him.

"You can bake it, you can slice it, and you can toast it," Les cajoled with a playful confrontation, "and then you can butter it and jam it, all you can eat."

"Whas dat?" the owner said.

"That's the bread baby, pay me! Where's my money?"

"Aint got it," said the proprietor as he avoided eye contact.

"You mean to tell me you still can't pay me for a gig that was six months ago?"

"What ah-moan pay you wit?" the owner snapped.

"Dog," Les persisted. "We had a deal. Why didn't you stop us from playing if you couldn't pay us?"

"You was doin' so well I didn't want to disturb you."

"Tell you what," Les bartered, "I won't disturb you while you're out there washing my cab."

There was a long wait for someone to laugh. Myles didn't mean to, in case it was no joke, but he couldn't help it. It had been so long since he'd seen anything like it. A foreign anomaly.

Myles and Les found a table after civil introductions and hatchet burying were done.

"If the Urban Cab Quartet had a singer, who would it be?" Myles asked. "What about *Spoon*?"

"Shirley Witherspoon? She's singing in heaven," Les lamented.

"Bless her," said Myles. "I dug her when she was a kid."

"We all did," Les confirmed, "But for the right now, other vocalists are out there. I just have to beat the bushes to see who would be willing and able."

"Sounds good," said Myles, "and I'm sure we'll be revisiting singers, but we need a good piano. What about that Lawrence noise you were talking about?"

"I was just kidding," Les said. "Him? He plays piano like he's wearing a catcher's mitt on each hand."

"No way."

"No lie," Les said. "He needs them, though. What else is he going to use to catch the tomatoes that people throw at him?"

"Alright, alright, forget it," Myles said. "You know this town, man. Who's still around?"

"Now that you reminded me, I've got a card from another drummer, a brother, about a piano player." Les took the card out of his shirt pocket and handed it over.

Myles was studying some writing on the back, moving it close and far from his sight as he tried to make it out. "It says here he's 84D. What's up with eighty-four D?"

Les took it back to read the un-seen side. "Oh, that just reads, 'HE'S BAD'," he said. "The guy who referred him has handwriting issues."

"Well, if he's all that *good*, I assume he's playing a lot."

"You'd be surprised at how many good cats are wasting away at home and just playing a stray precious gig every now and then. They're all under the heel of oppression."

"Who is he?"

"Weston Everson, an older player who fell on hard times in Denver and came here a few months ago to live with his daughter. He drives for Checker Cab."

"Can he still play any piano, man?" Myles kidded.

"Can he still play?" Les echoed in a higher voice. "When he plays, the spirits of dead elephants giggle as he tickles their ivories. On top of that, he can play in every key including Florida Key."

"Can we get him?" Myles calmly asked. "Old players know more tunes."

"We've got his number. We can try," Les said. "He's one of those drivers who work the eleven-to-seven shift, trying his best to keep the evening hours open in case of gigs."

"Sounds like a winner," Myles said "I'll cold-call him in a day or so. It would be a pleasure to do a gig with him."

"Don't look now, but guess who just walked in," said Les out of the corner of his mouth.

"That piano player?" said Myles with his back to the entrance.

"No, it's the gnat."

"The gnat?"

"Yeah, the union man," Les said dryly. "He's been after me, but I'll join the union just as soon as hell freezes over."

The direction of the footsteps was predictable. The union man was now at their table, standing over them authoritatively and looking straight at Les from under the brim of a shady black hat. "How about it?" he said in a gruff manner.

"How about *what*?" Les snapped. "Do I have to be in the union to drink beer?"

The union man was stumped into a bubblehead shake as his baleful face turned to Myles. "Whadda you play, bub?"

"I play the *miendeenma*," said Myles.

"What this hell is a miendeenma? One of them polka instruments?"

"Miendeenma own business," Myles said. "I'm over here on loan from Copenhagen, and it's an ax I brought over here with me."

"Well, where *is* it?" the union man's patience was wearing thin already.

"It's in my soul," Myles said with serenity.

The union man's head continued to bobble as he tried to think of an appropriate amount of union dues for the soul.

Myles had no idea that he'd come all the way from the other side of the world to watch a cartoon. He glanced at the popcorn popper. It was cold and empty. His eyes followed the union man's path far across the room to the couple of other fellow conversing over some brass instruments on their tabletop. The body language over there said it all, that the union man was a menace. Words could not be heard, but those musicians were seen putting their instruments back in cases.

"You'd better be nice to him," Myles smiled. "You might need him to go to bat for you some day in a tough workplace dispute."

"Can a toothless lion chew a tough steak?" Les queried.

"Not that I've ever heard of," Myles said.

"Thank you."

They left the place and moved on down the road. Les suggested stopping at the Rainbow Coffee House, a long stones-throw away. It was Jazz talent night as billed by a scrawled sign taped to the front door of the mortar brick storefront. The young musicians playing on the stage had the sounds of escapees from a monster called practice. Only the future would hold the outcome of their musical lives through the tune they were playing, *How High the Moon*. They were youngsters learning to swim, one toe in the water at a time. It was a toe jam, an interested breeding ground for the future of jazz.

Myles and Les exchanged looks of raised eyebrows and nods.

"It's good to see," said Myles, "because it gives you the feeling that someone will always be there to carry on this beautiful, jet-black color music long after we're gone."

"Amen to that," Les said.

When the tune was over, they approached the fledgling fellows, three eager Blacks and two courageous Whites, with introductions and encouragement. Myles sang the melody of their "*moon*" song by using the bah-bah method. "Play it slower," he said between phrases, "to feel it, live it and really hear it. You're doing' good. Keep it up."

They showed signs of teachability and openness for guidance. While Les demonstrated for the drummer a more relaxed grip on the sticks, saying that White guys may not be able to jump, but they sure can relax. Myles turned to the horns. "I think it would help to put more air in those horns," he said, "and I didn't say play louder. I said put more air in your tone. Give that ax some of your life. Another thing that's helpful is to wear yourselves out practicing scales, all keys, up and down, over and over every week," he said proud to be looking at such a promising group of sponges. "Good luck, guys."

As Myles and Les moseyed to the door, peers of those musician walked in and sat down to listen. They were the only other fans in the room thus far, but they were witnesses to the beginning of some kind of greatness up on that stage. They would definitely have the time to see it come to fruition one day, and when they're old and gray, each can look back and say, "I was there." If the world is lucky enough, *their* kids will either be able to participate in this wonderful, cherished musical style, or say the same thing, "*I was there when that musician first started playing.*"

It was nearly a week later, and Myles was crashed in his servant's quarters after a fulfilling day. Hours at the flower shop with his siblings was rejuvenating as usual, and the stops of the day with Les turned up a blind-side gig, and that was great. But it was the call he got from Yvonne in Copenhagen that stirred the winds of jet engines in his mind. She too had just landed a booking for a girl-singer gig and invited him to join her. It was tough to beg out of it, but he had to. Her gig would be starting the same night as the *Urban Cab Quartet* gig, and he was already booked. Myles assured her that he would be winding things down and returning across the ocean after a little refresher course on American gigging. Yvonne was very cool with the experiment and promised to keep the soup hot and the champagne cold. Their exchanges spoke for themselves, expressions of mutual, patient love, and before the transoceanic connection was lost, she teased him with some airy scat singing in his ear. It was bittersweet because she didn't even have the decency to give him time to pick up his bass. But he was all smiles, nevertheless, affectionately patting his airline ticket.

The day of a first gig back in the states, for comparison to Europe, couldn't have come soon enough, but now it was upon him. Myles spent his pre-execution time practicing what he preached, running up and down scales in all keys. The callouses on his fingertips were beginning to crack from under-use, but the actual playing of a job would be a much-needed cure-all as the butterflies in his stomach were being chases out by bats. It was enough with the scales already; it was time to play tunes! He dressed spiffy with tie and jacket before loading the car with his bass and a borrowed amp, not to forget the magnetic pickup. As he headed for the Tyrone Stagehouse Restaurant by the river, Myles was mentally reviewing Lester's briefing on the management turn-over, that the manager who booked the gig left for a better opportunity in Hawaii, and the new Stagehouse manager came in off the street from a bartending job in a Lake Street dive with an employment application that most certainly must have been a pack of lies. When he arrived, he found it to be a place that was as elegant as duck under glass, and as good a fit for a kind of fine music which soothes the delicacies of the inner ear like fine dining romances the tastes of delectable cuisine. It was a short haul from street parking to the interior of a futuristic, bustling room filled with well-dressed, spendthrift diners. Les and pianist Weston Emerson arrived minutes earlier and were beginning to set up. Handshakes all around was a good warm-up.

"This new manager," Myles said under his breath, "does he know our music? Is he a jazz fan?"

"I've heard a little about him," said Les, "because as you know, the grapevine gets around pretty good in the taxi business especially if it's the jazz grapevine."

"Who knew?" Myles kidded.

"Lots of folks," Les chuckled with his bulging eyes like nightlights on the dimmed stage, "they say the only thing he knows about music is how to whistle Dixie, and he does that very well."

"I get the picture," Myles said. "Let's just rise above him."

They started the music on time, and the trio played a marvelous first set of familiar love songs while learning that Weston Emerson was truly a gem at the keyboard. He was definitely *eighty-four D.* Myles played with a perma-smile on his face as he realized that this gig wasn't going to be a fight, including the way Les wove it all together with a tasty thread of excellent subtlety and restraint. He was a real-deal pro. As Myles occasionally glanced around the room, it was difficult to tell if some nods of approval were because of the music or the food. He would prefer not to ask, but instead, let this bubble of bliss grow and burst only if it felt like it.

Near the end of the set, a chubby guy wearing a suit and a gold manager badge appeared on the stage, and with suppressing hand motions, urged them to pipe down. "The diners can't hear themselves chew," he said in an angry whisper.

"Begging your pardon, sir," Myles said, almost as quiet, "but who needs to hear their teeth working on expensive mashed potatoes, soft rolls, and butterknife steaks? Our job is to spare them of that kind of agony."

"We're not paying you for that," the manager whispered through the bulging veins in his neck. "We're paying you to not disturb the diners."

"Interesting," Myles whispered back. "how much are we getting for this?"

"At the moment, fifty dollars each," the manager said going from a whisper to under-the breath audible.

"Wow," Myles exclaimed aloud, "with European tips like that, the paycheck must be wonderful!"

"Hrumph," said the departing manager.

Myles turned to Les, whose shoulders were already shaking with laughter. "Did he say *bah-humbug*?"

Weston Emerson was already into a light, sweet intro with a samba feel. Myles picked it up and put some bottom in it, a half-step up and down, back and forth with the bossa beat. To the surprise of nobody on the planet, the extended intro gracefully swung into Antonio Carlos Jobim's *Corcovado*, all for the purpose of giving the manager *quiet nights*. A lady from a nearby table of affluence scurried to the bandstand and complimented them by neatly laying a twenty-spot at their feet.

Myles already decided before the gig to go *pro bono*, doing the job and splitting his share between the other two. It was just a pleasure to do some American gigging for laughs, and besides, an eighty-five dollar night was the least that these outstanding jazz-playing cab drivers should go home with. As they were playing, Myles joined the others with nods of appreciation for the lady's tip. She did the samba back to her table like someone who had been to Rio de Janeiro a few dozen times, almost as if unaware of being so light-footed to the music. Manners prevailed as all the gentlemen at her table stood until she was seated. The tune played out with a swaying samba tag of diminished volume, bringing the set to a close.

Myles secured his bass and followed the leaders off the stage to a light smattering of dignified applause. "Very nice guys," he said to his long-lost colleagues as they walked to a table in the corner. "I'm honored to be among greatness, and I think we got through to a few people in spite of the manager."

"That's the way it is all over," Les said. "The people are fine. Our problem is managers."

"Only in America," Myles said.

The evening went by fast enough to be earmarked for the list of keepers. Myles didn't know what to expect, but he was thankful that a full house of civilized diners didn't inconvenience themselves by applauding after every single tune, but instead they spent the evening patting feet, rocking shoulders, and swaying heads in time to the music. Those were the true affirmative notes that mattered, if only management could see. Satisfied from their bellies all the way up to their eardrums, those favorable votes were almost all gone except for a couple of lovebird stragglers. The musicians leisurely finished packing up and loading their gear out to the cars before returning inside to tell stories and bullshit around. Any American jazz player worth his salt knows all about the art of waiting to get paid. Patience has to man up and grow the callouses of a fiddler's fingers. After a while, the jokes ran out of gas and their only entertainment was watching the bartender stack chairs on top of the tables.

"Pardon me," Myles said to him, "would you mind telling the manager that the musicians are still out here waiting to get paid?"

"Certainly," the bartender said and went to the office area to deliver the message. He came back in a few minutes saying that the manager would be out shortly, but the jokeless waiting continued into the wee hours. The bartender was finishing up and tried to help out for a third attempt to lure the manager out. He came back with an apology, a twisted mouth, and a wide-armed shrug. Then he put on his be-bop hat, slung a jacket over his shoulder and headed out the door with wishes of good luck. At the musicians table, Weston Emerson was falling asleep with his chin in his hand.

"I'm embarrassed about this," said Les. "I'm sorry bro."

"Don't be," Myles said. "I guess I talk too much about the other side of the ocean. Otherwise, there must be a good reason for it."

Les was slouched down in his chair for comfort. "There may be a reason for it," he said, "but there's no excuse for it. Should we just leave?'

"No!" Myles said abruptly. "Let me try it." He rose from his chair and strode towards the office door. On the way, there was a tune running through his head. From his army band days, he never forgot the finale of Tchaikovsky's *1812 Overture.* In front of the door is where he started loudly vocalizing if not singing *Marche Slave*. Then it was time for the cannons. Raspy or not, he kept the bombastic melody going while he gave the door one-two punches with his fists. It was enough to wake up the dead. The opening door was stopped by the sound of a chain lock and the sight of complete darkness inside. It was the kind of darkness from which no light could escape, like a black hole. There was only the nothingness of a nobody — nobody eyes, nobody ears, nobody mouth, and nobody nose.

"Hey," said a voice through the crack, "what the hell do you mean pounding on my door like that? Are you nuts? Now get the hell out of here before I call the police." A hand reached out of the slit of darkness and tossed an envelope to the floor before the door slammed shut and locked again.

Myles never felt more like a panhandler in his life, but he bent over and picked it up. "Thank you, sir," he said to the door. Chin up, chest out, Myles pulled some dignity from his inner reserves and walked the envelope back to the guys. Inside the envelope was one hundred and fifty dollars in cash which he split between them, taking nothing for himself. He was glad they didn't count it because for the time being, they didn't need to know he was folding and putting an empty envelope in his pocket. They were out the door and at least a dozen paces away when two uniformed security guards ran after them.

"I don't know what this is all about," one of them said, "but the manager needs you guys to leave immediately."

Myles took the document the other guard handed him and stared at it under the streetlight. "'*Please be advised that you are no longer employed at this establishment'*," he read aloud. "By golly, that manager," he said with a knee-slapper of mock disbelief. "How did he ever know we were already gone?"

"Beats me," one of the guards said as they both shrugged and walked back to the entrance.

The players stood and watched them until they were back inside. "I just know you're gonna say this would never happen in Europe," said Les, nipping it in the bud.

"No, I wasn't going to say it this time," Myles chuckled, "but it's true. This was just a big mistake, as big a mistake as a cockroach walking on a white wall in a discount shoe store. But without us, they'll need to put more tenderizer on their steaks."

A few days later, Myles was just leaving another satisfying green thumb shift at the flower shop when he got a surprise call from Weston Emerson. A one-night gig on the Hennepin strip opened up when the regular bassist couldn't make it. Myles appreciated Emerson's recommendation and had only one question. "Yeah, they do play jazz, between legs and tits and comedians," was his answer. Myles welcomed the challenge of playing universal music with strangers, even in a house of burlesque. He was no stranger to back in the day when the music of good quality cats was the pajamas of strip joints. With potluck, he would at least be able to feel the true pulse and see how alive it really is out there. The job description was one elongated set starting with quartet warm-up music for a funny lady billed as *Blue Mime Hein*, this only pantomimist in the world who could make Moms Mabley blush without saying a word. That alone was enough to make him run by the servant's quarters to pick up his bass. After all, a little levity in the mix was just what the doctor ordered. But first, the quartet had a chance to get down with the alto sax playing leader wailing away on a medley of tunes which started with *Embraceable You* and ended with the national anthem of strip clubs, *Satin Doll.* Myles dug into his bass and played that thing with growls for envious alligators.

It was nearly an hour since the musicians finished the opening segment and brought up Suzie Hein with blues in C with a backbeat. As Myles watched from off-stage with the others, he tried to pretend he was in Copenhagen, a place where the gyrations, gestures and eye play of *Blue Mime Hein* would be considered more of a work of art than an obscenity. Wolf-whistles, whoops, and marriage proposals prevailed over minimal laughter while she did her thing. Myles was only there to take the pulse of the jazz scene, but his heart began to beat faster and faster. His eyes widened and his jaw dropped. He was out of his seat and taking tentative steps toward the stage. She had a whole lot of shaking going on, and that shaking was too close to his upright bass for comfort. He wasn't sure, but he could only guess that she must be demonstrating either how to do straight-legged toe touches during an earthquake or how to strum a fiddle with an over-active posterior. Myles stopped in his tracks with a sigh of relief when her performance moved away from the bass. All he knew for sure was that it didn't survive a long flight across the ocean only to be obliterated by an out-of-control booty in a strip joint.

In a while, the group returned to the stage and played a chaser while Suzie picked up her discarded skimpies and took bows to a smattering of applause. She was a step ahead of the vice squad when she closed and locked her dressing room door.

As scheduled, Myles packed it up with the others and hung around for a minute to be sociable even after gratefully accepting the forty dollars pay and thanks from the hornman leader. The stories were the same, only the names were changed to protect the innocent. That old feeling persisted, that the more things change, the more they stay the same. Myles could identify with them as older players, and old players, they don't die, they just played away. After a mellow chat and the exchanging of numbers, Myles resurrected his snoozing fiddle and rolled it to the door, hoping over his shoulder that paths would cross again. On the way out, he slipped the wadded forty dollars in the garter belt of a surprised cocktail waitress. After the door hit him in the butt, he had a sneaking feeling that she would appreciate the extra grocery money.

Myles rolled to the car with some satisfaction about the music part, but he had a tongue-in-cheek thought that one has not lived until seeing dirty jokes by *Blue Mime Hein. Suzie Blue Mime Hein*, he concluded, was a piece of work. For the musicians, the only reason his mind was laughing was to keep from crying.

Time is airborne, and when the earth made two more complete spins, Myles was helping out at his brother Al's carwash as a hand on the drying crew. His last car of the day was a beautifully restored 1970 Chevy Impala with an eight-cylinder 454 engine, dark green exterior, tan interior, and black vinyl top. The customer's radio was tuned to a jazz station which was playing something with the ultra-familiar alto sax style of Cannonball. He thought it was Sam Jones playing the bass, but he wasn't sure, and he hoped he had time to find out as he laid across the front bench seat, putting some extra elbow grease into wiping down the dashboard. His concentration was interrupted by the sound of someone deliberately clearing his throat. It was the car owner, anxious to get going. Myles got out thanking the man profusely for his business.

"That's about as clean as this radio has been since this thing came off the factory assembly line," the man said as he reclaimed his Impala and drove off.

Myles could only conclude that the bass player had to be Sam Jones with that plunky style, because a Ron Charter tended to hold certain notes longer.

"How're ya holdin' up, man?" It was his beaming brother Al.

"Best workout I've had since I was here a few days ago," said Myles with smiles of his own.

To the amusement of the other workers, they playfully snapped their wipe rags at each other like back in the day when they were a couple of kids washing dishes in their mother's kitchen. At the end of a brotherly rag scrap, there was a little lull in business.

"It's all mine now," Al said contently. "Paid it off, baby."

"You're doin' great," said Myles. "I'm proud of you, Bro."

"Thanks, and just to let you know, partnerships are available," Al said in a hinting tone.

Myles folded his arms in thought. "You know, Al, your business could become one of the sponsors of a youth jazz program to encourage young and promising talent out of the closet of fear and into a world of fulfillment by way of available practice facilities and qualified instructors," he said in one amazing breath from a poker face.

"I could be into that in a heartbeat. We're brothers," said Al, "but it could take a while to get enough sponsors to make it work. Me? I try not to look a gift tax write-off in the mouth."

"It's certainly something to think about, isn't it?" Myles smiled.

"I'm sure we'll be doing plenty of that," Al said as he spotted two more dirty cars rolling in and started toward them. Shine was his passion.

"See ya in a minute," Myles said with a wave as he slowly retired his rag, stretched, and headed for his car.

After a quick stop by the servant's quarters to freshen up and grab a ham sandwich, Myles was back out on the town growing more amused by the hour at the scene. He likened it to being back in grade school when they herded all the kids into a dark gymnasium and turned on the movie projector. Mickey Mouse's face suddenly filled the entire screen as childhood cheers filled the gym. There wasn't a single kid who wanted the cartoon to end. Myles was starting to do a sardonic comparison between European and American gig hunting, but the American scene was only a continuation of a long-ago cartoon. He's certainly come to the right place for a laugh after a funeral. For more laughs, he pretended to be pulled around by a divining rod in search of precious jazz, but he was afraid he was going to find water first. But for the kids, the musician cartoon would be much too spooky, like watching musicians-turned-zombies, walking around looking for good gigs until their feet became dry and scaly, similar to walking around on two music schools. Myles snapped out of it before he started scaring himself.

As his ride laced the downtown streets, he caught sight of a recommended hotel and pulled into a convenient parking spot. The recommendation, he recalled, was for other musicians of color to chip away at gaining entrance to the lounge in the Evergreen Hotel, a high-end place with African doormen, East Indian bellhops, Mexican and Somali maids, Middle-eastern room service workers, Chinese laundry skills, French cooks, African American desk clerks, and an all-White jazz group. Myles walked casually through the entrance and to the lounge. To his own ears, there was something odd about the music coming from within. When his eyes focused through the dim lighting, he could see that there was no bass player with the accordion and trumpet. It wasn't too loud, but he immediately felt sorry for a lot of eardrums which deserved better. From the visual ambiance of the room, he figured it didn't take a rocket scientist to see that management certainly could afford to do better. The accommodating lady at the reception stand went to summon the food and beverage manager as he requested. After a few minutes, a man with the posture and look of a praying mantis appeared from behind some tall potted ferns and extended one of his prayerful hands to shake.

"May I help you, sir?"

Myles introduced himself, game for another stranger-on-stranger meeting with another food and beverage honcho. "Yes, I'm in the music business," he said, "and I'd like to get an appointment to discuss getting a real nice group a spot on your music rotation."

"Rotation? Rotation?" the manager laughed. "Did someone tell you that we have a music rotation?"

"No, but you *do*, don't you?" Myles probed.

"Newww," the manager said quietly with the head-shaking emphasis of a sledgehammer. "These musicians are the best. They don't need any rotation."

"Yes, well y' see, that's what I'd like to talk to you about," Myles said. "Rumor has it that those guys haven't had a vacation for ten years. We could fill in with a fresh, ear-friendly breeze off your stage until those guys get back. How about a two-week gig? We're reasonable."

"And what do you play?"

"I play bass fiddle," Myles said proudly.

"Bass fiddle?" Bass fiddle?"

"Yeah."

"Oh, no, absolutely not! A bass fiddle is an obscene instrument," the manager said. "We have nice ladies who come in here. They would be offended by the sight of one of those things and the vulgar sounds that it makes. Nope. I couldn't permit that. This is a *family* rated place, sir."

Myles was rocking back on his heels with dumbfounded amazement. "You bite your tongue about my axe, sir," Myles said with his anger on a short leash. "You are talking about one of the most regal and friendly instruments ever invented and furthermore, your . . . ladies . . . must lead very sheltered lives."

"Have a nice day, sir," the manager said as he disappeared somewhere back behind the potted ferns.

It was a no-brainer. Myles already decided that it was somebody else's turn to try breaking down the Evergreen stage door. He surmised with a smile of resignation that breaking a barrier at the Evergreen was an on-going musician joke that he unwittingly walked into. The truth was staring him right in the face. Hell would freeze over before a Black musician would ever play the room. On his way out of the hotel, a smiling uniformed African doorman swung the huge glass panel open for him.

In stride, Myles nodded and slapped a buck in his big open palm. He had a burning wish to be a fly on the wall in the upper-management penthouse office where music decisions are made. But it was probably one burning wish which might become just another smoldering pile of cinders by the time he got back on an airplane. Myles could take some comfort in believing that before hell freezes over, it would at least be a great place to keep a hell of a lot of irons in the fire. He remembered Lester's booking from weeks ago at another place, and tomorrow was that day. The musicians were already contacted into agreement and the Urban Cab Quartet would converge on The Wishbone in the warehouse district for a gig he was looking forward to with great anticipation. The seed was planted to motivate the other quartet members to go out with their own chisels and hammers to relieve their own gigs from the granite block of stubborn venues.

The next day, Myles thought he would be the earliest, but he arrived in front of The Wishbone at the same time as the others. With the first of their equipment loads in hand, they couldn't make it to the front steps of the place without a couple of jokes. Weston Everson the piano player meticulously laid out the set-up for an x rated bit about a guy walking his ol' lady's dog. Myles was only laughing because of father time's failure to bury a joke he'd heard thirty years ago on the way to another gig, but he would keep that fact to himself without ruining it for Weston Emerson.

"Hear me out, hear me out. You're going love this," Weston said as the siren of an ambulance put the punch line on hold.

With their equipment getting heavy, they waited out the distractive whoops, wails, and light show of the ambulance by starting up the seven steps to the front door. Myles set his bass down, gripped the door handle and pulled three times. They gave him a little ribbing for being too old and weak to open a lousy door. He pulled again. The unmistakable sound of the deadbolt was a punch in the jaw. The orange page taped to the glass suddenly had fine-line pencil writing on it. If it was a snake, it would've bitten them.

"*'We are closed for good,'*" Myles read aloud. "*'Thanks for your patronage.'*"

The ambulance, the jokes, and the inside lights were gone. All was quiet. "Well, boys, looks like this wishbone broke the wrong way," Les said with dejection. "And what really bothers me about this is that this fool had my phone number."

Myles saw the situation as the punch line to a dirty joke he'd heard many times before. "Don't worry about it," he comforted, "it won't be the last."

"I know good and well that it won't be," Les agreed, "but it sure makes you feel like it's the last."

"Maybe they think they're funny," Weston said.

"Yeah, well this is about as funny as a rubber crutch," Les said. "Look, let's all forget about this and go down the street to this soul food place. I'm buying."

Myles loaded up and followed U-turn taxis to a soul sulk.

They made it down the road to the restaurant, *The Down Home Diner*, tried the door and found it open, and settled into a booth in the corner. It was like coming from a battle in the gremlin war and landing in a safe foxhole.

"No matter the country we're in," Myles said, "we're still colleagues of a culture, we're brothers pulling for each other. When these things happen to us in America, our music cries out in pain in Copenhagen, China, or wherever we are around the world. But all it's doing is making us stronger in our resolve to not be forgotten,"

"Myles, my alien colleague," Les said. "You're pretty good at saying grace. Let's eat."

The server, a middle age soul sister with a smile returned with the beer they ordered and backed off to give them time to decide.

"What's good?" Myles said as he scanned the menu. A puzzled look slowly clouded a previously upbeat face.

"Everything, everything," Les said reassuringly.

"I thought you said we were going to a soul food place," Myles inquired.

"That's exactly where we're at," Les said as he pointed directly at a string of entrees in plain sight. "See right there you have pan fried sole, baked sole, broiled sole, breaded sole. It's all good sole food."

Trying to maintain a decent deadpan. Myles looked him over like a hawk eying a desert rat. "Have you ever thought about auditioning for the Gong Show?"

"I tried out. I didn't make it," Les said with a grin. A laugh could always kill the taste of the lockout fish.

"It reminds me of when I first arrived in Europe through Amsterdam," Myles fished his memory, "and I found out that *Dam* became known as a safe haven for Black Panthers. The people of Holland knew that the panthers weren't like today's murdering gangs of the hood, but instead, just standing up to protect Black folks from murdering rogue police officers. Amsterdam embraced them as heroes, protected them from American persecution and false prosecution. I wasn't a panther, but I felt that embrace when I first got there. That umbrella of protection was in the air for a brother with an afro. American news photos showed the panthers with all the guns and bandolero, but they forgot to tell people that it was only a symbolic show of strength. All the way across the pond. Dutch people didn't have to be told that rampant mass shooting sprees were not really part of the program. I hooked up with some jazz musicians right away, Black and White players. Gigs were plentiful. They wanted to show me the local ropes and started out by inviting me to a restaurant where you could get free cash. 'You mean real free cash?' I asked. 'Yes, real free cash,' they swore up and down it was true. Well, this is a country that helped the panthers? And now restaurants are giving away free money? I pinched myself asking, 'Tell me for real, where am I?' I thought, what the hell, what could be better than picking up a pocketful of them ol' Dutch guilders to tide me over until I got a gig. Needless to say, they talked me into it because I was also hungry. When we got there and took our seats, my head was on a swivel looking for somebody to start passing out Dutch greenbacks. As visions of solvency were building up in my head, the server brought the menus, and that's when Red, a horn player who became one of my good musician buddies said to try what he was pointing out on the menu. I guess it's an international thing, musicians pointing out things on a menu. I gotta tell ya, I was so deflated when my eyes focused on the words at the tip of Red's finger. It read, *freak hash."*

The others woke up with a laugh.

"They didn't mean any harm," Myles said with a tone of fraternal supportiveness, "and besides it served me right for foolishly presuming the growth of money on trees. So, everyone ordered *freak hash*, and by golly, it was the best hash and coffee I ever had. Later on, I learned to navigate those Amsterdam canals and kept coming back for take-out orders of *freak hash*. The only thing getting rich was my belly."

After orders were taken, it wasn't long before the waitress brought them some sole. More told and untold musician stories came up for enough air to blow The Wishbone out of mind. The silver lining of it was the camaraderie for a next time. Myles felt right at home with the universal cohesiveness of the art and the artists. Being in a country that played by a different set of charts didn't diminish the important thing of togetherness. On a day to remember, they ate sole for the sake of the soul.

Myles agreed to join them the next afternoon for another Lester Ride gig. Taxicabs from various companies lined the curb in front of a south suburban residence. The drivers, all ten of them, answered the call and hauled instrument cases from their trunks and assembled efficiently on the front lawn, being careful not to step on the flowers. Shining instruments were mated with mouthpieces while sticks and fingers waited for the cue. Sitting with one cymbal and one snare drum, Lester gave pianist Weston Emerson the finger-snapping tempo to start some intro chords on his battery-powered keyboard. Softly and harmoniously, they swung into Cole Porter's I love you. Stroking his bass with feeling, Myles excavated the tune with enough bottom to fall into.

The front door of the home opened, and a well-dressed, white-haired man walked out cautiously and leaned on his front porch railing with both hands. Neighbors on both sides of the house and across the street were lured out of their homes by the sounds, chairs in hand, and sat down to listen to what was to be an extremely short concert. With a puzzled look on his face, the targeted man on the porch listened patiently to the whole sweet tune, and when it played out, the air was open for discussion. Myles agreed to come along on this outing after hearing about the plight of musician-cabbie Birchwood Winters at yesterday's fish fry. Birchwood lost his driver's license on a DWI, and recently suffered a fall from a ladder which broke both ankles, all of which caused him to fall far-enough behind in is rent to be facing eviction. He was laid up and unable to make the gig, but they were all there on his behalf. They were brothers.

"Please mister landlord," Les stepped forward and pleaded, "can you find it in your heart to give Birchwood Winters a little more time before you kick him out? We're sure he can work something out with just a little more time, right guys?"

They all agreed with a *yeah* in unison. It was pure theatre for the neighbors.

"Well," said the man, still leaning on his rail, "I've owned buildings and rented units for a lot of years, but this is the first time I've ever seen anyone serenading their own eviction."

Myles started the chant, and the others picked it up, *"Give him some more time, sir. Give him some more time! Give him some more time, sir. Give him some more time!"*

The man raised his hands, more for the sake of quiet than for sweet surrender. "It's too late," he said, "eviction papers for Mr. Winters have been filed and are already in the works. I'm sorry, but we all know it's just a pay-as-you-go business. I've got a waiting list."

"Can't you give him 'till the end of the month?" asked a voice from the ranks.

The landlord put his head down, hands clasped behind him. Then he lifted his face. "Tell you what," he said, "for the song, I'll put him up for a week at the Francis Drake Hotel. It's the best I can do." He left his card on the rail and went back inside.

The audience of neighbors couldn't complain, because they didn't have to buy tickets to the event. Their chairs followed them back indoors.

Being only a guest in town, Myles deferred to Les to pick up the business card. "We'll think of some other options for Birchwood," he said.

There were handshakes all around and the musicians packed up and headed back to their cabs. There was still a living to be made.

Myles had world-class experience putting a cased bass fiddle into a regular automobile by lowering the backrest of the shotgun seat so the instrument can slide body-first into the back seat while the fingerboard and scroll pointed the way, blues. He followed the direction pointed and cruised around until he found himself at Snoose Boulevard on the West Bank. The sign of a place caught his eye, and he pulled into a near-by parking spot and observed the doorway of the place for a couple of minutes. Black and While people mingling around looked like remnants of the *hippy* era with ragged blue jeans, afros, long-hairs, beards, and beads. They were the ones who had already taken their turn to give peace a chance. They asked nicely, but it never came. Myles knew he had enough gray hair to blend in with these people, so he used his fingers to puff out his thinning afro as much as possible before putting some hipness into getting out, locking the car, and a strut down the sidewalk like a man with a new spring in one leg.

Amplified live music was coming through the propped-open door of *The Broken Drum Bar*. It was a throwback to when he first arrived in Amsterdam all those years ago, once again giving them the feeling that the more some things change, the more they stay the same. Myles stood just inside the door and glanced around the crowded, hazy room. On the shallow stage, bluesman guitarist known on posters and sandwich boards as *Crazy Bill*, strummed and wailed the I-*Didn't-Know-It-Was-You -Till-I-saw-Your-Shoe-Flyin'-Blues*. Myles found a standing-room listening spot, sipped a beer and kept time with the music by patting the pocket with the plane ticket inside. *Crazy Bill* was good listening for ageless ears.

Myles made his last stop in the area with a raid of some minds at the West Bank School of Music, in an attempt to scrounge up any and all information, rumors or scuttlebutt about the latest on fiddle strings. "Stay tuned," they said. He was feeling like an astronaut on the moon, running low on oxygen, but determined to turn over a few more rocks of green cheese before his return home.

It was after nine-thirty before Myles was back at the servant's quarters with his bass, relaxing by practicing the head to *Green Dolphin Street* while thinking about missing Yvonne and the home they built with the brick and mortar of togetherness. He thought of calling her but didn't want to awaken her at four-thirty in the morning. Noon tomorrow would be perfect. His stomach was still full from the planned fried chicken and barbeque ribs dinner at his mother's house with his brother Al and sister Althea. After a satisfying session with the tune, he and his fingers agreed it was time to put the bass down and crash on his bed of creaks. When the noise settled down, he could hear his memory playing some of the favorite tunes of his far-away, golden-era record album collection. He imagined playing footsie with her as they lay side-by-side on the floor, flickers of light from the fireplace dancing on the ceiling. His mental stack of vinyl would continue to drop down the spindle to the spinning turntable and caressing needle, until there were no more grooves to conquer. With fondest thought of Yvonne, Myles kissed his pillow's lip and succumbed to the sweet intoxication of sleep.

His early-morning phone talk with Les gave the rising sun a chance to brighten the blue sky, but it was Les' voice which carried a dark cloud of bad news. Myles got ready within an hour and headed to the entrance of the Southside Hospice of Greater Minneapolis. Les was waiting there with gloom in his eyes. "It's Royster Bottoms," he said.

"I know, you told me," said Myles, "and I was trying to remember the last time I saw him before I left the country."

"Good bass player," Les said, "but he hasn't been on the scene for quite a while. He's an old man with a liver ruined by years of being a serious alcoholic, and his time is almost up, so the doctors and social workers had him transported here to die."

"Didn't anyone ever try to help him?"

"He dried out a few times," Les said, "but he just couldn't stop having harder and harder falls off the wagon. Right now, he's too old and too Black to get a new liver, so he's a goner."

Myles shoved his hands in his pockets and looked at the floor. "I wish I could wave a wand and make him better," he said.

"You're waving a wand just by being here," Les said. "I wanted another bass player to come by and talk to him. Somebody he could identify with. Thanks, man. You guys speak the same language through your strings."

"No problem. Where is he?"

"Follow me," Les said as he got the nod from the desk attendant to go down the hall and up some stairs.

"How should I act?"

"I don't know if you remember," Les said, "but he still tells corny jokes. Just play along with it and let him tell his corny jokes and laugh if you possibly can. It would make him feel good to have a last shot to entertain somebody."

"I understand," Myles said as their hike brought them to room eight-six where Royster Bottoms was being made comfortable. Taped to the door was an oversized musical score sheet with the notes of a tune written out in detail. They both saw it simultaneously and stopped on a dime. Myles counted off with his snapping fingers, and they started scatting in unison.

> "*Sha-dahba dop doo-dobba doo-dop!*
> *Sha-dahba dop doo-dobba doo-dop!*
> *Sha-dahba dop doo-dobba doo-dop!*
> *Sha-dahba dah, sha-dabba dah . . .*"

They fell against the wall with laughter, mostly because they read it right. "Yep, that's Monk," Myles said.

"*Well, You Needn't*," Les pinpointed with a grin.

"The musician who hung that up certainly did it to suggest that Royster Bottoms needn't leave planet Earth," Myles said.

They gathered themselves and entered the room with semi-somber looks on their faces, but a laugh was just a stone's throw away. A doctor wearing a smock and not stethoscope greeted them solemnly. The sight of Royster Bottoms was shocking. One side of his upper lip was frozen with a nose-crowding sneer and his eyes were two white orbs with the irises rolled out of sight.

"He's in what is known as a *chordotonic stupor*," said the African American doctor. "His mind was functionally blocked by one-too-many extraordinary musical chords, and the last one just blew him away," he said.

Myles and Les exchanged looks of horror.

"We have his bed speaker on several hours a day with computer-generated chords," the doctor continued, "and none is the same. Maybe one will snap him out of it."

"Is this all on the level?" Myles asked incredulously.

"It's all in the chords, and it was one that was just too much for him."

Myles was running a lot of weird composers through his mind. "What do you suppose it was?"

"Well, I think it was a C-seven," the doctor said.

"Boy! He really must be super sensitive," Myles laughed apologetically.

"It don't make no sense to me either," said Royster Bottoms, his face re-aligning properly as he weakly joined the laugh from his death bed. The snickering doctor removed his smock, busting himself down to just another fellow musician of the slush pump variety. He introduced himself with sincerity before leaving to attend to his double-parked taxi.

Royster Bottoms looked pale, but he was still smiling about another one of his little home-spun antics.

"I want you to meet another bass player," Les said as he introduced him to Myles.

Royster's hand was weak, but they did the secret everlasting bassist handshake. They were brothers of tamed catgut.

"Good jazz musicians are like sparkling gems," Royster Bottoms said, softly enough to draw ears closer to his words, "so at sessions or gig, you just have to listen for the glisten."

"I agree," Myles said as he pulled up a chair to be closer. "We're listenin' for a good horn, and lord knows a good horn is hard to find."

"You from around here?"

"I was born here, and I used to be from here," said Myles, "but I've lived in Denmark half my life, and I'm here now visiting family."

"When I die, I'll give you all my gigs, but only if you promise to get a day job to live on," Royster said.

"Well . . . that's . . .that's generous of you," Myles said trying to play along, "and I'll be sure to make you proud of me."

For a sick man, Royster Bottoms reeked of mischief. "Say, man, what's this? *Squeedly-deedly wop! Soo-beeo. . .".* His eyes were closed, and his hands mimicked the fingering of an instrument he did not have. "*Squeedly-doo, whee-deedly wop! Squeedly-wop, whee-deedly wop! Squee-wop, squee-wop, Squeedly-wop!"* He stopped and opened his eyes widely, anticipating a sure correct guess.

Myles pondered the question and hung his head, pretending to think. He then shot a glance at Les who shrugged his eyebrows instead of his shoulders. "Is it an Italian trying to play the sax?" Myles answered.

"Naw, man," Royster Bottoms said slightly above a whisper. "You know what I mean."

"Sorry," Myles said, "but maybe it would help if I knew who was playin' those licks."

"Him? Oh man, he plays a mean horn."

"What kind of horn?"

"A car horn."

"Is that car horn in the union?" Myles asked with a reserved smile.

"It'll never let you know," Royster said, reserving his own smile.

"Now there's a car horn with a future," Myles said as he got an A-OK sign from Les for being a good actor.

Royster beckoned Myles to lean closer. "Say, man, what did the hooker do when she ran into the medical examiner at the end of the block?"

"I don't know. What?" asked Myles with mild curiosity.

"Sh. . .sh. . .she turned a coroner."

"That's terrible," Myles blurted out before correctively remembering his role, "terrible that is for all those people who didn't get to hear you tell that."

It was too late to wait for a crowd. Royster Bottoms was already cackling away like a man in pain but with a spirit of gold, and he wasn't through. "Say man. What 'cha call a hooker who retires to go an' live in Alaska?"

Myles let out a long sigh and thought about the higher, but unmentionable regard that people of another country have for ladies of the evening. "What?" he finally said.

"Nome whore," Royston Bottoms groaned.

Myles had a sympathetic look on his face like he was bulldog-certain that the medication was causing this as Les demonstrably mimicked a hopefully contagious smile. It was enough of a hint to get Myles to put on his good-sport hat by showing some, but not all of his teeth. "So . . . how about this nice weather we're having," he said trying to forge a new avenue.

"Yeah, it's just the opposite of one time back in the day," Royster Bottoms said with a slightly stronger voice as a nostalgic look tickled his white-bearded black face. "It was cold and snowin' outside, a day before Thanksgiving. My girlfriend had a live pet hen in her house for a couple of years. She called that hen *Bestyke*. Good ol' *Bestyke hen* turned out to be a great Thanksgiving dinner. We had *Bestyke hen* stew and high-yellow salad. A day after that, we took off for New Orleans. Them was the days, boys."

Myles and Les were left sitting there with the smiles of two well-fed Cheshire cats. "Are you into Dixieland jazz?" Myles asked.

"Oh, I'm modern," said Royster, "but I do love Dixieland."

"You're better than me," Myles said. "I only like Dixieland."

"Northern blood needs to love Dixie," Royster insisted. "We're from down there."

"You got family roots down Dixie way?" Myles asked politely.

"Yeah, my family roots are there, and so are yours, my brothers," Bottoms said. "From way down there to way up here to all three of us, we're family . . . jazz family."

"Good point," Myles said as he joined Les' nod of agreement.

"Oh yeah, man, there's a lot to love about the land of Dixie, named after the *dix*, the ten-dollar bill," said Royster Bottoms, his eyes drifting off dreamlike while he used a sweep of his hand to accentuate his words. "It's Louisiana, the land of the Spanish moss, the gray beard mushy strands hanging from the trees."

"You're scaring me Royster," Myles said.

"I'm sorry," said Bottoms. "I didn't mean to remind you of a lynching, but other things really do hang from trees, you know. Dixie is also the land of Cajun, one-pot cooking," he said with a sweep of his other hand. "The beautiful Black, Spanish, French, and Mexican mix of Creole."

"I'm feeling better already," Myles said.

"I knew you would," said Royster as he placed a hand on his chest as if he was about to sing *my country 'tis of thee*, because it was a land that was spared from Civil War destruction right down to the last parish, to become a place where nobody goes to hell, even though some should." Now his arms were extended wide. "Because everybody is buried above ground," he said.

Myles was trying his best to remember who's show it was, he could only drop his head in sorrow at one man's irreverence for the angels. "If it's that good, why did you leave?"

"It's a nice place to visit, but I'm up here because a Black man down there has a better chance of getting beat to a pulp by the police just for being Black. A good innocent, upstanding friend of mine with a wife and three kids was pulled over one night on his way home from work. For no good reason, he was tenderized to death under a barrage of police night sticks. So, you see, I ran a long, long way for a long, long time trying to get away from that, but as I look back, I haven't gotten very far, have I?"

"I guess none of us have," Myles said.

"But that doesn't mean we have to forget where it all started," Royster Bottoms said, "*The Big Easy* was the start of Dixieland carved in stone. Actually, it's a cement square in the sidewalk, a plaque honoring Buddy Bolden. He's the turn-of -the -century trumpet player who invented the art of jazz."

"Scott Joplin just opened one eye," Myles said.

"Maybe," Royster said, "but he would understand that the more honors given to the origins of a wonderful music, the better. They deserve some love and some light."

"Absolutely," Myles said.

"The *Beethovens* of the world got carved in stone for classical," Royster said, "so pass the chisel and hammer. Hell, Beethoven could be a colored man from down home. He got some rhythm."

Myles glanced over to see Les nodding for him to play along. "I feel ashamed that I didn't know that before now," he said. "Tell me more."

"Beethoven must've been a colored man," Royster Bottoms claimed, "because he understood syncopation."

"Nah, German," Myles said.

"Whaddya want? Beethoven had to be a colored man. His head was nappy."

Myles had his eyes closed while shaking his head very slowly, "German," he said as calmly as he could.

"Look, as famous as he still is, Beethoven didn't get paid much money, so he *must* have been a colored man."

Myles was growing roots as the Rock of Gibraltar, "German."

"Beethoven probably threw the ball that Scott Joplin caught," Royster Bottoms persisted.

Myles still had his eyes closed with his head still slowly shaking negatively. "Hard to believe," he said, open-eyed and ready for the wind to blow open some more pages of a comic book.

"I've got an idea how we can settle this," Les said, nipping a bitter stalemate in the bud. "Let's do some research to find out if Beethoven ever ate chitlins, because if we find out he ate chitlins, it's a good bet that Beethoven is a colored man."

The sound of tiny crickets was a laugh from the throat of Royston Bottoms. He grabbed both of them by a sleeve and pulled them closer. "We would know for sure Beethoven is a colored man if we find out he puts hot sauce on his chitlins," he said under his frail breath. "A White Beethoven wouldn't have the guts to put hot sauce on his chitlins."

For a change, Myles laughed of his own initiative. "I'm glad there's a way to put it to rest," he said standing for a solo ovation.

"Say, man," Royster continued, "What 'cha call a boxin' match between two hornets?"

"It's probably way over my head," said Myles full of smiles. "What?"

"*Bee-Bop*."

"In what key?" Myles countered.

"Whiskey," Royster played.

"I'll drink to that," said Myles trying to stay with him. "But tell me, Royster, what was your best gig?"

"Royster Bottoms took a deep breath and rolled his bag-laden eyes in thought. "I guess I've had a lot of best gigs," he said, "but when I was a much younger man living in Washington D.C., I got in with some players who had contacts for grass roots functions. You know how those people like to party. It was a blast, man especially the time we played at one of President Kennedy's inauguration parties."

"Impressive memory," Myles said.

"Well, the party was great even though the president was a no-show. Still, it was pretty cool just being there," Royster Bottoms recalled with pride.

"That's good," said Myles, "because it was probably the president's idea to include some jazz. He probably thought jazz in America is like the canary in a coal mine, and that there's a connection between the health of jazz and the health of American society."

"In that case, I'm glad I'm going to be leaving this life," Royster said with a sigh.

"Why?" Myles asked.

"Because I don't want to be around when the only place you'll be able to hear jazz is on the elevators, and that day is coming soon," Bottoms said.

"Not if I can help it," Myles assured him.

"Git 'em tiger," said Royster.

"By the way," Myles blind-sided. "Who is your favorite drummer?"

"Chano Pozo," Royster said without hesitation. "He was spectacular! Mentored a lot of people before he was killed in a 1948 street attack. Look, don't call him anybody's angel, just call him a *dynomite* Cuban drummer. Oh yeah, when I hear Cuban or Afro-Cuban drumming I always listen for his influence," he said.

"I never heard of him," said Myles.

"Maybe it's just that you think you never heard of him," Royster Bottoms said. "He reminds me of the tribal war drums and communication drums with all the tribal and territorial chants and dancing from the jungles and plains of Africa to the shores of North America and Cuba."

"I get it," Myles conceded. "You're sayin' it's in our blood."

"I'm sayin' all those talents started to come together from a heritage of bondage," Royster said. "For something so ugly, slavery laid a golden egg called jazz. Carry it on, boys, if you can."

"Your wish is our command," Myles said with a promise that was durable as a bubble. He couldn't help noticing Royster's fingers laced across his tummy while his thumbs twirled around each other like the rotor blades of a lawnmower. It was either the sign of a thinking man or the devil's workshop.

"Say man, what 'cha call a hooker who tries to be a model on top of a block of ice?" Royster queried.

"Not a clue," Myles said.

"*Ice-pose ho*," Royster said from the bottom of his heart.

Myles blubbered his lips like a man on the tundra. "Why do you s'pose you're so cold to *working girls*?" Myles probed.

"I know 'em, I don't hate 'em," Royster Bottoms said. "But hookers have played a big part in shaping the public image of our venues."

"You mean to tell me hookers need to learn how to be better architects?"

"Only if they want to," Royster said. "But when people hear the words *jazz club*, they think bad things. They think the jazz club is at the top of the list of where hookers hang out. I've never liked the association. Because of them, conservative politicians are always trying to find ways to shut us down. In fact, this shit goes way back. Before the turn of the last century, a fella named Sidney Story sponsored a bill to limit prostitution by clamping down on jazz. Around New Orleans, they called it *Storyville*."

"Really? What happened?"

"The law didn't work," Royster said. "Jazz and hookers just kept on going until death us do part."

"What about all the ladies of the evening who show up at symphony concerts or rock concerts or ball parks?" Myles asked kindly. "Do politicians try to shut those places down too?"

Royster Bottoms was speechless as he pondered the question. "I guess you got me there," he said.

"All the more reason why they should be legalized like they are in Copenhagen," said Myles. "Over there, ladies of the evening and politicians are good friends."

"And bedfellows?"

"I don't know," Myles said, "it was never my day to watch them, but before I forget, I'd be interested to know who your favorite sax player is?"

"Trane," Royster Bottoms said quickly in an ever-stronger voice. "John Coltrane is the best thing that ever happened to the saxophone since Adolphe Sax invented the damn thing in 1846."

"God bless Adolphe's parents for not blowing it," Myles said with a smile that was causing *mother* Les to relax.

"You've got that right," Royster said, "but you've also gotta bless John Coltrane for being able to carry a tune on a golden platter."

"Amen," said Myles. "So, tell me, what's your only regret?"

"My only regret? My only regret is that marijuana didn't get nationally legalized while I was still alive."

"Are you a ghost?"

"Not a chance," Royster winked, "but I couldn't' wait to see how many hundreds of cops started smoking joints and inhaling, talkin' 'bout '*Schooop! You're under arrest, man.*'"

"Lord help us," Myles said.

"I also wish I had tried it just once," Royster said, intermittently swooping air while trying to talk through a held breath. "Just to see what all the fuss is about, you know."

"I know, I know," Myles said.

"I'm old, but maybe if I had tried it, I'd be living longer," Royster said with tiny words barely escaping his throat from the same held breath of a veteran weed head. His liver loved it when he finally exhaled and resumed breathing. The walls of the hospice room could only smile.

"If you had one last wish, what would it be?" Myles asked. "What do you wish for our music?"

"Two wishes," Royster Bottoms said. "First, I wish the record companies weren't callin' the shots. They don't care about ten million true jazz fans out there. Jazz is real music. Instead, record companies want everyone to believe that there are a hundred million rap fans and a billion country western fans out there, so that's all they promote.

Myles couldn't help it. "Only in America," he said.

"Be honest," Royster said, "Is rap real music?"

"It's hard to say," Myles answered, scratching his head. "It might be greener, but it's not my kind of pasture."

"I rest my case," said Royster," and that's only because I'm a dying old man. But, like Duke Ellington once said, 'Jazz is music, swing is business.' Well, we might as well be saying rap is business, never mind the music of jazz."

"How did it ever get like this over here?" Myles asked, as if he didn't already know. He would rather let someone else say it.

"It's a wide conspiracy with evil motivations, but hear me out," Royster said, wagging an index finger. "When the big shot recording industry decides to pull the plug on jazz, it's like major league baseball shutting down all levels of the minor leagues. In either case, it's the youngsters who are left high and dry. They'll lose interest in studying it because they'll think it's not relevant, you know what I mean? So, who replaces the departing jazz superstars?"

Myles could only do a slow and continuous nod in agreement.

"My second wish is for somebody to make sure after I go, to please get me those famous Nairobi grave guys to bury me."

"Oh? Who are they?"

"*Kenya Dig It*," Royster Bottoms said with a face as straight as an arrow.

"Sure, just for you," Myles snorted.

They were politely interrupted by the attending nurse. It was time to give Royster his pain meds, and it was time for visitors to go. Les and Royster did the thumb-clasping handshake, but it was humbled by the more complicated and involved shake of two bassists, which was kept secret by a cocoon formed by each other's free hand. They were true brothers of *boom-boom*. There were no good-byes because there would be a next time.

"Interesting guy. Thanks for inviting me," Myles said as they walked down the hall towards the exit.

"Thanks for coming," Les said. "He appreciated it a lot."

"Have you done a lot of gigs with him?"

"Oh, yeah, and he can play some bass," Les said. "One of the best."

"That's what I would've guessed," said Myles.

"Yeah, he's been playin' for a long time, but his roots in our world run deep. His grandfather had the experience of blowin' a tuba in a Dixieland band on them riverboats runnin' up and down *Big Muddy*," Les revealed.

"That's nice. I can only envy his family history," said Myles. "Can you imagine rubbing shoulders with the fathers of jazz music?"

Les was already shaking his head. "Only in one of those beautiful hindsight dreams about the glory days of the Mississippi River," he said.

"Well, something that *just keeps on rolling along* doesn't have any need for glory days," said Myles, "and that's where we come in."

Les looked at this watch. "Speaking of rolling along," he said as he headed for his cab. "I'd better get my meter rolling because that's what pays the rent, not my drums. Catch you later,"

Myles was back in the car checking his messages. If the visit with Royster Bottoms was a soulful sundae, the lovely and patient voicemail from Yvonne was the cherry on top. He exhaled a deep, relaxing breath and started the engine, knowing he would call her when he got back to the quiet of the servant's quarters. But first he was determined to run by the flower shop for a couple of hours, just to get his fingers dirty with Minnesota potting soil.

Days later, Myles didn't have to look to know he was still well-situated with money, but he was serious about getting another gig or two, just for laughs. It would be just a little something to keep a smile on his face during the eventual flight back across the Atlantic Ocean. Les was feeding him advice on who the good players were and where to find them. On successive evenings, Myles was gassing up his car and making stops at some suggested venues, a few far between as they were. Low to no-paying sessions were all that most of the locals had to hang their hats on, but he didn't care. With him, it wasn't about money as much as just hanging with some colleagues on another side of the planet. Myles saw and heard a few players, most coming off their shifts as cab drivers. Some had pure talent and genius while others had enough on-stage work ethic to get to play jazz professionally. For those who had neither but were interested in the art, they could still close their eyes tightly, clasp their hands together and pray hard for chops. If nothing else, novice brothers in their basement woodsheds could put their horns to their mouths to idolatrously emulate the famous jazzmen.

The trail continued to a place downtown Minneapolis called *King Solomon's Mines*, highly regarded on the list as the musician's place of tolerance for low pay. As soon as he walked through the door he thought he had lived and breathed and died and gone to hell. There he was, another graying relic of a brilliant pianist who was his old buddy from light years ago.

"Hoddis! Hoddis Hervmore," Myles said with a handshake that collapsed between a mutual back-slapping hug. "What a surprise! I thought they said you left here after I did."

"I did," Hoddis Hervmore said with a smirk. "But at least I was still in the country, you turncoat."

"Just following my light," Myles said, laughing it off.

Hoddis Hervmore sported a thick, white moustache which he tweaked subconsciously as he absorbed the surprise. "How have you been, Myles? You look fit."

"Thanks, back at ya," Myles said. "I'm just here hanging out a little bit after my mother's funeral a short time ago."

"I'm sorry for your loss," Hervmore said after turning off his smile. "I know the feeling after losing both of my folks fifteen and twenty years ago."

"They say you went to San Francisco," Myles recalled. "When did you move back here?"

"I didn't," Hoddis Hervmore said, "that's my retirement home. I don't play as much as I used to, but I still get some good gigs out there. I've been here for a few days after attending the funeral of my grandson's wife."

"I'm sorry, brother," Myles said. "And she sounds a little young to be dying."

"She was a young adult who was killed by a stray bullet during a drive-by shooting."

Myles could feel his pain. "My prayers are with your grandson," he said. "I'm sorry."

"I am too," Hoddis lamented. "She was five-months pregnant and died of a severe belly wound. They're calling it a double homicide, and nobody has been arrested."

"There's gotta be some justice for your family, and soon," Myles said with genuine concern.

"Somebody saw something," Hervmore said, "but lips in the hood tend to stay pretty tight."

"Well, maybe we'll have to go up in there and audition some singers," Myles suggested. He was standing near the bar and ordered two ice-cold beverages, handing one to Hoddis Hervmore who accepted it graciously. *King Solomon's Mines* had its fair share of lounge lizards who were currently in a chatty limbo between musical sets. Myles observed a group of musicians near the stage who were engaging in some kind of coin-flipping contest. He could only guess that they were either trying to supplement their incomes or gambling for the privilege of being the next in line to play. It wasn't exactly *Charlie Scott's* in Copenhagen, but he would think of a good reason why his hometown needed to be cut a little slack.

"How ironic is this," Hoddis said, shaking his head. "That we're both back in this city for sad reasons."

"Yeah, it really makes us think about our own mortality doesn't it?" Myles said before he took a sip from his can of coke.

"How long have you been gone?" Hoddis Hervmore asked.

Myles smacked his lips and shook his head. "The last time I was here, this was in glass bottles, and the gulp of a coke would light a fire in your sinuses and bring you to tears," he said. "That's how long I've been gone."

"You must be livin' good. I've heard cats out west talking about the *Copenhagen Jazz Festival*, but I haven't made it over there yet."

"You'd love it," said Myles. "It easily draws a quarter of a million people and I've played it a few times over the years. Yep, in Europe, jazz musicians have so much less to complain about."

"Welcome back," said Hoddis Hervmore, "but over here, what you see is what you get."

They glanced at the source of some warm-up horn toots where the musicians were preparing to end their break and go back on stage. The trumpet player was beckoning from across the room. With raised eyebrows, Hoddis Hervmore was pointing questioningly at his own chest. The trumpet player nodded affirmatively with a come-on windmill sweep of his hand. Another piano player deferred to the signals and gray-haired seniority, got off the stool and walked back off the stage knowing there would be other sets.

"You're on," Myles said.

"I guess I'll run up for a tune or two," Hoddis Hervmore said. "Why don't you come too."

The question was too late. Myles was already cracking his knuckles and flexing his fingers with eagerness. He followed Hoddis onto the stage and grabbed someone else's bass. His guilt for such as act of piracy evaporated when he was assured by a keen observer that it was okay, because the instrument's owner was still at the bar trying to get to first base with a nice lady. Myles was very understanding of the Don Juan syndrome as he lightly plucked each string to test their truth. They weren't lying. He was open-minded and open-eared as he surveyed the up-tempo intro Hoddis Hervmore was laying down. There it was, in the first four bars, the Coltrane thing, *The Night Has a Thousand Eyes*. Myles smiled at the selection and glided right into a walk that was actually a medium run. He kept an eye on Hervmore's right hand, a hand that was a scared mouse being chased up the keyboard by a posse of low-brow, disgustingly funky chords. This pianist was a head-turner for everyone in the room except for a little old lady seated near a corner of the bandstand. She was concentrating on a scarf she was knitting, but her patting foot kept a more Perfect time with the music than her weaving needles. Myles could feel a groove happening as early as the tune's melody phase. It was a good set-up for the up-coming rounds of improvising waiting in the wings. It was all about universal professional know-how, and bona fide proof that birds of a feather flock and fly together irrespective of geographic boundaries. Myles held the tempo together while the brother on drums dropped a stick and bent over to pick it up. He felt obligated to keep the old lady's foot going while the drummer recovered and caught up with him. But it was Hoddis Hervmore who humored the very human mishap by missing obvious notes while not missing a beat. Myles thought he had died and gone to Copenhagen, and it was a small confirmation of the rumor that players look forward to coming to *King Solomon's Mines* because it provides a variety of talent levels, a chance for the rich to mentor, and a golden opportunity for the poor to learn to be professional. As Myles plucked the strings of a strange bass and listened to the procession of plaintiff horn solos, he could only feel empathy for the state of incarceration of American jazz. He found a good spot for a four-beat rest to feel his back pocket to make sure his plane ticket was still there, then resumed plucking right on time. The tune was playing itself out, and before the very end, Hoddis Hervmore seemed to be feeling in a medley mood, throwing a smile over his shoulder as he usurped the same tempo to start the familiar intro to the Miles Davis tune, *Seven Steps to Heaven*. It was a long walk, but Myles was up to the task, picking up the back-and-forth fifths and then those statement seven notes before the four-bar drum solo.

The drummer dropped a stick again.

Myles saw it coming and finished the drum solo by slapping the rhythm on the wood shoulders of the bass. The same seven notes repeated as composed and Myles subbed again by doing a four-bar hambone off his thigh and chest. With the tune still going on and the horns harmonizing the next melody phrase, Myles could only plunk the strange strings as he watched apparently the only other drumstick in the house being brought back on the stage by the little old lady who was knitting. The drummer rose like a gentleman and stepped towards her to accept the stick and thank her. Myles kept the bottom tempo going as he saw the little old lady do a snatch move and a sidestep maneuver. Suddenly she was in the drummer's seat with both sticks while the butter-fingered drummer stood over her in total disagreement with the take-over. He urged her with all his heart to go right ahead and make a fool of herself and then huffed off the stage with full confidence of an impending disaster. The musicians drove the tune to the next station, pulled it over and parked it, then casually slinked off the stage. It wasn't the end of the ride, and it wasn't the departure out of disrespect for the drummer. It was only the drummer's turn to take a long solo, and it was an old trick somebody picked up from the real jazz clubs in New York, were the rest of the musicians hang the drummer out to dry until his expression cries uncle, at which time they would all come back to finish the tune. But now it was an unusually confident little old lady picking up a tempo embellished with seven-step accents like the musicians were still there. Myles was too paralyzed by amazement to go with the other musicians. He held the strings quiet as he marveled at her ability to hear a tune in her head. Her ride cymbal was in the driver's seat, her rim shots were a pop better than bubble gum while her tom-tom accents were a mere thunder dance from afar. But it was her energetic high-hat work that was lighting the place up as she turned that thing into an unforgiving fly catcher. Heads were already turned to her, and now chairs around the room were turning to face her brilliance. She had it all, throwing in a luscious crescendo-to decrescendo press roll which brought the crowd's attention to its feet. Myles was totally mesmerized along with everyone else. This was a little old lady! How could this be happening? She was no nonsense for real and in complete control of the tune's backbone. Her flamadiddles jumped up and rang the bells in the center of the cymbals while her timekeeping was stiffer than a convent laundry room. This lady had more independent coordination in her limbs than a box of aloof cats, and tonight, she could send an angry Elvin Jones out for cigarettes. Myles watched with inner amusement as a contingent of Asian tourists moved in a crouched, single file column toward the bandstand where they huddled on their knees taking pictures and notes. Their enthusiasm for jazz talent reminded Myles of his many gig trips to the orient, where jazz had grown the roots of sequoia trees. He could see it in their eyes, a *Godzilla* movie most certainly would have taken a backseat to this little old lady's act. They were looking at each other with glee and nodding profusely. *Ah-soul*, they seemed to say. The lady squelched the ride cymbal with her hand immediately after she gave it a spank with a stick. End of solo? No. Her sticks galloped a steady paradiddle on the closed high-hat as she gave Myles a wink and a nod. Myles read her like a book and returned to the tune's beginning riff, those familiar fifths going back and forth. It was an open door, a door the two of them would hold open until the masters of the melody returned to the stage. Amid wild, standing applause for the drummer lady, the other players returned with their horns and spit out those seven notes of the head. Without dropping a stick, the little old lady did the four-bar solo to set up the repeat. She then had no problem laying down a nice ride for the bridge phrase before returning to extremely soft paradiddles on the closed high-hat. The horn players followed her light touch to the tune's conclusion, and Myles claimed the last two notes, a long, low slow fifth. He then joined the explosive standing ovation and cheers from the room and other musicians for the smiling, humble drum lady. With a bath of camera flashes, she stood and bowed modestly to the continuing raucous acknowledgement as she sheepishly surrendered the hummingbird wings she was using, which were once again only a pair of drumsticks. But there was nobody to take them, so she laid them neatly across the snare drum.

Myles was closest to her and introduced himself. He looked her sideways with a frowning smile as he wagged a playful finger at her. "You've got that album, don't you?" he said.

"I do," the grandmotherly lady laughed. "I love Miles Davis, and I'm so glad he hired Tony Williams."

"I would love to know your name," Myles said respectfully.

"My name is Enola Adams," she said.

"Where did you learn to play like that?" Myles asked with awe. "I mean, I've known some drummers who think *time* is a magazine, but Enola, you're the bomb. You blow a lot of people out of the water, and your time is magnificent!"

"Oh, no-no," she cooed, "but thank you very much. My time is limited, and I'm just marching to the beat of my own drum," she added, obviously down-playing some serious past formal training.

"I admire you," Myles said as he shook her hand again.

The crowd wanted more, but she was done. The other musicians lined up to shake her hand before she retired to her ringside seat to finish making her scarf. Never in a million years would she ever drop a loop or a needle, and never in the history of jazz did a drummer ever wish that a lady would've minded her own knitting.

The next musicians on the waiting list hurriedly took over the stage, hoping to piggy-back the room's fever created by a little old lady with a pair of drumsticks. Myles followed Hoddis Hervmore and two others who were headed to the back stoop for a break and a breath of fresh air. At the far end of the parking lot they saw a man bent over from the waist.

"Is he throwing up or tying his shoe?" Myles asked.

"Neither," said Hoddis Hervmore. "I know him. That's the drummer His name is Corky Woodsong. Trust me, he's cryin'. The brother is very upset because he couldn't hold a candle to an old white flame."

They walked over and consoled him.

"Can I make a little suggestion to you?" Myles said after an awkward introduction.

Back upright, Corky Woodsong dried his eyes knowing he'd better take all the help he could get for free. "What?" he asked with a sniff.

"I don't think anybody would blame you if you wanted to use a little pine tar on your sticks," Myles coached. "That way, nobody would wanna touch 'em."

"I'll keep that in mind," Corky Woodsong said.

Suddenly out of nowhere, a mosquito was flying around them, masquerading as a joint. Its sting spared nobody, including a deposed young drummer who could appreciate a little pick-me-up. There would always be a day of redemption for the downtrodden. For the others, it was a commemorative toast to the woman who just shattered the glass ceiling of drumming superiority. After so long, the least they could all do was exhale.

A few days later, Myles' early morning phone talk with Lester Ride gave the rising sun a chance to brighten the blue sky, but it was Les' voice which carried a dark cloud of bad news. Myles got ready within an hour and headed to the entrance of the Southside Hospice of Minneapolis where Les was waiting with gloom in his eyes.

"What is it, Les?" Myles asked. "You look terrible."

"Our friend Royster Bottoms just died," he said quietly.

"Rest his soul," Myles said from the healing depth of his own recent loss. "We're all soldiers, and our ranks just got all the more thinner with his passing. We're getting so endangered that the next cats coming along to replace us need to bring nine lives with them."

"The good thing is that he lived a good, long life," Les said.

"I should be so lucky," Myles said. "Maybe I should go up and salute him goodbye."

"They already took him," Les said. "I just talked to some relatives of his who said that his final plans have already been made. Would you want to come along to his memorial next Friday?"

"Certainly," Myles quickly said. "I wouldn't miss it. Bass players are all joined at the bridge by the G-string."

"Good. We'll go down and see him off-key," Les quipped in honor of Royster Bottoms.

The coming Friday was a sad but blessed day at the Riverton Funeral Home. Inside the door, Myles could feel the flavor of old home week for old players as he noticed the respectable showing of gray heads. The notoriously reliable musicians' grapevine always draw them together, especially after a death. He could only see that as the sad blessing. People lined the walls and overflowed into the lower lobby of the funeral chapel. The soul of Royster Bottoms had already been released to the heavens through cremation, and like a firefly, rose up to find its place among the stars. All that remained up front were his urned ashes and the kind words of his friends and colleagues. Somehow, it seemed, he deserved an even better send-off, but love was in the air even through a belated postmortem of ribbing.

"Just look yonder at him," said an irreverent mourner to no one and everyone as he pointed a backhanded thumb at the defenseless urn holding Royster's ashes. "A long time ago, he hung out on the corner. It ain't no different. Now he's hangin' out on the coroner."

Myles closed his eyes tightly, but the man's pummeling never materialized, because it was one of Royster's own jokes.

"Pay him no mind," Les said out of the corner of his mouth. "He means well."

"Seems like it," Myles acknowledged with a very reserved grin.

"But just so you know," Les continued, "Royster Bottoms wants it known that his ashes are to be driven to the cemetery in a long, black, well-polished rehearsal."

"I imagine he does," Myles twinkled.

"Can't believe he's gone," Les said with a sigh. "He was one of the building blocks of what we've had around here for a long time. Part of our fabric is torn away."

"Naw, he didn't just die," Myles said, "he was promoted to glory."

"Well, with a promotion like that, I hope they give him a big fat raise," Les said.

"He's getting it right now," said Myles. "He's getting raised up to however high heaven is, and he won't even have to go to Colorado."

"Well then, that must be the universe I hear singin' *amen*!" Les said.

"If we keep this up, we're gonna have to start taking up an offering," Myles joked with assumed permission from the urn.

"No way," Les said. "He'd like it better if we just sold tickets outright."

"I'll bet," Myles chuckled as his eyes scanned the very decent turnout, "but seriously, I wonder what happed to his bass?"

"Why? Did you want to confiscate the strings?"

"No," Myles assured in no uncertain terms. "Used strings are against my religion."

"Good," Les said, "because someone just told me he donated it to a high school band room."

"What a guy," said Myles. "Hopefully it still has enough good vibrations in it to get some youngster's interest in studying and playing jazz."

Les' backbone went rigid as he turned away. "Oh oh, don't look now, but here she comes," he said through his teeth.

"Who?" Myles asked, heeding the heads-up.

"It's Alberta Clipper our excuse for a newspaper jazz reporter," said Les. "Unfortunately for us, she was reassigned from the sports desk."

"Oh?"

"Yeah, and she really lives up to her name. She's cold," Les said like he was a weatherman. "Now we're the football that she loves to kick around, so don't encourage her."

"Sorry to hear that," Myles said.

"Probably here doing research for another of her slights and bold-faced lies," Les added.

"Do I detect a slight case of sour grapes?"

"Hell, no!" Les fumed under his breath. "What could she ever do for me?"

"Do you love her?" Myles pried.

"I can't tell ya," Les said, almost inaudibly.

With a kibitzing smile and eyes rolled towards the ceiling, Myles softly sang a few words from that little song about trouble in paradise.

She was upon them, and Les was her target. "Wasn't Mister Bottoms a wonderful man?" said albert Clipper, shoulders draped with a pretentious ruby red silk scarf which matched the full lips beneath unseen eyes hiding under a wide-brimmed, floppy hat from the realms of Churchill Downs.

"He was a good man and an even better bassist," Myles said, falling on the grenade for Les.

Alberta Clipper tilted her head back far enough to show a fluttering of eyelashes. "And who might you be, sir?" she inquired.

"You can call me Myles," Andrews said, "and I'm in love with jazz."

She extended a limp hand and introduced herself unnecessarily. "Don't worry, it will pass," she said. "It's a phase that we all go through. Where are you from?"

"Copenhagen," Myles said with pride.

"Get out."

"No, really. I'm from Copenhagen. Ask Les."

"He's from Copenhagen," Les confirmed as he fidgeted, "and he plays a mean bass too."

"I beg your pardon, brother," Myles said without hostility," my bass is not mean, because I've taught it to be nothing but gentile."

"You're just as bad as the urn," Alberta Clipper said as she gave her filmy scarf an extra toss around her shoulders and drifted away, her big black hat seemingly guiding her like the sail of a wayward ship.

"Go for it, man. What's to not like about her?" Myles said, all smiles.

"She doesn't sing," Les said.

"Well, can't she even . . . hum?"

"I don't know. I didn't ask her," Les said as his eyes followed her black hat through the crowd.

"That's quite an aroma she was wearing," said Myles.

"It's Old Spice. Probably a carry-over from her locker room days," Les said.

"Man-o-man-o-man! She's got a lot of vas deferens," Myles said.

The murmur of shared Royster Bottoms stories could have gone on until the moon turned blue, but for the moment, they were interrupted by a soft bell in the hand of the resident minister who stepped up behind the alter to deliver the eulogy and prayer. The man of the cloth would be forgiven for preaching to the choir about Royster Bottoms, but there was a sneaky feeling in the air that if Royster Bottoms knew about it, he wouldn't object. After all was lovingly said and done, Royster Bottoms didn't get a ride to the cemetery in a rehearsal. No, he rode to a resting place in the real show, as Myles drove in the second line of the procession just behind Les' taxi. The entire jazz community would wholeheartedly agree that good memories can't be buried, but ashes must rest in peace. They would also agree that a new spirit of inspiration would rise from those ashes like a phoenix, only to create another player to cherish. The thirst was present and accounted for.

GETTING TO THE POINT

That one last hometown gig was out there somewhere, and Myles was determined to find it, just for old times' sake. He derived some obscure kind of joy from having a belly full enough to look for a gig without a feeling of desperation. It had become a fun sport in which he knew from deep down in the marrow of his bones that they needed this music more than he needed them. The fun part was watching them deny it. After all, he thought, jazz music was something with Black roots, something for the American establishment to resist on general American principles. Myles figured the least he could do for posterity was to put his best foot forward as a foreign agitator.

Time was still flying as Myles was becoming a welcome fixture at the flower shop and the car wash, but he still reserved some space over the passing days, which turned into unintentional weeks to snare a few word-of-mouth substitute gigs. Between *urban cab quartet* gigs, he played a date with the Brazilian pianist *Joao Donato* at *King Solomon's Mines*, and another Brazilian keyboard artist *Festado Frayman* at the suburban *Whitehouse Restaurant*. Then it was two weekends at the elegant *Carousel Restaurant* atop the *St. Paul Hilton Hotel* with the *Sam Hammond Quintet*, whose bass player was injured in a car accident. Next, he did a temporary job at *The Impala* out south on the beltline strip with a sultry singer named *Bertha Paradise* who fired her bassist for inappropriately touching her. All this didn't just fall in his lap from out of the blue. Lester Ride was the one working overtime to throw him all these bones. Myles was just thankful that he had the teeth to catch them like a leaping, dreaming dog. He continued to return to his servant's quarter retreat with a feeling that this midwestern scene was showing signs of a pulse and enough compensation to at least keep the chickens from starving. But since he owned no chickens, he got a lot of satisfaction out of dropping off his earnings at various food shelves.

Myles also took time to reflect. He was doing a lot of thinking about it, and the tune running through his mind was *The Night We Called It a Day*. The night before, he took his hometown family out to dinner and discussed it with them and got their blessings and best wishes for his decision, that it was time to be getting back across the Atlantic Ocean. His good-as-usual talk with Yvonne a few days earlier left both of them with the mutual thought that it wouldn't be too much longer before they would be seated in their special booth at *Noma*, their favorite restaurant.

Myles was leisurely half-packed with a few more days to kill when the phone interrupted his dream. He answered and listened for an eternity. Then with a poker face, he slowly sat down and stayed quiet with the phone to his ear.

"Why, yes sir, Mister Persons," he finally said. "I'd be delighted to take the gig."

It was a call from a tenor sax player with a name familiar from way back in the day, Huey Persons. His long-time bass player was moving on to a gig and a new home in Sarasota, and he needed an interim bassist to do a rehearsal for his enduring job at *The Point Supper Club* out in *Golden Village* with his quartet and a singer. Huey Persons was a smoker, and he was out of breath after explaining it all.

Myles was flattered. It was a no-brainer. Yes, to go to the rehearsal in two days with Huey Persons, but it was something for which he would inevitably have some explaining of his own to do. He felt confident that he could make it right with everybody.

Two days was long enough to wait to find Huey's comfortable home in south Minneapolis. Myles hauled his bass to the elegant front door, but it opened before he could knock. He and his ax entered to the warm welcome of the graying, smiling and bespectacled elder statesman on the local jazz scene, *the* Huey Persons, who took his bass' coat and ushered him in among the fellows. The moment before introductions, they were all strangers, but nevertheless, Myles felt as if he had known them forever. They were the birds of a certain feather and flock, namely Noah Jameen on piano and Landil Hakes on drums.

"You're a veteran player and familiar with the old standards just like everybody else," Huey conceded, probably on the mere heresy of one Lester Ride. "We'll just be sharpening charts."

"I promise, I'll try my best to keep up with you," Myles kidded, which caused Huey to throw his head back with a cackling laugh. "Are we missing somebody?" Myles said of the dapper gentleman sitting off to the side.

"Oh, don't pay any attention to him," Huey said with his continuing smile, "That's just Noddix Hackley, our accountant. If anything goes wrong, just remember that he's the bean counter."

"How do," Myles nodded along with the kidding.

Huey's gorgeous, middle-age Asian wife came in with a tray of tall ice tea glasses, introduced herself, and left again.

"She's the greatest," Huey said proudly.

"She is, you lucky man," Myles said. "But who's doing the singing?"

As if on cue, she returned from the ladies' room. It was Bertha Paradise! Her angular brown face was framed by silky black hair and punctuated by a little rose blossom of lips. She was a solid platform from which to launch a tune.

"We've met," Myles said after a perfunctory introduction.

"I know," Huey said with a wink as he reconnected his horn to the neck strap. He inaudibly suggested a tune in Noah Jameen's ear and counted off a medium-slow tempo. Noah chorded beautifully into a blues intro on the baby grand. Myles walked the walk until Bertha Paradise picked up the mike to her mini-amp and swayed gently before she sang.

> *"I'm feelin' mighty lonesome, haven't slept a wink,*
> *I walk the floor and watch the door and in between*
> *I drink . . . BLACK COFFEE . . ."*

Huey blew his airy, supportive licks and waited for the swinging kitchen door to open just a little. It did. His wife peeked her head out and smiled at him with a sideways look, exposing herself as a lady who knows her tunes. It was the *Sonny Burke* and *Paul Francis Webster* thing, but he must've known that his wife wasn't about to throw on a pot of coffee after serving all that tea, just because she knows the tune. It was a nuance that Myles fell in love with, somewhere in the depths of his string plucking. It was also, he thought, one final gig that was intriguing enough to slightly delay his throwing in the towel on this American excursion. The coffee blues played out just in time for a sip of iced tea.

Huey Persons walked over and patted the bass, then bent over to speak to it. "Did I already tell you you're hired?" he said to the instrument.

"I feel honored," Myles said.

Huey slowly turned his head from the face of the bass to look up at Myles. "I wasn't talking to you," he said with an expression of phony seriousness — old school humor to the others.

Myles was nodding with a smile because the reason for Huey's unprecedented longevity on one gig was becoming abundantly clear. What fine-dining restaurant manager on the planet would have the heart to fire him? For the diners, it must have been so many years of being doomed with goodness in a place where indigestion must have been at an all-time low! The longer this session, the more it got Myles to thinking, "*with rehearsals like this, who the hell needs gigs?*" It was too easy for a cat with European deep pockets to say, and it sho-nuff wouldn't be a question he would ever ask an American jazzman aloud.

Over the next couple of hours, the thick walls of the mansion deprived the neighbors of some quality listening, but the time for the musicians to call it a night repeatedly came and went until collectively they finally convinced themselves that the gig was going to be just fine.

On the eve of his *Point Supper Club* debut, Myles was at the servant's quarters putting on his final touches — the tie, the jacket, and same color socks. As he hauled his wrapped bass out the door, he paused before he locked up. He could only chuckle that for an old jazz veteran, getting butterflies about going to a new gig was supposed to be a thing long in the distant past, but this time, the butterflies apparently didn't get the memo. They were busy tickling his growling stomach. It was just the elixir he needed to feel young after a good aging in America.

Myles was under way, instructions for directions firmly in his mind. The night was clear, and the traffic was sparse as he drove along Olsen Highway. He checked his speed and recalled the turmoil and changes in the neighborhoods over thirty years ago. The older near northside Jewish community fled their homes at bargain prices because they feared angry Black encroachment and the riots of the times, leaving houses that could be had for a song. Those were the times that tried men's souls, and exactly the time that Myles decided to try some soul in Europe. He was just another child of the town who followed the Pied Piper to a place where jazz has a right to exist, a fantasy world which turned out to be true.

Myles drove to the edge of town where the car started downhill and past a sign which welcomed the masses into *Golden Village*, a western lowland suburb. His headlights made up for the lack of streetlights along the highway as he drove into the darkness, bursting through low-hanging wisps of fog off the marshland. Myles had the radio tuned to the classical FM station and turned up the volume just in time to savor one of his favorites, a wild Stravinsky piece. Kettle drums rolled like thunder. Violins dashed by leaps and bounds like deer through the forest. Cymbals smashed and hissed like a barrel of rattlesnakes. Then from the darkness behind him, flickering red lights and bright spotlights filled the car like an open door to hell. Startled to the bone, Myles slowed and pulled over for a stop in the middle of a swamp. With his eyes riveted to his outside mirror, he turned down the volume to avoid a possible disturbing the peace citation, then rolled down the window and waited with a serenade of a million summer crickets. As the flashing red behind him continued, minutes were becoming more precious, and they were being wasted by waiting for someone to approach him. After a protracted amount of time, the mirror reflection showed a policeman cautiously approaching on foot like he was stalking wild game, one hand on his gun handle, the other holding a bright flashlight high. The crickets suddenly got quiet. The cop stopped short of the driver window and made a stretching peek-a-boo to shine the flashlight in.

"Is there a problem, officer?" said Myles, always the one to break the ice while squinting into a bright light.

"I recon you've drove too far, didn't ya?" said whatever unseen face there was behind that damn light.

"For a guy who came all the way from Copenhagen, you could be right, officer," answered Myles.

"See your driver's license, bub?" said the blinding light source.

"Why certainly, officer," Myles said as he reached in his jacket pocket, pulled out his international driver's license and handed it over.

"Boy, you've got to be kidding," said the voice behind all the light, "this ain't gonna fly. Let's have your *real* license."

"That's perfectly legal," Myles assured him. "Just ask the State Department."

"Sit tight," the cop said as he leisurely walked back to the squad car. The crickets had no comment while the red lights were speaking, and time was becoming a wicked witch.

After fifteen minutes, Myles was resisting the urge to get out of the car to go back and ask the officer to please hurry because he knew it would be a gimme merit of honor for a threatened cop who dared to take action and defend himself. Myles stayed put because he wasn't extremely interested in becoming a dead Santa Clause. A glance at his watch showed him that the stop was officially cutting into tune-up and warm-up time. He looked back to see his bass to see if there was any way he could take the cover off and save some time by tuning it while he waited. It didn't take long for him to abandon the idea when he remembered that his ax looked too much like a cannon when it was laying down, something threatening, something to defend against. The damn thing just wouldn't sound right if it was full of bullet holes. Myles could always take pride in being a veteran player who can tune up in the middle of a tune.

Finally, the door of the squad car opened and the cop with a flashlight for a face slowly approached. Two fingers appeared from the edge of the light with the international driver's license between them. "This is a nice clean community out 'char," the officer said with a very territorial demeanor, "an' we gonna keep it what way," the cop said. "Drive careful."

"I most certainly will, officer," Myles said as he pocketed the international driver's license and put the car in gear.

He pushed the gas down hard enough to catch up with the run-away clock but backed off so as not to push his luck. Getting to the gig was supposed to be half of the fun, but he would reserve judgement until the end of the evening. For now, he got some solace when he leaned over and patted his back pocket, finding that his airline return ticket was still there.

Near the end of the drive, the sign up ahead validated his good ear for following the directions. *The Point Supper Club* welcomed him into the crowded parking lot where the valets were shaking their heads about the availability of an open spot. He slowly drove along the rows, hoping and praying, until bingo! White back-up lights down the line were peeking out, signaling a departure. Myles stopped to let the car get out, then thankfully pulled into the vacant slot. He shut off the engine and got out then immediately snapped his finders, got back in and restarted. With the narrow spaces between cars, he needed to back out just far enough to open the door wide enough to get the bass out. Myles chuckled at the thought of passing up an opportunity to become a flute player years ago, but at the end of the day, he wouldn't have missed these character-building wrestling matches for all the tea in China. He waltzed his fiddle across the pavement and inside the door of *The Point* where he heard the group playing without him, and he felt punished when he heard pianist Noah Jameen playing the bass line on his lowest keys.

In the elegant foyer was an attractive poster about the entertainment, including a near life size cutout of the featured singer, a smiling Bertha Paradise, posing in an alluring, tight sparkling black gown as she sang into her hand-held microphone proudly displaying her ample groceries over a decolletage even for the beadiest eyes of old men. It was pretty good for a cardboard cutout, but as he caught a quick glance at his watch, he was bulldog certain there wouldn't be anything cardboard about facing the music with Huey Persons.

Myles politely declined an offer of assistance from the maître d' and proceeded into a packed and upbeat room of good live chewing and good live listening. He put on the brakes for a strong and lovely server who was shouldering a head-turning, nostril-teasing tray of salads with sizzling, succulent steaks including all the fine dining trimmings. The place was a magic formula of sweet music and murmuring conversation. When he made it to the stage and uncovered his bass, his embarrassment for the tardiness was amplified when he realized that he walked in on *Jimmy Mchugh's* tune, "*Where are You"*. It *had* to be coincidental, he thought, because nobody spanks *that* well.

Huey Persons was finishing up a solo just in time to acknowledge the grand entrance with a long, expressionless look at his watch while mentally buying a front-row ticket to the explanation. Myles caught the smile and sigh-of-relief from pianist Noah Jameen on his emancipation from the bondage of doing the bass line. Jameen was free as a bird, and deep down, Myles felt like Abe Lincoln. He also felt the turn-around coming, the full-band set-up for Bertha paradise to chime in with the head, and the plaintiff question she sang into her microphone, *"Where are you?. . ."*

Myles was with it, providing some bouncy boom to her silky lyrics, his strings seeming to say, *"Here I am."* All it took was the soft and effective stickwork of Landil Hakes to caress everything over for a smooth landing. The applause said it all, that people can eat and clap at the same time.

Myles didn't have much trouble catching Huey's eye. "I'm sorry," he leaned forward to say under his breath. "I was detained."

"Sure," Huey said without animosity as he popped his fingers and kicked off the next tune.

At the take five break offstage, Myles was in the process of draining his excuses and apology tanks down to fumes when Huey interrupted him. "Say no more," he said in a reassuring way. "I've been aware of that problem on the highway for quite a while. Been through it myself. Just don't do anything to get yourself hurt because you don't have to be a rocket scientist to see that it smacks of some kind of shooting waiting to happen. So please be careful," Huey said with sincere concern.

"Thanks for the heads up and let me just say that it's a pleasure to get a few tunes in with a hometown legend," Myles said.

"I'm lucky you were available," Huey said, "most of the good bass players are in and out of the airport day and night."

"You mean there are a lot of gigs out of town?"

"No-no-no," Huey said. "I mean they're in and out of the airport as cab or limo drivers on the night shift, where the money is."

"I see."

"But you know, I think I remember your name from back in the day when you were a neophyte," Huey bullied playfully.

"Thanks," Myles said all smiles. "But is this really America? Why can't there be more places like this?"

"Well, you see, this place is kind of an anomaly that has slipped through the cracks of oppression," Huey said, "but keep it quiet because jazz is still learning how to swim in shark-infested waters. Take away the sharks and jazz swims."

"Don't you think those sharks know that jazz has rights?" Myles was deliberately preaching to the choir.

Huey was nodding affirmatively with his eyes closed. "Let's just hope that one day, those sharks will find out," he said.

"Will you promise to write and tell me all about it?" Myles pleaded without passion. He silenced a laugh from Huey when he pulled out his airline ticket and put it back after seeing it.

They were on the clock, but the chat between them during the short break was solid gold. Everything was just turning into a big funeral for a hatchet, but nobody knew or cared why it was being buried. It must have been that they were professionals who were under the influence of their collective talent.

Once again, Myles was back on the stage of the *Hobre Room* where the atmosphere was maintaining its festiveness. He courteously waited until everyone was in place before grunting five times to count off the tune he called, Gershwin's *Our Love is Here to Stay*. Myles walked right into it, an ultrafamiliar tune that he'd played at least twice in his sleep last night. As he played, he dedicated himself to being true. He embraced and welcomed the commitment to being true. The melody deserves it. Keeping time, he put his ear close to the open G-string, frequently a part of his line of plucking, and sent out tones that were fur slippers for Bertha Paradise's lyrics. But what he was hearing wasn't true. His left hand reached up and turned the G screw slightly. The peg snapped with tension and the string was tighter. Now it was true to the melody and lyrics, but who knew? The drummer's brush job briskly washed the windows of tasty piano chords, but the bounce around tune came to an end too soon for the pavement. For the night, another gig at the *Point Restaurant and Lounge* was the rave on Valley Road, and the applause was robust and enduring. Eventually, the manager took a microphone and was profusely apologetic about not allowing yet another encore, and that the house was fresh out of second and third desserts anyway, so it was time to leave, he claimed, "*because we have to show our liquor license a little love.*" As the musicians started packing up, the manager was gracious enough to extend a warm invitation for tomorrow night, same place, same time, same group. It was too good a deal to turn down. It was the only decent thing in town blues, don't you know.

It was his third night of driving into Golden Village, but already he began to get an uneasy feeling about the posturing of police cruisers along the way. Myles kept an eye on his speedometer as his headlights picked up the white of a black and white which was idling on the median ahead. Suddenly, he was nearly blinded by a bright spotlight from law enforcement. He brought his speed down to five miles under the limit and braced for an encounter out of expectation. Sure enough, quick glances in his rearview mirror showed the squad car making a U-turn and closing on him without lights. Police car engines don't play around. Myles was aware of their approach, but he didn't think it would be safe to go any slower unless he saw some red lights. In seconds, the police car was side-by-side with him, and so was the bright spotlight. As he shielded his eyes, law enforcement inexplicably sped ahead into the darkness without headlights, turning them on after they were about a hundred yards away. Myles immediately recognized that life was too short to try and make sense out of American police. It didn't matter, because it was a night that he made it to the gig with time to spare. In twenty-four hours, it will have been forgotten, and he would still be a proud and thrilled sideman who had a decent American gig to go to, damn the distractions. This was a slice of the good old days, and it was the kind of distractions which made him want to enjoy the gig even more. And he did — his smile going from his face to his bass with no strings attached. His boom was his salvation. During a tune, it caused Huey Persons to twist backwards on his stool to deliver an appreciative nod. The night that has a thousand eyes also has a thousand ears that can clearly hear that jazz may not be on the throne, but at least it keeps a highly polished crown. It was an evening that played out with a sparkle.

The next night after a relaxing day of washing cars at his brother's place and helping with flowers at his mother's place, Myles got himself ready early and loaded his bass for the increasingly familiar westward drive. The radio was tuned to a classical statin playing the famous *William Tell Overture.* His car burst in and out of patches of fog in the cool calm night as he crossed the border into Golden Village. The fog grew heavier in the marshland, and he was able to follow the intermittent white lines in the road. A lower speed was a must with a fiddle aboard, so thirty-five miles per hour seemed safe and manageable for the moment. In the next fog clearing, the badge of a Golden Village police car reflected from his headlights like a giant one-eyed cat laying in the weeks. With *The Lone Ranger* music playing on the radio, Myles passed it and kept an eye on the rearview mirror of solid fog. A few seconds later, tail-gating headlights suddenly came on, winking back and forth. A super-bright, piercing spotlight warmed the back of his head before the red flashing lights came on scolding him to a stop. He turned the radio off so as not to encourage any unnecessary bad cowboy theatrics in the absence of the *real* Lone Ranger. Myles stayed calm with his heart pounding during the eternal wait for a cop to make an appearance. Finally, he heard a door slam and footsteps approach.

"Do you know where you are?" said a voice behind the flashlight.

Myles was playing it by ear, which told him that the voice of an unseen face sounded different from the last time. "The last time I checked, officer, I was in the United States of America. Ah . . . what can I do for you?"

"We've had reports about someone fornicating in a moving vehicle," the cop said resting a hand on the handle of his holstered gun. "I need you to step out of the vehicle."

"Fornicating? In this fog? Are you kidding me?"

"Get out of the vehicle, *now*!"

Myles got out carefully and stood aside as the policeman directed him to do and watched as the inside of his car was being scanned with a slow-moving flashlight.

"Ma'am," the cop said sternly. "I need you to hold that blanket around yourself and step out of the vehicle."

There was no response.

"Ma'am," he repeated. "I need you to cooperate and step out of the vehicle, *now*!"

"Excuse me officer," Myles interjected hesitantly. "May I say something?"

"Yeah, I think you'd better tell me pretty quick what this lady's name is."

"Officer, that's Mrs. Hofner, my bass fiddle."

"What? With a body like *that*?"

"I'm afraid so, officer."

"Are you callin' me a liar?"

"No," Myles said. "But I think you're a person who has led a very sheltered life."

"That's it," the cop snapped, "you're gonna hafta show me what's in there, or I'll run you downtown for obstructing justice *and* insulting a police officer."

With a sigh of exasperation, Myles complied right there on the side of the road. He extracted the fiddle from the car and unzipped its garment, then stripped it without privacy and held it upright in the wind, bare naked like a piece of meat. With the second half of a slow wolf-whistle, the cop tilted his cap back and leaned on the car, giving it a once-over like he was ogling Marilyn Monroe, his flashlight lingering on the G-string. "Turn it around," law enforcement said in a weaker voice.

Myles obediently swiveled his axe so that all the cop could see was backside. If basses could blush, it would be redwood.

"That's the way I like 'em," the cop said with great admiration, "big and brown and shiny and shapely." That was all it took to restart the chirping of crickets.

Myles was trying his best to hold himself in check. "Are you quite finished, officer? I do have a job to go to, you know."

"Cover it up and put 'er back in and sit tight," the cop said as he returned to the squad car.

Myles endured a long wait, entertained by the flickering red lights of a sick road show that was once again making him too late to be on time. Before the rising moon got too much higher, the cop ended the light show, pulled out and sped into the distance. Myles sat for a moment, stunned by what just happened. He then started the engine and took off, getting back to the speed limit with the partially opened window wheezing and rumbling with the speed of night air. His mind was working overtime to come up with a plausible story for Huey. The truth was going to be an excuse that nobody was going to buy.

Myles arrived and walked through the elegant door hugging his fiddle with a readiness to face more than one kind of music including another coincidental tune they were playing, *At Last*. He accepted it as a fitting that those retroactive meddlers Harry Warren and Mack Gordon composed it, and that the great Huey Persons called it. All he needed was a bottle of ketchup to eat it with. Myles hurried past full dining tables on the way to the bandstand where Huey was shooting him a smiling glare for his tardiness, which he would be more than obligated to explain. He unwrapped his bass and joined the tune in progress, hoping that *At Last* would last forever, but a break and meeting with Huey was inevitable. Myles was getting the feeling in his gut that he could be back on a trans-Atlantic plane sooner than he planned to be. The remainder of the set was good, with the players and singer settling in with the sound of a full group, and after a short chaser, Myles left the stage with Huey, whose hands were in his pockets and his eyes fixed pensively to the floor. They strolled shoulder-to-shoulder out of the dining area and into a small cozy lounge where they could talk privately. This was it, Myles thought. The ominous bomb was about to be dropped, and his only fallout shelter was an airline ticket.

"Look, Mister Persons," he stammered, "that scene on the highway tonight was so strange that I . . ."

"I know what's going on out on that highway," Huey interrupted, "and so do other people. But I'm just a guy trying to keep a group playing good music for a good restaurant. It's been my gig for over thirty years. You see, the owner and the manager really like this music, and as you'll see, they pay us good. Right now, they're only in the throat-clearing mode, but if we keep this up, though they're going to start talking to me about it. Can you kind of understand what I'm sayin'?"

"Yes sir," Myles said. "I totally get it."

"Good. So, with that and all of your problems with the police, I'm going to hafta tell you," Huey hesitated with reluctance. "You're not fired."

"Some of my best friends are believers," Myles said with gratitude. "Thanks."

"Just be careful," Huey said. "Take another route and throw 'em off your trail."

"Only in America," Myles said seriously.

In a few minutes it was time for them to go back up, and to a casual observer, it would have been difficult to decide which one of them was returning with the most buoyance.

Pianist Noah Jameen followed Huey's lead in setting up the tempo and intro for the set opener, a medium swing tune.

"...I Don't Have A Car . . .
I Walk . . .Everywhere I go . . .
Must Be . . . The Gypsum In My Sole . . ."

Bertha Paradise sang and turned around for a big wink to the guys. Landil Hakes the drummer did it again! He carried that tempo magnificently with the quiet power of a distant thunderstorm of lightning cymbals. It was easy to digest. Huey Persons snapped his fingers with a smile as he waited for his turn to solo. Myles pulled it all together by lacing up the strings for a walk deep in the valley, with sweet chords of the ivories. The nights to remember were adding up.

It was another day and had been several hours since the sun came up on a beautiful brightening of blue sky, but Myles lingered in bed at the servant's quarters before getting up and out to the pro bono jam session. The plan was to hook up with Les over there at two o'clock.

Myles found the joint, *Flamingo Alley*, a nondescript bar near a scrap metal yard. Once a week, jazz musicians had permission to come on in for a jam session with a potluck platter of varying talents. Sometimes it should be called a sports bar because the crowd tended to be good sports about bad players. It was a cozy arrangement, the bar owner profited from drink sales while the musicians had a place to play for free. On stage, two trumpet players get the call to play *Yesterda*y. One starts playing the Beatle tune, the other starts playing the Jerome Kern tune, and neither seemed to know the difference. They sounded like escapees from a monster called practice, and there was more chaos than a Chinese kitchen. Myles found a seat as the sun rose in his heart. He appreciated them because they were kids who were the young jazz trainees for the future, and they wanted to learn the art and develop their respective voices. There was a need for a light at the end of a long, dark tunnel. So, it was clear that the practice monster needed his ass kicked, so they can all say *Let There Be Light In The Key Of*

See. Until then, the eyes of Myles will cry tears of pain for his bleeding ears.

Les found his table and greeted him with the clasping bebop handshake and an introduction of a cat he dragged in. "Josh Winters meet Myles Andrews," he said. "Josh is a guitar player, and Miles is a bass man."

"A pleasure," Myles said accepting the firm handshake. "Strings are us."

"Especially when we're not strung out," said Josh, a middle-aged fellow with gray dreds flopping around his beard, black face of sunglasses, "and that's easy for me to say because I'm a recovered junkie."

"Congratulations to a saved life," Myles said. "I hope you're stayin' with your ax."

"Well, I'm sixty-three years old, and I'm getting a disability check that barely pays the rent on my downtown flophouse room, I'm living off food stamps, and I can't seem to keep my cardboard bottoms in my shoes. But you know what? I'm a dedicated jazz musician! That's me!"

"That's a good way to be . . . dedicated, that is," Myles said. "But we all worry about each other to avoid dying over being dedicated. Get yourself a day slave to help out, brother," Myles said with all due respect.

"I tried it and found out that a day job only keeps me from being dedicated," Josh joshed. "I'm too old for a day slave, but I'm just right for a gig."

Myles took a hand out of his pocket and shook hands with Josh again, this time palming off a twenty dollar bill or two.

"Thanks, you're kind," said Josh. "You the one they say is from some other country?"

"Copenhagen," Myles said, "the land where I went to fulfill my dreams."

Les had been fake drumming on his own knee with his eyes closed until a tune ended with more crowd chatter than applause. A fresh group of musician took over the stage and started right in with an off-the-wall *avant garde* number which lacked a specific beat for the knee drummers of the world. "Let's get in line to play," he said, eyes wide open.

"I'm ready," said Myles. "Who's that up there?" He was referring to the bassist who was cutting up with some attention-getting licks of virtuosity.

"That's Arco Bridgeland, and he's a bitch," Les said.

"Uh-huh," Myles said transfixing by Arco's fingers flashing up and down the fingerboard like a cat on a hot tin roof, and he loved witnessing a player that could bring a room's chatter to a screeching halt. Arco Bridgeland's brilliant talent humbled him, but he would bet his bottom dollar that he could out-walk Arco any day of the week and twice on Sunday, and he would go up and play anyway when his turn came up, mainly because jealousy is for the birds and the bees. Anyway, he thought, who the hell needs fingers like a centipede?

After a mind-bending set, Arco Bridgeman and company relinquished the stage to a warm smattering of appreciation. Myles followed Les and Josh up to take over the community instrumentation. Another horn and piano man joined, potluck. A B-flat blues thing was getting the consensus can-do nod.

"Don't look now, but here comes the union," Les said out of the corner of his mouth.

The man wearing a black Stetson mounted the stage with a toothpick in his mouth and an eye out for strangers. There was no telling what he had under his long black coat. "Hodd," he said as he extended a hand to Myles, "Rathig Hodd. Are you, ah. . .in the union?"

Myles looked pleased to be asked. "Am I in the union? Why of course I'm in the union, Mr. Hodd. The union is mob hitch because I'm not too fond of being found floating face-down in the Mississippi River, don't cha know."

Rathig Hodd was the only one on the stage who wasn't laughing about what the customers couldn't hear above their own conversations. His toothpick slowly worked itself to the other side of his mouth. "Got a card?" he said with a poker face.

"The police took it and wouldn't give it back," Myles said leveling with a tilt.

Emerging sweat on the union man's upper lip had a tell-tale Nixonian shine. "I'll talk to the boss and check with the police," he said as he backed off with the grin of a Cheshire Cat and disappeared into the shadows.

"They're always trying' to sting you like a cagey bee," Myles said. "And I've been to a lot of places, but that's why I never wanted to go to Russia. Let's play instead."

The blues had a tempo that was fast enough to run away from trouble, a tune called *"You Ain't Gone Yet?"* They played it only as long as they wanted to.

The clock was cherished as he burped and excused himself to his reclining bass. It was a great time he had with Althea and Al, siblings *ala carte*, who treated him to a fine dinner at a downtown place called *The Monaco-Ville*.

It was too much fun for the pavement, but not for the highway leading to the Golden Village gig. Fog from the marsh was thinner than usual so he couldn't help noticing a pair of off-the-road headlights turning on and doing a little rumba as it rolled over the curb and onto the highway. Myles was forcing himself not to worry about it because it could always be just a couple of lovers who just finished a hot parking session, or some nighttime anglers who just caught more than their limit. He adjusted the rearview mirror to keep an eye on that long vehicle which was about one hundred yards behind. He then glanced at the dashboard clock and saw that there was enough time for some fun fact-finding. Down the road, he skipped his usual right turn at

Douglas Drive and kept going west to the Highway 169 cloverleaf. That car was still back there and maintaining its distance, but he was confident that no one in his right mind would copy what he was about to do unless he were indeed being followed. He signaled to take the south bound loop and saw that car do the same while closing the distance a bit. He could only think of it as an honest coincidence as he completed the loop onto southbound traffic. He then immediately signaled and turned onto the exit loop leading back to eastbound Highway 55. He now had a broadside view of that car and all its glory as it traversed the curve. It was a police car, and it was also signaling to go eastbound. There nothing to it, Myles thought, just a cop turning around to make sure he stays in his jurisdiction. Myles drove the short distance to Winnetka Avenue, under the speed limit, and the squad car did the same. Myles turned on the green left turn arrow and drove two blocks to Golden Village Road where he turned right, finally pulling up in front of The Point. The cop must not have been in the mood for fine dining and music because the squad car slowly rolled on past, ending the dogged pursuit. Myles shut off his engine and watched in wonderment until the cop was out of sight. "Only in America," he said aloud.

It was a renewed privilege to get inside with his ax and be a part of the setup and warmup with time to spare. He savored another consecutive night where a full grand dining room of people came for the food but lucked out by having the best music to eat it by.

Then he watched a smiling Huey Persons, seeing that everyone was ready and doing a circular, finger-snapping motion with his hand, "Let's knock 'em dead," he said kicking off the opener with a peppy intro which lured Bertha Paradise into those questioning lyrics of Cole Porter's *What Is This Thing Called Love*. Scores of diners were destined to know the answer by the end of the evening.

The three sets flew by on a night which belied a lot of wild rumors that jazz is dead. Diners again lingered well beyond strawberry cheesecake and table-clearing. What kind of people are these who can't be driven out the door by the sound of jazz? It's so un-American, Myles thought sardonically with a microscopic grin. It was over for the night, but that was only because the owner insisted on their quitting at quitting time despite the urging and begging of the die-hard listeners. Myles did the musician pack-and-chat thing before heading for a highway to the servant's quarters.

Myles was still beaming as he got up to speed on eastbound Highway 55. He couldn't help thinking of Yvonne and how great it would be to return to her, coming from an unusually good American gig. The deep breath he took in came out as a sigh of satisfaction, because he knew in his bones that it wouldn't be long. He turned on the radio and hit the FM jazz station. An unfamiliar group was playing that soft, swaying bossa standard by Michel LeGrand, *Watch What Happens*, a cool melody conducive to relaxation. His drive reached the Wirth park area where the fog began to thicken, but Myles felt blessed that the white road stripes would be his gentle guide to the other side. He bobbed his head slightly to a tune he'd played many times over the years as he watched what happens when youngsters played it. It took discipline, but most of them stayed awake until it ended, he recalled.

From the darkness, flickering red lights from behind jolted him. With the accompanying bright spotlights blinding him through the mirror, it took two-handed concentration to pull over to the side of the road without going into the swamp. He stopped and turned off the music with its timely message. Myles was already watching like a hawk. It must be the car, he thought. Even in a *fog*, his vehicle must have arrived on the radar of recognition becoming known by the police as *that* car carrying that Black man who plays *that* music. He would have to talk to his brother Al about spray painting it a different color. The possibilities were limitless, starting with fog gray or a midnight camouflage. A tap on his window brought him back to reality.

"Yes, officer," Myles said with as much pseudo-cheerfulness as he could muster at such a late hour. "Was I driving too slow?"

"Where you comin' from, boy?"

Myles could only think that this cop was presenting himself as a step down from the last one either by design or by ignorance. "I'm coming from my job, officer."

"Where's your job?"

"At *The Point Supper Club.*"

"What are you, boy, a dishwasher?"

"Not quite," Myles said, ignoring the obvious age demotion. "I'm a musician, sir."

The cop pointed his flashlight through the window and snooped his eyes out. "Ah ha! Is that a bag full of stolen silverware?" he was focused on the bass case.

"No, officer. It's my instrument. An innocent bass fiddle."

"Get out and show me."

Myles was all for keeping an American cop happy by getting out of his car, extracting his ax, unzipping, and peeling back the cover for the swamp-side inspection. "See, it wouldn't hurt a fly," he said calmly.

The cop nodded with approval and asked for a drivers' license.

Myles was more ready than last time, producing his international driving permit and his passport.

"Put it back in and wait," the cop said on the way back to his highly illuminated cruiser.

Myles could only feel thankful that this stop wasn't on the way to the gig, because at least there would be nobody at the servant's quarters to call him on the carpet for tardiness. But these cops, he thought, they wanted something, or they wanted to keep an eye on something. What? Could they be doing surveillance on part of the contraband that he personified that valuable and illicit commodity called jazz? Do they think this is something innocent families with children and house pets need protection from? What is this anyway?" The guessing cap on top of Myles' head was about to implode when long minutes later, the cop returned with his documents and a ticket for speeding.

"But officer," Myles said calmly, trying not to whine, "there must be some mistake here. It's way to foggy out here for speeding."

"Take it up with the judge," the cop said and went back to his squad car only to drive off with squealing tires and the smell of rubber.

Myles started the engine and drove eastward out of the fog, eventually making it to his place while still in a state of disbelief. The incident took him back to his childhood and the rural amusement park he went to with his siblings. They never missed the Fun House, that dark, scary, jerky tunnel ride full of screams, sobs, and pop-up monsters around every curve. But he had to look on the bright side. After all these years, he would've expected serious inflation costs for admission tickets, but it didn't cost him a dime! He just got a Fun House on the house!

As the world turned, Myles was up at the crack of noon, as he promised to get over to the flower shop and help Althea unload bags of potting soil from a truck. They joked their way completely through the task, which was what made it much easier to do than it sounded. His time back in the states was giving him a chance to reconnect with her after decades of sibling estrangement.

After that, he just knew that brother Al wouldn't mind if he dropped in and stole a free workout washing cars.

But he mainly wanted him to be a sounding board about what was going on out on the highway.

"Maybe if you didn't tell 'em you're a jazz musician, they'd leave you alone," he had said just a few hours ago.

Myles forgave him for having lived such a sheltered life. "Jazz is my bitch!" he had said with playful grit. Now he was on his way out to yet another date with his *bitch*, and it was a fine romance. A double-dog good time.

Myles drove across the Minneapolis city border and into the suburban village of bogs with the radio blaring out that good old *Duke Ellington* big band standard, *Satin Doll.* His patting free foot was keeping good time with music until suddenly, there was a silencing swipe noise like a phonograph needle being unceremoniously removed from the record.

The announcer would surely explain. "Well, dear listeners, we've heard your demands, and we are happy to report that this station, as of this minute, has switched over to a country music format, and we'd like to start things off with a Johnny Barns tune, *'Weird Weasel, Walk on out The Door'*. So welcome aboard buckeroos!"

"What?" Myles said to the radio. "Did I demand that? Nobody called me! I didn't tell 'em to do that, oh no, not me."

There was only one solution to the startup of incessant listening for a moment. A Bach chorale became a musical life raft.

The evening was clearer than usual, which allowed him to see far into the distance of his rearview mirror. Some sort of an emergency vehicle the size of a dot was on a run and getting bigger with each glance at the reflection. He saw the headlights winking back and forth while the flashing red lights grew brighter as the distance decreased, and now he could hear the wailing siren, royally fucking up Bach's chorale. Myles thought it just had to be an ambulance in a hurry, and he was prepared to do the obligatory pullover for an emergency vehicle. He came to a stop with his tires against the curb, a safe enough distance to let it pass. He watched in disbelief as the emergency vehicle slowed, pulled over and came to a stop almost directly behind him, the siren still blaring. It was an ambulance that somehow morphed into a police squad car. The siren finally went off and the wait began. Myles loved the silver lining in all of this. The next time he ever went gig hunting in America and the club owners asked if he had a following, he could look those club owners straight in the eye and say in all honesty, "Yes, I have a following." When the cop was good and ready, and not a minute before, he got out of his squad car and approached, apparently the same old talking flashlight.

"How are you, officer?" Myles asked. "I've missed you so much."

"What's your name, wise guy?" the talking flashlight said.

"My name? Why do you ask, officer?"

"I'll ask the questions, you'll give the answers, but first, turn that goddamn thing off," the cop said with no respect whatsoever for Bach.

"But officer, it helps me relax. Isn't that legal?"

"Look, boy, you can turn it off yourself, or you will get out of the vehicle, and I'll turn it off. Now what's it gonna be?"

His bass was taking a nap and Myles didn't want to wake it up with a lot of commotion, so he pushed the button and cut Bach off at the knees.

"One more time," said the voice behind the light. "What's your name?"

"Sure. My name is Myles Andrews, officer. What on earth is the problem?"

"I know everybody out here, and that name just doesn't ring a bell," the cop said.

"Wow," Myles exclaimed. "You must have a mind like a steel trap."

"Trust me," the cop said menacingly, "we've got a steel trap for troublemakers like you."

Myles bit his tongue with a gut feeling that this thing was headed south on a fast track. Caution was going to have to become his ally against an apparent loose cannon cop. He saw an urgent need to become an absolute miser of reasons to shoot and reasons to die the American way. "How can I help you, officer?" he inquired as he squinted up at the bright light.

"What brings you out here?"

Myles was thinking to choose his words very carefully. "My car, mister officer," he said.

"We don't need troublemakers out here. Git my drift?"

"Well, if I see any, you'll be the first one I'll call," Myles promised, "and you don't even have to give me a reward."

"Where you from, boy?"

"Madagascar, sir. You see I'm just a tourist over here checking out all the wonderful sights," Myles said while handing over his passport and his international driving permit.

"You sit tight," the cop said on his way back to the cruiser.

Myles waited long moments with his heart pounding and thoughts of survival, but this wasn't anything he remembered from army basic training. With this kind of cop, it could go either way, even with an ill-timed sneeze, and then he could instantly become just another unfortunate statistic of the swamp. His world travels were too long and extensive to wind up having the angels singing that he traveled a valley too far to reach heaven before his time.

At last, the cop returned to his window and handed the documents back while wearing light blue wrist-length rubber HAZMET or crime scene gloves.

"Ya can't be too careful," the cop said. "Move on."

Myles drove away while quietly whistling a little tune, but it chilled him when he realized he was in the wrong part of the country to be whistling *Dixie*. He kept an eye on the diminishing headlight of the immobile police car. The next time he looked all he saw was two distant orange parking lights, and he tried not to entertain any thoughts that the cop would be waiting right there to escort him home after the gig. When he was quite a distance down the road, Myles drove through an intersection with green lights while consciously holding his speed at fifty, five miles-an-hour under the limit. Another police car was sitting at the crossing, its turn signals flashing for a left turn back in the opposite direction. Myles was feeling relief as he kept one eye on his mirror. The cop car was in the intersection preparing to go the other way, both of its taillights showing, but it stopped, and now its back-up lights were showing. Myles didn't miss the cop's knowledge of the standard celebrity limo driver's escape tactic, skidding a smokey one-eighty spin and headed west after him. Myles saw the flashing red lights come on and rolled the window down a couple of inches, but he didn't sear a siren. The sinking feeling in his gut was enhanced because of being so close to *The Point*. That police car was closing on him at something looking like seventy miles an hour. Myles thought he could just get a grip on his bass and step on it, beating the cop to the restaurant, but it would look too much like fleeing. He simply pulled over and waited, foiling the cops desire to engage in a chase. Sure enough, the cop car, ablaze with flickers of red, breezed silently in behind him and came to a stop like a bunny at the end of its hop. The policeman used up precious minutes before he finally approached the car.

“I already did this a few miles back,” Myles explained. “What’s this for?”

“It’s for your own good,” said another cop who was less afraid to show his face from behind the dimmer flashlight.

“Officer, can’t you guys change up a little and do this for somebody else’s good?”

“Yours first,” the cop said. “Let me see your signal lights.”

Myles pulled the lever down, and the cop merely turned his head both ways to see that they were working.

“Now the other side.”

Myles pushed the lever up while the officer stood flat-footed and watched as the green dashboard dot winked at him.

“Now let’s see your emergency flashers.”

Myles pushed the dashboard button hoping the cop would take a walk, but he didn’t. He seemed to be getting a vicarious thrill from being in the midst of flashing lights. Sigmund Freud would probably conclude that he was deprived of Independence Day fireworks as a child, and that it would be the very reason that this policeman joined the force.

“Now let’s see the windshield wipers.”

Myles turned the knob, and the wipers smeared the guts of bugs into two golden arches across the glass. The last thing he needed was to come to America and start doing commercials for McDonald’s.

“Let’s hear the horn.”

“Are you sure, officer? I mean wouldn’t you rather hear the radio?”

“You *do* have a horn, right?

“Yeah, I do,” Myles said. Obediently abiding by the order to honk, Myles used the heel of his hand to become the world’s first African American honky, certain to become a distinction that would live in infamy.

Myles was looking at his watch and fighting himself to stay calm. "Why yes, officer, this most definitely is my car."

"Got any drug paraphernalia?" the cop asked as he shined his flashlight down into Myles' lap.

"No, officer. I haven't made it to the Rocky Mountains yet."

"Umm-hmm," the cop muttered as he finished up his flashlight intrusion. "Turn off your vehicle and hang loose." He was gone back to his squad car.

As Myles waited, he saw the clock and could only guess what tune they were now playing to open the first set. Sooner than he expected, the squad car drove up to his window where the officer rolled down his passenger window and dismissed him with a warning before driving off.

Myles arrived shortly and waltzed his bass through the door and into the quiet din of dinner, but there was no music in the air. The group was standing off to the side of the stage chatting. Myles sought out and caught the eye of Huey Persons, then nodded profusely with affirmation that, yes, it had happened again. The easygoing Huey, suave and debonaire in his pinstriped suit simply returned a nod of understanding about the hushed highway atrocities. "We're taking five waiting for another drummer," Huey said. "Landil Hakes got sick at the last minute and couldn't make it tonight. But hang loose, a good sub is on the way."

At that moment, a fellow walked in burdened down like a pack mule with black cases and rollers of drum gear. Huffing and puffing, he set it all down and extended his hand to everybody. "I'm Max Roach," he said, "at your service."

Myles exploded with a guffaw, fulfilling a need for something to laugh about, the fact that there is really only one Max Roach.

Undaunted and looking like he was thoroughly used to the drill, the fellow reached under his jacket and extracted his wallet from a back pocket. He willingly flipped it open and showed his drivers' license. It clearly showed the same blond crew cut, the same black horn-rimmed glasses, the same cheesy grin, and sure enough, his name was actually Max Roach. The only thing the license didn't show was the high pants and white socks.

"Well, well," a smiling Huey Persons said. "The musicians union said they were going to send me a drummer, but I didn't know it was going to be . . .a Max Roach."

"The pleasure is all mine," Max said as he swung into action setting up his traps. He was a plumber and an erecting mechanic with logistical speed, and in a flash, he was ready. It seemed almost too easy to deduce that good set-up skills means good playing ability, but it remained to be seen. Myles joined in with the tune-up, and when they were stoked and ready to go, Huey took the microphone and greeted the contented diners, then kicked off the first tune, a four-four thing, kind of up. Bertha Paradise happily stalked the spotlighted microphone in her sparkling gold dress of neck-breaking contours and sang out those old familiar lyrics, "*It's you or no one forrr meee...*"

Myles was all in with the tune, and it was about to get beautiful, but he was a patient man. Max Roach played the wire brushes like tennis racquets on the sidewalk while his bass drum started knocking like the hammer of a master carpenter, on every single nail, on every single beat. Myles heart sank as the incessant knocking rendered his cool *Ray Brown* walk useless. He tried to throw in some accented syncopation to break it up a little, but the only thing that was breaking up was a good groove. With all that knocking, the diners were fixing their full mouths to ask, "Who's there?" Myles couldn't see Huey's face, but he could see dejection in his shoulders with a resignation that this was going to be a night to tough out to a bitter end. Everything was going to sound like the drumbeat for Buddy Holly's *Peggy Sue*.

Myles was fighting with the time, trying to restrain and reel in the rushing drummer like *The Old Man and The Sea* with a big, feisty marlin on the fishing line. While he fought, Myles saw Huey summon a waiter to the edge of the stage and whisper something in his ear. Within a few moments, the waiter left and returned with a few bar towels. Huey hung them on the back of the bass drum to muffle the knocking, but Max Roach didn't know the difference because his eyes were closed while he thought he was being creative, but just look at Huey throwing in the towel to get the right sound. Myles felt the relief of springing *Ray Brown* out of prison, it was quieter, but he knew the parole would last only until a hole was knocked in the towel. It would be in his best interest, he thought, to double as a towel boy for the rest of the evening.

Professionalism carried the night as the veterans in the group found a way to make it fly for three sets with a busted cylinder. They broke camp for the night a little more subdued than usual, but there was silent optimism for the next night, when their machine would be back from the repair shop. Myles was wrapping up his base within earshot as Huey Persons was talking to Max Roach.

"Man, . . . don't you *feel* nothing'?" Huey asked.

"Oh, yeah, I'm doin' that all the time," Max said. "Don't worry about me. I've got lots of girls."

Huey played like he believed him, thanked him for coming, paid him, shook his hand, and wished him luck in the future. Myles wished him the same, thinking that Mr. and Mrs. Roach couldn't have known what they were doing by naming their son Max, but the kid really dodged a bullet. . .or a shoe. . .by not being named Cock, because if he had been, everyone would be trying to stomp on him, and only then could the real Max Roach stop spinning in those little graves in people's minds.

Myles was packed and out the door after a comfortable hang with the guys, but before he drove a mile, he was kicking himself for taking the wrong road home. He immediately saw the error of his ways for his lapse of fortitude in avoiding Highway 55 by doing a cowardly detour down Glenwood Avenue. Next time, he vowed to stick to his guns and be himself on Highway 55. He would have to dig down deep within himself to come up with his best Alfred E. Neuman persona. The situation, he surmised, was not his problem, it was a police problem.

The days sprinted by while Myles was pulled over twice again by village law enforcement, but his chin was held high in the clouds of righteousness. It was a lift to be with his siblings at the beloved house of Isabelle. They were sitting around the table over the spoils of another wonderful, killer fried chicken dinner. Lingering with the taste of strawberry ice cream was a genuine concern for their brother, Myles.

"It sounds like some very crazy stuff going on out there," said Al. "And I never heard that it was like that."

"That part of America is like a broken record," Myles said. "The more things change, the more they stay the same."

"I just don't want you to wind up getting shot, you know how they are," said sister Althea.

"Shoot me?" Myles scoffed. "Nah, I just speak softly and carry a big bass."

But Althea wanted to keep it serious. Her brow was furrowed with worry. "Can't you just tell 'em you're a visitor, a guest in the country? It could get you better treatment," she asked.

Myles leaned back and laced his fingers behind his head with a half-kidding smile on his face. "If this land that you guys live in is so great, it shouldn't matter," he said.

The cat had their tongues. It was too true to refute. Myles wouldn't have had the time to argue the issue, even if he wanted to. He hugged them both and hurried off to get ready for the gig out in the sticks, because experience taught him how much of a glutton Highway 55 cops were with other people's time – a routine that was definitely showing signs of old age. It wasn't long before Myles was leaving the lighted city limits and driving into the darkness of Golden Village. A medium fog slightly shrouded his view of the road ahead while once again the friendly oncoming intermittent stream of reflective paint stripes on the highway guided him. Suddenly his eyes widened as he passed through the lake and swampland of Theodore Wirth Park. He was startled by a moving greenish carpet on the road ahead and turned on his high beams. There must have been thousands of frogs leaping their way through the mass crossing! He laid off the gas and brakes, and with a white-knuckle grip on the wheel, he tried to steer straight but the car fishtailed and skidded and swerved around as the tires popped and squished the migrating horde of amphibians. Myles was fortunate to regain control of the car when he passed their crossing route, and he let out a sigh of relief that he and the bass didn't do a roll. As he resumed lawful speed, he heard the tapping of tire debris hitting the wheel wells, and he thought it was clear sailing to *The Point*, but he couldn't have been more wrong. Frog legs never were as lucky as rabbit feet, because from out of the darkness he spotted those confounded flashing red lights in his rearview mirror. He pulled over and came to a stop, and so did the police car. Moments later, Myles heard the croaking of shoes as the officer approached the car, and once again he squinted to protect his eyes from the intensity of a flashlight.

"Are you lost, buddy?"

Myles thought of the question as not only tired, but it was exhausted. "No, just going to my job," he answered.

"You were observed swerving and driving recklessly back there," the faceless voice said. "Have you been drinking?"

"No! Frogs! It was the frogs," Myles insisted, "check my tires. The frogs definitely had a hand in this."

"Step out of the vehicle," the cop ordered.

Myles got out and blew a kiss in the direction of punctuality at *The Point*. He squinted again as the cop closely checked his eyes for redness.

"Tell the truth for a change, boy," the cop commanded. "You have been drinking haven't ya?"

Myles quickly made the honorable decision to come clean. "Why yes, officer. I have been drinking," he said.

"How much have you had to drink?"

Myles looked at the ground as he searched his memory. He then tweaked his chin as he gazed at the heavens while trying to recall correctly. "Well, it wasn't three, but it was actually four glasses of lemonade that I had with my fried chicken dinner."

"Wise guy, huh? Okay. Let's see you walk a straight line with your arms out."

Myles heeded the order and started walking a straight line that would have been the envy of *Karl Wallenda*. He did an about-face and returned with an almost straighter walk.

"Alright, alright," said the disappointed cop. "Knock off the showboating and get back in the vehicle and sit tight."

"That's far from showboating, officer," Myles assured him. "Because if I was showboating, I would take a knee like Al Jolson and start singing *Mammy*. That's showboating."

"Al *who*?"

"I rest my case," Myles said as he got back in his car to wait out the enforcement of the law of the land. He surrendered his international driver's license and turned on the radio for a little detention music, cutting in on the oldies R&B station playing James Brown's *Hot Pants*. It was a tune which took him back a few decades to the discos of Copenhagen where he danced. Myles started bobbing his head with the music and the memories were so contagious that he started making moves like his feet were in the seat of his pants. It was nasty. James Brown was allowed to finish the entire super-funky tune before the cop finally showed up, and appearance that Myles greeted with gratitude because his butt muscles were getting sore from dancing past his prime.

"I would take care of that soon if I was you," the officer said as he handed a ticket and the international driver's license through the window and left without taking questions.

Myles turned on his dome light and read what he was stuck with. "Careless driving on an international driver's license?" he yelled back at the flashing lights. "Is that all? What about the frog slaughter? I know, I know, tell it to the judge."

After the cop doused the lightshow and drove off, Myles followed at one mile-an-hour under the speed limit with his eyes peeled for road creatures big and small.

When he finally got there, Bertha Paradise was on, and Noah Jameen was going some extremely hip bass work with his left hand, but he nodded with relief when the boom of real fiddle strings took over. The music was the restaurant's laissez faire affair, subtle and unobtrusive, but good. It simply belonged, and even the cooks knew it was that last seasoning for a fine dinner of succulent prime rib with buttered mashed potatoes and tender asparagus. It all worked out well with a few shakes of Bertha Paradise and a brass ladle of Huey's soft, seasoned notes of nectar. It was home far away from home, but through it all, Myles could feel Huey mentally sharpening his hatchet. Between notes, he patted the back pocket containing the folded airline ticket. This could be it, the end of an extended American visit, and he plucked each note of each tune with a melancholy sense of farewell. Too soon, they were playing the chaser to end the first set.

"I need to have a word with you," Huey said with a summoning index finger.

Myles followed him to the calm privacy of the small lounge with visions of a three-thousand-mile journey dancing in his head. He braced for the ultimatum from a straight shooter, that the gig had run out of last chances. "I'll make it easy for you sir," Myles said bravely.

"No, I'll make it easy for you," Huey said. "That third note of the bridge on that second-to-the last tune, he pinpointed, "you played a B where it should have been a B flat."

"Oh, well . . . I mean, how could I be so careless," Myles stammered. "I certainly will be more careful next time."

"Please do," Huey said before being tracked down by a restaurant employee with the message of a waiting phone call. For Myles things were suddenly shaping up like the evening a bullet was dodged, which would stall off just a little longer the day he would be warming the seat on a trans-Atlantic flight.

The rest of the evening's gig played out like hot buttered okra with no friction whatsoever, and a decent substitute drummer to boot, but not to boot around. Each tune Huey Persons selected to call was another layer of mellowness for all within earshot. Such love, this music.

Afterwards, Myles made it back to his pad without a highway misfortune to burst his bubble of bliss. It felt so much like an inalienable right.

It was three weeks into a good gig at *The Point*, but Myles was once again feeling that hollow spot in his gut, a yearning for the little land of thousands of kilometers across the Atlantic, Denmark. Over the years, the place cured him like a slab of bacon, and he missed it, and he longed for the presence of Yvonne. He just finished an intercontinental phone call to her which lasted longer than the usual thirty minutes, and their feeling of absence was mutual. By the end of the conversation, they talked each other into a plan that the end of *The Point* gig would be the right time to return. Their afternoon soup dates were scheduled to resume and continue for eternity. His ear was still warm after he dressed himself and his ax for the elements. This time, the weather forecasters didn't lie. The pouring rain could stop neither a mailman nor a jazz musician from delivering. His windshield wipers were working overtime as monster drops pummeled the roof and hood of his car like Max Roach. His speedometer was reading forty-five in a fifty-five zone, but flashing red lights bloodied the water cascading down his rear window. Myles pulled over and came to a gradual stop. The hard downpour didn't have the look of letting up as he waited for a wet-behind-the-ear cop to show up. He didn't have to think back too far to recall that stops like these were something completely unheard of on the highways and byways of Denmark or any other European country. This is an exclusive canker sore on America's butt, a country that apparently takes it sitting down. Myles didn't see him coming and was startled by the cop tapping on the window with a night stick. He rolled the window down and took in a cool shoulder and lap shower.

"Somethin' I can help you with out here, buddy?" The voice behind the dripping flashlight was surly and menacing.

"Well, you might want to help me stay dry," Myles said with a dry tone.

"Alright wise ass. I'm gonna need you to step out of the vehicle. Let's go!"

Myles was puzzled. "You. . . mean. . . after the storm?"

"I mean now, move it, bub," said the ego-soaked policeman.

"But you don't understand," Myles pleaded. "I'm a musician and the musician's union won't let me go out in the rain before a gig. It's all right there in our bylaws. You see, if they catch me playing all wet, I could get hit with a pretty hefty fine."

The cop was drenched with something more than water. He stepped back, drew his gun and for the moment, held it pointed at the ground. "It's up to you," he said through clenched teeth.

Myles again was thankful that his momma didn't raise him to be no fool. The sight of the lethal hardware prompted him to get out of the car with raindrops falling on his head. The cop made him turn around and place his hands on the car, then kicked his feet apart for a wider stance. Still holding the gun, the officer of the law began frisking him with his other hand, upper body first, then the legs. The cop's groping hand arrived at the groin and stayed there too long, squeezing and kneading.

"Do I have a right," Myles said with his eyes blinking rapidly from exploding rain drops, "to ask what the hell do you think you're doing, officer?"

"I'm lookin' for drugs," the cop said, still squeezing.

"I'm sorry to know that you need drugs this bad," Myles said of the repulsive invasion of privacy. The rain was coming down harder and the cop was finished getting his jollies just as a bright arc of lightning rolled a clap of thunder across the angry sky. He ordered Myles back into his car, holstered his weapon and sloshed back to the squad car where he turned off the emergency light and took off.

Feeling violated and shaken, Myles sat for a moment trying to chase the elusive sense of it all. He was running late so he stepped on it and was lucky to make it to the gig with two minutes of green time remaining. Carrying his bass in front of him, he did the steering tango through the front door and among the tables, avoiding serving trays and eye contact. He was on stage out of breath, wringing wet and ready for the first note, but by golly, he made it. Huey Persons tried not to notice, maintaining that all the other bass players in town were booked, so go with the devil you know, so he moved on to a special introduction and explanation over the microphone. The regular singer Bertha Paradise was a little under the weather tonight, so he asked for and got a warm round of applause to welcome to the stage, substitute *Button Heckett*! The diminutive cutie pie bounded in stage, grabbed the microphone and waited professionally for the intro to be played. When her time came, she belted out the lyrics to an old familiar tune. As he played, Myles smiled to know that a singer like this could be a breeze who could speed up the evening, maybe enough to dry him out. If she was as big as a minute, her voice was as big as an hour. She was no Bertha Paradise, but Bertha Paradise was no Button Heckett either. Whatever she was selling, the diners were buying it and paying for it with hard-earned applause. Huey Persons would definitely be able to redeem his image as a great leader since the disaster of a player mis-named Max Roach, which is why a sly smile was included in Huey's embouchure. Here is a man who truly enjoys what he's doing, which is the main ingredient that has fueled his grand longevity at *The Point*.

The set completely dried Myles out and on the break, he headed straight for the bar to get a little bottle of sparkling water. Huey Persons was going in another direction but veered out of his way to approach him. He placed a fatherly hand on what just might become his *former* bass plyer's shoulder. "It's happened to me before," he said. "But I got pulled over on Highway 55 tonight, about an hour before you."

"You're kidding," Myles said. "You?"

"Yeah, not far from here."

"But you've been out here forever, Mr. Persons. Don't they know you by now?"

"I don't know, but to them, I was violating the rule."

"The rule? What rule?"

Huey looked both ways as if what he said would matter to anyone else. "Driving while Black," he said out of the corner of his mouth.

"That's pretty sad commentary on America, isn't it?" Myles lamented, "but to be honest, I really didn't think I was the only one of us getting pulled over in a driving rainstorm. The question is, does city hall know this is going on, and if so, what are they doing about it?"

"They do know about it," Huey said. "They've known about it for quite some time. Sometimes city council meetings tend to get publicized in the newspaper, and I've read a few times about attempts by city hall to defend the cops against complaints."

They were simultaneously distracted from their conversation by two elephants in the room, the rarely seen owner of *The Point*, Horace Leary, and the infamous Octavius Killjoy who was rolling one of his little devilish upright player pianos right square into the path of the surprised Mr. Leary.

Myles and Huey were well within earshot and watched the upcoming incident with rapt attention to a blatant display of audacity.

"What is this?" the owner said waving his arms like he was directing the New York Philharmonic Orchestra.

"This, Mr. Leary, is how you are going to eliminate those horrific expenses of owning a piano," Killjoy said with all the cheer of a bouquet of plastic flowers. "Hear me out."

The scowling Mr. Leary was resting his tightly coiled fists on his hips as he pondered the legal expenses of assaulting this clown in front of witnesses.

"Let's talk about your piano on that stage," Killjoy said winding up for a pitch like he thought he was Cy Young in the World Series. "Here's what you could be lookin' at. First, you gonna need to check the soundboard. Over time they can warp and lose resonance, but you might be able to avoid that cost it and only if you don't have a fire."

Myles glanced at Huey who was starting to smile as he read the boiling expressions of irritation on the owner's face like an old familiar music chart.

"Then you gonna need to restring it," Killjoy continued, "an' da restring gonna cost ya da thirteen hundred dolla," he said, counting items by clutching each of his fingers for emphasis. "Then you gonna need new hammer heads. "It never felt so good," Killjoy said with a devilish smile, "but thas agonna cost ya da eleven hundred dolla."

Myles was buying into the joke with a few smiles of his own as he watched Mr. Horace Leary's anger slowly turn to shock.

"But before you do all that, you gonna needa da pin block cuz dat's what holds your tuning in place, but we'll get to tuning in just a moment," Killjoy promised. "Are you wit me?"

Mr. Leary extracted a handkerchief from his pocket and biting his lip, slowly wiped some beads of sweat from his forehead.

"One pinblock job is gonna cost ya da eight hundred dolla. Then you gonna need da regulating job," Killjoy proceeded with his finger counting, "because dat's what gives a piano da action, and you wouldn't want a piano around that ain't got good action, would you? Well, dat's gonna cost ya da five hundred dolla."

Somewhere over the last few decades, Myles concluded. Huey Persons must have seen this con attempt before because the bandleader's laughing shoulders indicated a good outcome as the owner acted out a good play along.

But Killjoy wasn't through, "Then you needa the refinishing job to make your piano pretty. It'll cost two thousand dolla."

Myles saw that Huey Persons didn't have the slightest hint of worry on his face. In fact, he had the look of a man who just came back from watching twenty cartoons. But the owner was still reeling from sticker shock as he tried to wring sweat out of a damp handkerchief. He then started slowly pacing around this atom bomb of musician unemployment while he weighed the screaming bottom line of running a restaurant.

"How many of them repairs," Mr. Leary asked. "Can I get away with not doin' every month?"

"All of 'em," Killjoy pounced, "cuz that's a lot of money all together, ain't it?"

Now Mr. Horace Leary was sizing up Killjoy's toy with visions of a fatter wallet dancing in his head. "Well maybe you're right," the owner said with a tone of caving in. "Repairs do cost a lot of money. So . . .what's your deal?"

"Got it right here," Octavius Killjoy said as he opened a little trap door on the back and plugged it into a nearby wall socket. He then pushed a button on the side. A flip top keyboard appeared. Killjoy was counting his chickens as he pushed another button. The keys started moving as an invisible ghost started playing *My Wild Irish Rose*, honkytonk style. Killjoy smiled like a proud father while the owner winced.

"How much?" Mr. Leary asked.

"Give me one minute," Killjoy said as he opened yet another trap door and pulled out a soft plastic blob which he unrolled across the top of the piano. It was attached to a little electric box with a cord which he hurried to plug in and turn on. The little noise it made sounded like a compressor, and it started inflating the soft plastic mass. In a few moments, a full-blown well-built woman in a tight green evening gown rose from the piano top like a phoenix, a gaudy replication curled and cuddled on its side, head propped up by the hand and elbow as it supposedly admired the music. "It's a one-time thirty-five hundred dolla, and I'll throw in the goil for free. Whaddya say?"

Mr. Horace Leary's eyes were riveted to the seductive landscape above the Irish waltz going on below. It stopped him in his tracks. "Can she sing?"

"Well, no, but she can hum with the best of 'em if you don't put the plug in too tight, otherwise, she's a good listener," Killjoy said sheepishly.

Myles and Huey exchanged eye-rolling glances but continued to listen like two files on the wall.

Now the owner was scratching his head. "Do you play piano?"

"Nope, never learned," said Killjoy, "but I do know they're more trouble than they're worth."

"I'm gonna keep my piano," the owner said, "and this is a respectable place of business, so you need to remove this from the building immediately."

"Your wish is my command, sir, but think of me when you sit down with your accountant." Killjoy said while snatching cords, depositing a business card in the owner's hanky pocket and rolling the whole musical burlesque show out the side door, much to the amusement of everyone in the lounge except the owner who stormed away to his office.

"I feel guilty," Myles said.

Huey asked why.

"Because I didn't pay a cent to get into this show," Myles said, and they both cracked up.

"Think of how many of us would be out of work permanently if that clown gets his way Johnny Appleseeding those things all across the land?"

"I can only think of how many of us wouldn't be out of work for long if he gets his way," Myles said, "because that mess could get older than Methuselah so fast that people would be rioting for our return."

"Well, speaking of riots," Huey said after composing himself, "we'd better get back out there to keep one from happening here tonight."

They were back onstage accompanying Button Heckett on some scat-singing blues with an appreciation of something not to be taken for granted. Playing a gig was not just a livelihood, but it was something to be protected from being undermined by the invasion phony substitutes. They backed up the talent of Button Heckett who could sing well and didn't need to be inflated for attention. Through her fine voice, she must have been lobbying to Huey and the group and the diners for the job while at the same time being realistic enough to know that Paradise is hard to displace unless Paradise is under the weather. On this stage, the forecast for a substitute was never going to be good. To her credit, Button Heckett ignored the weather and sang her heart out, letting the chips fall where they may.

By the end of the night, the monsoon rain had stopped, and Myles was back on Highway 55 headed to his pad from yet another rewarding night of playing the music he loved. He blindly reached for one of the CDs on the darkness of the passenger seat and inserted it in the player, whatever it was. The car reverberated with the bodacious sound of the Buddy Rich big band, a good choice for his mood, and the bass in his mind played along. Suddenly, a bright, white shaft of light penetrated the darkness of his rear window. He slowed and prepared to stop. Flashing red lights came on and gave the music a disco feeling as the big band played Cannonball Adderley's *Mercy Mercy Mercy*. The cops turned off the flashing red lights and abruptly sped past, but not before hitting him in the eyes with two bright flickering spotlights.

As Myles resumed his journey, he turned the music down and pondered a certain curse that seemed to be consuming him, and he had to ask himself aloud, *"Am I getting used to this?"*

He had been away from it for enough decades to be objective about it, and if the answer was *yes,* he would be a walking, living, and breathing goddamn sinner of human dignity to call himself *used* to this kind of police behavior. *The Keystone Cops* were notorious for keeping people awake with laughs in movie theatres, but this was like watching a bunch of uniformed guys who must've fallen asleep during training. Hopefully, he thought, someday after he's gone, somebody will give them a wake-up call. That was a thought he could sleep on tonight.

There were two more evenings of highway hell being soothed by the delights of Button Heckett before Bertha Paradise finally returned. It was Huey Persons' gig, but it was Bertha's show. She was gorgeous in a very enrapturing way. Aside from all of her glitter, hers was a voice that grabbed listeners by the lapels and sat them down for a good taste of ear candy. They were getting ready to play again. Huey Persons was setting up the charts as Bertha Paradise picked another sideman to tease. Her low-cut, purple sequin even gown was the perfect mold for her to be poured into. Her hazel eyes and hair were accentuated by the thin shaft of a spotlight as her full ruby lips commanded him.

"Play me a tune," she said, her head tilted back and sideways as she looked up at him.

"What do you want me to play?" Myles asked game for anything.

"Silent nighty," she said without blinking.

"Silent nighty?" Myles said while being respectful of another person's untimely observance of Christmas.

"Yeah," she said, her head unmoved from its teetering angle of playfulness.

"What key?"

"F," she said, her eyes closing only halfway.

"I can see right through that one," Myles smiled.

"Does that mean you can read the music from the beginning *through* the end?"

"With big ears like mine, somehow I'll find you," said Myles with a laughing appreciation of her sense of humor.

Huey Persons finished lining up the charts with rolling and smiling eyes. He'd certainly been around long enough to have seen it all. The joking was over when he raised his hand to kick off a tune that was becoming more familiar over the weeks. Everybody loved *The Night Has a Thousand Eyes*. It was a semi-up tempo that Bertha Paradise swung right into with Noah Jameen's hip block chords and Landil Hakes' ever present adept subtleness on drums. Waiting patiently in the wings, locked and loaded, was a sugar water solo from the sweet horn of Huey Persons.

Myles plucked his bass impeccably and thought he had died and gone to heaven until his eyes picked up an incongruous sight among the diners. His string skipped a beat when three uniformed cops stopped approaching at the edge of the dance floor and stood with their arms crossed, casing the stage with more authority than a New York port. Myles couldn't tell if they were staring at him or at Bertha Paradise, a few diners in the room who knew the tune viewed it as a well-produced theatre; the rest were startled and unnerved by the rude intrusion. The musicians exchanged glances but continued to accompany hundreds of chewing jaws, playing the tune through to its near-conclusion, and for effect, they ended without playing that last, highly anticipated note. It was that old, tireless, lowdown, sneaky jazz trick. The police officers, the only ones not applauding, turned and walked out, but they knew the tune all too well. As any laxative could attest to, the cops were trained to have eyes in the back of their heads for one false move. Myles could clearly see that a thousand eyes was a bit too much for one night, but not nearly enough to catch one false move on his bass strings.

But that was all yesterday. Myles had a great following day, including the great trans-Atlantic phone conversation with Yvonne in Copenhagen and the great lunch with siblings Al and Althea, and now it was nightfall again. The treacherous road to a gig in the valley must belong to the people, he thought. He felt a need to test his inalienable right to go to a dinner club forty acres away in the mule he was driving. Something was telling him in his heart and soul and gut that if there was an answer to this road misery, it wasn't going to be coming from the street. He turned on the radio and lucked out on some relaxing Brazilian Bossa music and rode along with the samba, which took him to a place he'd never seen in all of his travels. He recalled agreeing with Yvonne that it was one of the destinations on their bucket list which they will eventually get around to, but for now, he could just feel the pulse of Rio and dream. The sky was star studded and the moon again beckoned human footprints. A quick glance in his rearview mirror completely blew all that tranquility to smithereens. It was nowhere near Christmas or December, so he knew that the object approaching him from a distance couldn't be just a flashing Christmas tree out for a jog. A few more seconds proved him to be right. Myles slowed and braked to a stop, then rolled down the window to wait, reluctantly turning off the samba. He braced himself when he heard two squad car doors slam and the slow crunching of pebbles under approaching footsteps. The cops split up, with one on each side of his car aiming bright flashlights in his eyes. Blindness seemed to be their main goal.

"Well," said the cop in charge, "what do you have to say for yourself?"

"You've got the right guy," Myles squinted, trying to shield his eyes with a hand. "I confess, I'm a serial rat killer."

"We'll certainly investigate that" said the cop, "but I don't remember seeing you around here."

"Why not, officer? Didn't you know we all look alike?"

"Show me your driver's license, and I'll be able to tell ya."

Myles could feel his heart pounding, but he was trying to stay cool. "What did I do wrong? What's the reason for stopping me?"

"In case you were not aware, I'm the one wearing the badge, and I don't need to give you a fuckin' reason for nothin'. Get my drift? But I'll just let you know, you were speeding, boy."

"It's just as easy for you to call me sir as it is to call me boy," Myles said. "It's still only three letters."

"That's right. Just like the KKK," the cop taunted. "Now let's see your license."

"If you can't give me a reason for stopping me, then I'm not going to show you my driver's license," Myles said defiantly.

"Okay, you're under arrest. Step out of the car, now!"

"You've got to be kidding," Myles said calmly.

Both cops drew their weapons and aimed at his head. "You'd better get out of that car, boy. I ain't playin'."

Myles was busy having an affair, a love affair with the life he didn't want to have taken from him. It was a no-brainer. He got out of the car, hands raised. "I do have some rights, you know," he said. "This is not about speeding, and you know it."

The cop in charge holstered his gun, spun him around and slammed him face down on the side of the road and kneeled his full weight on his back as he prepared to put on the handcuffs. "You think you know your rights?" he smirked incredulously.

"Yes, I do," Myles gasped and strained under the weight.

"Well, you know some of your rights, but you don't know all your rights," the cop said almost in the tone of a guarantee.

"What? Do you want to get into a pissing contest over this?"

"One thing's for sure," the cop said, "you're gonna be doing your pissing in jail tonight." They hoisted him to his feet and led him to the dreaded backseat of the police cruiser.

"Hey," Myles said with a panic of reality, "what about my car and my bass? I'm a musician, and I've got a job I'm supposed to be at."

"Well, you ain't got no job tonight because you're goin' to jail, and the car is goin' to impound." After shutting him in for a ride downtown, they drove away, passing his car and leaving it vulnerable to the goblins of the swamp.

"But you don't understand," Myles said looking out the back window and seeing only the diminished reflective license plate on the front of his car. "That's a valuable instrument in my car. Who's going to be responsible if something happens to it?"

"We're gonna have to hold your musical instrument," the other cop spoke for a change.

"Why? What do you mean?"

"We'll have to keep it for evidence."

Myles could feel his temples throbbing. "Evidence of what?"

"In case any crimes are involved, we'll have a source of fingerprints," one of the cops said.

"But what am I supposed to use at my gig, man?"

"You're just gonna have to sing along, boy," said the cop who was driving, "but that's only if you get there tonight. If this thing gets cleared up by tomorrow, you should be able to pick it up at the property room after you properly fill out and sign all of the required forms before five o'clock."

"Nobody would know how to handle it but a bass player," Myles insisted. "What about damage? What if they drop my sound post?"

"Simple," the cop said with a tongue-in-cheek glance at his partner, "just fill out a damage claim, turn it in, and don't hold your breath."

"Thanks a hell of a lot, officers of the law," Myles said with sarcastic emphasis. "So where will my car be?"

"Your vehicle will be at Tundra Towing way up on the north side," said the officer of seniority. "Just hitch a ride up there, pay the towing charge plus the storage fee, and last but not least, c'mon back downtown and pay the no-parking ticket."

"That's cold," Myles said without a shiver. "Gigs out here could get pretty expensive." He rode in silence for a few minutes, hands shackled behind his back while thinking about what he would be doing at this very moment if he hadn't come to America. It was a schedule etched in his mind that he would be on a swift train with a great jazz group headed for a two-night concert in Stockholm. Tonight, those lucky guys are truly free. On that crazy northbound train, he would have still been wearing the freshness on Yvonne's see-you-in-a minute kiss on his lips, which was something he never took for granted whenever he left the comfort of their home. Myles traveled a long way to experience the surrealistic juxtaposition of his birth country throwing him in the slammer just for going to a jazz gig. As he peered at passing scenes through the window bars of the rolling cage, he searched his soul for some newness in all of this, but he came to the sad conclusion that it was as old as the victimizations of middle passage. Bondage of Black men was a hip thing to the White man. As the ride downtown neared its destination, he could clearly see that the more things have changed, the more things have stayed the same. With his hands cuffed behind him, he could conveniently feel his wallet which contained his folded-up airline return ticket. He didn't need to check the expiration date. It was still good. Moving forward, it was just a matter of time. He could hear the intermittent babbling of the squawk box, but he wasn't listening. His eyes studied the only little part of a cop's face that he could see in the rearview mirror.

He couldn't help asking, "Why did you guys become cops?"

"I became a cop in order to get to know some blackface people, boy."

"Really," Myles said without question.

"Yeah, with you setting back thar in the cage. I'll ask the questions, and I'll get the answers and then we'll know each other a lot better, right?"

Myles' jaw dropped. "Well, shut my mouth," he mocked. "The last time I heard that line in a movie was way back when I only paid a dime to get in."

"Don't worry," the cop said, "these days we don't say our lines for free. It'll be included in the towing fee. Think of us while you're payin' it."

"For sure," Myles said. "But tell me, be honest, do you ever stop any White people?"

"Honestly? I never notice what color you are. I just notice bad driving habits," the cop said.

Sore ribs kept Myles from laughing. "Try stopping some White people," he said. "Who knows, you just might like them better."

"We'll run it up the flagpole," one of them said.

"In my experience, things that get run up the flagpole usually wind up flappin' in the wind," Myles said.

"That just goes to show you, ideas that flap in the wind ain't all that important, right? You got any more ideas, boy?"

"Not at this time," said Myles, "but stay tuned. I'll think of something."

Before long, the squad car made it to the heart of downtown Minneapolis where officers of the law who were sworn to serve and protect were about to serve their prisoner into the Hennepin County jail, all for the protection of the law-abiding citizens. The police car arrived at the night-lighted ancient gothic red shale courthouse and slowly rolled down a ramp and waited for the huge metal doors to open. They drove a short distance inside and parked in front of a sign which read: *Intake Only*.

Myles swung his legs out and stood up when they opened the door. With one cop on each arm, they escorted him through a door leading to the booking desk. Myles summed it up without asking, certainty they made some kind of deal to share the collar. Brownie points are a big fucking deal in the police department. As officers from other jurisdictions walked by, they craned their necks to catch the shoulder patches of their arresting colleagues. It was hard to tell if the righteous nod of approval were for Golden Village or the arrest of another Black man.

At the desk, Myles was photographed, fingerprinted, booked, and stripped of his belongings. They got his wallet, but they missed the airline ticket. He was then taken to the infamous holding cell known as *the tank*. The door of the iron bars slammed behind him. It was real. He was in jail. The tank was half full but was sure to fill past capacity with an influx of Friday night misbehavers. His suit and tie were like the bullseye of a red-and-white target. He was asked, but no, he didn't have a cigarette, and no he didn't have any spare change, nor did he know what time it was, and no he didn't want to talk to the incoherent Native American who had nose-curling halitosis from the depths of the Rippo vinelands. Across the cell, he saw a fellow who was already sick of incarceration, doing the Technicolor flash by throwing up his latest meal with a big splash on the concrete floor, followed by convulsive heaves. Myles turned away and removed his tie, wadding it up and stuffing it in his pocket, then took off his jacket and slung it over his shoulder just in case his own urge to vomit got any stronger. He observed that Native Americans dominated the population of the cell followed by many fewer Blacks and a sprinkling of Whites, one of whom was staring at him through bloodshot eyes.

"What're you in for?" the man asked.

"Me? I'm here for the improvement of White America, don't you know," Myles said. "I'm here because the powers of intolerance, without due cause, plucked me off the highway with a fishnet and threw me in here. I'm here because I've got a lifetime reservation in the *house of limbo*. But what it all boils down to is I'm here because a suburban government has been looking the other way for *years,* man. That's what *I'm* in here for," Myles said with a sigh.

"Sounds like you been doin' a lot of white-collar crimes, pal," said the man as he rose to his feet and walked an imaginary tightrope to the community toilet in the center of the cell, unabashedly pulled down his pants and seated himself rigidly. He was a guy in a fishbowl, forced to have his innermost business scrutinized. It gave a whole new meaning to being locked in the bowels of the county jail. The transparency of the fixture's placement was no doubt intended to be a humiliating deterrent to ever again becoming a jailbird. Myles could only speculate about whether or not that theory was working because it would depend on how many repeat jailbirds were in the house of detention. All he knew for sure was that the fellow on the john couldn't have summed up the Golden Village highway situation any better.

Myles clutched the cold iron bars and looked up and down the empty hallway for a jailer he could pitch for his rightful turn to make one phone call. Thirty minutes later his name was called, and he immediately raised his hand like a school kid. They let him out and showed him the way to the operator and then *The Point Supper Club.* He explained the situation to the first person who answered and then got put on hold. When a jailer told him he was taking too long, he held up a calloused index finger, begging for a few moments. When another unidentified person picked up, he explained who he was and desperately asked for Huey Persons. While he waited, the jailer was clearing his throat and looking at his watch. Finally, it was Huey on the phone, and he again explained and listened carefully for anger in his voice for the tardiness, but the anger in his words were directed at the police. He breathed a sigh of relief when the boss assured him that someone would be there as soon as possible to bail him out. Before Myles could finish thanking him profusely, the controlled phone went dead. He was led back to the jail cell and locked up the American way, where iron bars had his back. While he was gone, the population increased to standing room only. He found a spot in the corner and tried his best to mind his own business, his thoughts concentrating on the gig and all those wonderful tunes carrying on without a foundation, missing the boom of his kidnapped bass. His soul harbored a terrible frustration of letting down great musicians and a fabulous singer who all bent over backwards to take in a foreigner. His mind was racing with ways to make it up to them, especially Noah Jameen, the pianist whose lower keys must have been working overtime to carry the load.

After nearly an hour, Myles heard his name again and pressed through the crowd and to the door. The jailer let him out and into the custody of two strange men who showed up to bail him out. Both wearing suits and stern faces, familiar but forgettable mugs.

"The owner of the restaurant sent us," said the one with a toothpick directing traffic from the corner of his mouth.

"I'm so glad," Myles said. "Thank you."

After a laborious walk, they were out of the jailhouse and into the transport vehicle, a double-parked sleek black limousine. Myles was in the back seat, squeezed between two massive bookends of beef who were dressed to kill. It was an obvious requirement for getting him out of jail, but the question was asked anyway.

"What's your name?" It was the bullfrog voice to his right.

Myles' eyes were fixed on the huge diamond pinky ring which illuminated with a dazzling sparkle every time an overhead streetlight passed by. On the first try, his vocal cords were tied, and he said his name in a whisper. "My name is Myles," he said audibly, "and I – I don't swim very well with my feet set in cement, and I'd be more than happy to carry your violin cases if they're too heavy, and in conclusion, I didn't do anything wrong, so if you don't mind, I'll just get off at the next corner."

"Relax, my friend," the big mug laughed with a wheeze. "You're goin' back to the restaurant. We're friends of the owner, and he told us to look after you,"

The other one, humorless and stony faced, stared straight ahead as the driver negotiated traffic along the route. In a few minutes, they were passing the ass-kissing welcoming signs of Golden Village. In a few more minutes there were flashing red lights from the rear. The driver pulled over and stopped on the road diving the swamp. The lone cop approached the car with his flashlight high, cautiously peeking into the driver's open window. He then stood straight, relaxed and put the dark flashlight back on his belt. "You're good," the cop said, "just wanted to tell you how nice your limo is. We always compliment good things, it's policy. Have a good night." He was gone.

"We never miss putting the check in the mail, do we, Guido?" There was no reply. Myles could swear on a stack of Bibles that the check in the mail was in the form of white skin.

After a swift ride, the limo pulled gracefully into the parking lot of *The Point*. Myles thanked his rescuers and hurried in, living the nightmare of showing up at the gig without his bass, and running smack-dab into the owner, Mr.

Leary. "Got an extra microphone?" he asked, as if trying to change the subject.

"Sure, you can use my personal mike that I need to direct people in case of fire," Mr. Leary said as he pulled a fat fountain pen-size microphone from a pocket in his suit coat. "It's wired to the room, so just turn it on."

Myles was blown away that his request was so quickly fulfilled without question. "Thank you, sir, and by the way, I've been meaning to thank you for sticking up for a *real* piano. I really appreciate it."

"Yeah, that gizmo salesman is a pretty *stockitz* character," the owner said.

"Sir?"

"Well, the cops told me that they arrested him in the bushes outside."

"Did I miss something?"

"We all did. They caught him under the bushes committing indecent acts with his blow-up dolly."

In the face of his situation, Myles almost choked on something to be happy about, but it was welcomed.

"But they said he had an alibi," Mr. Leary continued. "He was only layin' on top of his dolly and squirming around because he was trying to let the air out of her, so she'd fit back in the piano. Well, they hauled him in because he couldn't explain why his pans were down around his ankles."

Myles' belly laugh was sputtering like the starting of a cold jalopy, waiting for the punchline to floor it, "So they arrested him for indecent exposure?"

"I guess they were going to, but after a little investigating," Mr. Leary shrugged, "there wasn't anything to charge him with except disturbing the peace."

Nothing else needed to be said. Myles was already rolling on the floor with laughter. "He didn't get the sale, so he figured he'd better get *something* out of it, boy, you can't get any more *stockitz* than that," Myles laughed holding his aching gut. In a minute, he was back on his feet but there was a serious look on the owner's face.

"On a serious note," Mr. Leary said in a subdued tone. "I'm aware of the trouble you're having on the road out there, and just so you know, we'll do everything we can to support you."

"I appreciate it," Myles said. "Thank you." He heard the sound of instruments preparing to play. It was time to go up, so he excused himself and headed for the stage. They opened the last set by playing *How High the Moon.* Myles pulled out his borrowed remote microphone and did the bass vocally by singing *Boom de-Boom de-Boom Boom Boom Boom.* He always knew his lower vocal strings could get the job done as an emergency ax.

Huey Person's had been around for a long time, but never in his career had he seen anything like this. "Where is your bass?" he mouthed with a roar.

"The police had it towed away," Myles said between breaths, but he boomed on. "If *Manhattan Transfer* can do this, so can I."

Huey Persons was a good-enough sport to let it pass, turning back to the oblivious diners and blowing his airy horn with nods of approval from the other players. The vocal bass notes and intervals were true enough for Bertha Paradise who was smiling as she sang. It was a night to remember.

Myles elected to call a cab after his abbreviated part in the last night's gig and it just happened to be Lester Ride who was willing to pick him up and drop him off at Tundra Towing to spring his car out of impound. It was best that he did it in the wee hours before the sun came up and baked his bass alive, melting the glue and undoing the strings. He didn't need to look to know that his finances were still very good, even after having to shell out more than two C notes to get his car out, but he would've preferred to give that money to a musician's charity fund if he had the choice. The sun and Myles were up at the same time, but a fair night's sleep hadn't relieved him of anger about the whole of last night, including going to the towing lot and finding his windows wide open, leaving his precious fiddle exposed to thieves and bad weather —a tired towing trademark.

He and Lester were into a half-hour of a strategy meeting at the counter of Al's Breakfast in *Dinkytown*.

"You know what those bastards need," Les said, clearing his mouth to talk as he held a syrup-dripped forkful a couple of inches from devouring it. "Those damn Golden Village cops need to be taught a lesson." He stuffed a wedge of stacks in his mouth and shook his head, either about the badness of the cops or the goodness of the pancakes.

"You're right," Myles said. "There comes a time when a man has got to stand up and fight police abuses, but that time has come and gone many times. What's changed?"

"Not much," Les conceded, "but somebody's got to make them really *hear* what innocent people don't like, because so far, those sons-of-bitches act like they don't have ears *or* brains."

"I heard that," Myles said, "and before I go back overseas, I'm gonna find a legal way to shout out a Black man's right to go to the gig in peace. American jazz is depending on it."

"Here-here," said Lester, raising his coffee cup in a salute before taking a swig. "I've got a friend who works in an office near the capital in St. Paul. It's the A.C.L.U. office."

"I don't know what that is," Myles admitted.

"Of course," said Les to a foreigner, "it's the American Civil Liberties Union."

"What does that mean?"

"They're kind of a watchdog for people's rights, among other things," Les explained. He started rummaging around in his shirt pocket and wallet, and there it was — the business card he sought. "Call him," he said, handing over the worn-out card. "He can point you to someone who would love your situation."

"How can I thank you?" Myles asked appreciatively.

"Pay for the pancakes, Dog," Les said sneering.

"Done," Myles said with conviction.

It was only the next night before Myles experienced another cop stop on the way home from the gig, although he slept a little better knowing that the calvary was sharpening swords, and he made it to St. Paul in a flash to challenge this A.C.L.U. outfit to see what they were made of. He followed the directions of three office officials until he finally located the man on the card, Starkey Mathews, introduced himself and spent an hour explaining his problem in sordid detail. Starkey Mathews was a patient man with calm furrows in this brow, his ruffled reddish hair accented his wrinkled brown suit. He listened, nodding as if he'd grown quite used to a broken record, taking notes in his head with his fingers laced across his belly. There was a grand pause after the story was told.

"Yes, we've had quite a few complaints about police activities on Highway 55, but your take on this problem suggests something fishy about your repeated encounters," he said. "We'll get to the bottom of it through the legal process."

"I don't mind speaking for others," Myles said. "We're all in the same boat."

"Well, we work with a different breed of lawyers," Starkey Mathews said. "They wouldn't lower themselves to become ambulance chasers unless their superiors insisted on it. Instead, they live and breathe to find civil rights cases. Call me tomorrow, and I should have someone."

"Thank you so much," Myles said. He accepted the extended business card and left the office with a handshake.

There was time to pass, and Myles did it by drying clean vehicles and clowning with the crew at his brother Al's carwash, then making it to the gig and back without road hassle and crashing for the evening with an impatient eye on the clock. Tomorrow couldn't come faster as Myles tried to fool himself that he was sleeping, lying in bed forcing his eyes to stay closed, like the anticipation during a childhood Christmas Eve, wishing for the Earth to please turn a little faster into the sunlight of tomorrow.

THE TRIAL

Myles was up early having a cup of tea and pacing as he waited for business hours to roll around. A half hour had passed since he made the call to Starkey Mathews and got a lawyer to take on the mess of Golden Village. Don't bother to call, he was told, just go there, because an open door had already been arranged. At Zero hour, Myles bolted out of his pad like the Kentucky Derby horse gates sprung open. His car didn't dare to not start, and he rode it with a lead foot and one eye glued to the rearview mirror until he reached the downtown brownstone warehouse district of buildings with beautifully renovated interiors and old, weathered exteriors frozen in time by historic preservation mandates. Myles lucked out on a parking spot directly in front of the target address. Out of the car, he bounded up the stairs of the Modern Law Offices and opened the third mahogany door down the grand hallway, which was the well-furnished office of Merle Williamson and Associates. The elegantly attired, attractive secretary was expecting him and showed him into Mr. Williamson's suite.

"Come in, come in, Myles," Mr. Williamson said as he was just getting off the phone. "Would you like some coffee?"

"No thanks, I'm fine," Myles said as the secretary left them and closed the door.

"Starkey Mathews gave me a briefing on your situation, but I'll want to hear more from you." Merle Williamson stood up from behind his desk in a crisp white shirt and colorful tie. He was a tall but portly man with a kind demeanor and the handshake of security blanket. "One of my associates is at city hall as we speak getting this on the municipal court docket, but after thinking it over, we're going to refile this case in the U.S. District Court under the provisions of the Federal Civil Rights Act of 1871. Isn't that nice?"

"Sounds real nice to me," Myles smiled, "but don't you have an act that's a little younger?"

"You would also be covered under the Civil Rights Act of 1964, but you need protection just in case the Ku Klux Klan jumps out of the swamp at you."

"In a way, it feels like they already have," Myles said.

"I understand," Merle Williamson said, "but let's just take things one step at a time, and rest assured, we're always trying to stop the boogeymen of injustice and intolerance in their tracks."

"That's good to hear," said Myles. "Just curious, where are you from?"

"I'm from Georgia," Merle said, almost standing at attention with the sound of his own words, "and I am respectfully not an apologist for the law, it is what it is, and I'm here to weed out and prosecute those who dare to violate it whether you're wearing a badge or not."

"Just checkin'," Myles inquired, "does that mean you're a tireless advocate for the downtrodden?"

"Well, I've been known as a pro bono champion, but don't hold your breath on this one," Mr. Williamson laughed, "we'll just try to finish what the police started."

"Why did you decide to practice law?"

"Oh, I always wanted to see social justice in a land where at one time there wasn't much," Merle said. "I was just plain lucky as a young college student because I was able to go from Minnesota to Montgomery, Alabama to help support the bus boycott caused by a fellow named James Blake."

Myles was scratching his head. "Who the hell is he?"

Merle Williamson laughed. "That was my exact sentiment at the time," he said. "I know you remember he was the bus driver who couldn't get Rosa Parks to give up her seat to a White man."

"Sure, I remember everything but his name," Myles said, "and he had her arrested, can you imagine that? But what kind of a man would ask a woman to get up so a man can sit down?"

"The word for that hasn't been invented yet," Merle said, "but that's what he did. I'll never forget cutting classes at the University of Minnesota and hitchhiking to Montgomery. It was such a pleasure, but my folks back in Georgia were having a fit because a group of us White kids chipped in and bought a bunch of poster board and paint. When we first got there, we were greeted by a group of people giving us the thumbs up when they saw our signs, like they were really glad to see us coming to help out. But the reality hit me like a ton of bricks when I put my glasses on and was able to see that all those people were only giving us the finger."

Myles shook his head as he smiled at the floor. "They were either showing their ages or their IQs," he said.

"One or the other," Merle confirmed, "but we found a spot in an alley and kept working on our boycott signs for lunch counters and bus stops, and we also made sandwich board signs tied together with strings for gray-haired African American guys to slip over their heads and wear proudly with front and back messages which read 'I Am A Man'," Merle Williamson recalled with sorrow.

"What was it like?"

"I gotta tell ya," Merle said, "aside from the dumb Klux Klan who didn't have a clue, the name calling, bumps and bruises, dog bites, a broken tooth, horse manure, spit, and just plain old seeing the heartfelt hate that there was for people of color? It was sad. I was sick to my stomach the whole time I was there because I could've been killed at any moment for being a meddling northerner, but I just needed to be there."

"Glad you're still here," Myles said.

"I can be thankful for that too," Merle admitted, "but it was like having a front row seat on the cutting edge of change, and I wouldn't have missed it for anything. With our help, the world witnessed the owners of lunch counters and bus lines begging for mercy. The boycott was killing them, but it took too long for the world to finally see diversity at those lunch counters and Blacks finally riding in the front of buses and not having to step off the sidewalk to let a White person pass by."

"Only in America," Myles said.

Merle Williamson unbuttoned his cuff and rolled up his shirtsleeve to his forearm. "See that? They're still there. Bites from the vicious teeth of public safety commissioner Eugene *Bull* Conner's police dogs."

"Did you say *public safety . . . commissioner*?" Myles asked incredulously.

"That was his job," Merle said, "keeping all the White people safe from Black pigmentation. It was these bites from way back then that hurried me through law school, and to answer your question, that's what made me want to practice law. What do you think of that?"

"Well, you're hired, I guess," Myles said

Merle Williamson rolled up his other sleeve, showing an unblemished forearm. "What do you say we get to work?"

"I'm all in," Myles said. "Let's do it."

"Good. What you have told me about your plight is appalling for sure," Merle said as he took a fresh yellow legal pad and pencil from a shelf and plopped it on the desk in front of his new client, "but I'm going to need you to take this home and write down everything you've experienced on that highway. *Everything!* I don't care if it's ten pages long. Write it down."

"I can do that," Myles said, "because I think you really do care."

"Of course, I do, and I'm not alone," Merle said. He went to another shelf and pinpointed a folded newspaper which he pulled out and unfurled with a few shakes, laying it out to show a frontpage story in *The Village Sun* newspaper. "See this? This is about discussions that the city council has been having about improving race relations in Golden Village. Some are concerned that not enough is being done to address questionable incidents between the police and Black citizens."

"Interesting," said Myles as he scanned a reporter's lengthy coverage.

"We're not going to change the world," Merle Williamson said, "but we have an obligation to air this issue in the courtroom. It all boils down to human rights, and it's not much different now than when I was a kid in law school. For instance, back then, I organized a demonstration to help free an exchange student who was a political activist and was jailed for several days. His name was Journ Hudsov, and he was of Swedish Russian descent. It was during a period of renewed efforts for social justice in these United States, so it was quite remarkable to see a kid from totalitarian Russia coming to this country and joining in with a movement against fascist police tactics. There was a ground swell of student participation from which Journ Hudsov was plucked off the street, handcuffed, and jailed for what the police trumped up as disturbing the peace and being a foreign agitator. Hundreds of demonstrators showed up at the front steps of city hall in the bitter cold with signs and banners and featured bullhorn speakers. Most of the signs read and all the crowd chanted, '*Free Journ Hudsov! Free Journ Hudsov! Free Journ Hudsov!*'"

Myles was trying hard not to laugh at another man's plight. "So, what happened?"

“Well, they finally let him out because they couldn’t stand the exposure,” Merle said.

“You mean they warmed up?”

“Yeah, they warmed up and let him out, but threatened him with deportation if he ever did it again,” Merle recalled with a smile. “But at any rate, I digress. We need to take care of our own business at hand here. I’ll get your written statement back in a day or two, I trust, and then we can get you scheduled for deposition.”

“Deposition?”

“Don’t worry,” Merle assured him. “That’s just a session or two where you and me and the attorney for the police will sit down in a conference room and grill you in the presence of a court reporter. It’s a record that both sides will have access to for the case I’m going to build and what the other side is going to try to refute, so again, I need as many details as you can provide.”

“You got it, Mr. Williamson. I’ll get right on it,” Myles promised as he stood and shook hands. “Nice to meet you.”

“You’re a jazz player, right?” Merle asked.

“Yes, that’s my cup of tea,” said Myles.

“You know, I play a pretty mean horn,” Merle said with his hands in his pockets and a twinkle in his eye.

“Really?” Myles said, pleasantly surprised. “You’ve been holding out on me. What horn do you play?”

“A telltale twinkle lingered, but with a straight face, Merle said, “A car horn.”

Myles was deflated. “Oh well,” he said. “I’ll settle for a good mouthpiece any day.”

Merle Williams threw back his head with a good laugh. “We’ll do our best,” he said as he placed the legal pad and pencil in the hands of his client and saw him to the door with a conflicting reminder to take his time but hurry back. Myles was out of the office and halfway down the front steps before he stopped in his tracks and took a deep breath. There was a smell of justice in this American air. He pinched himself.

Hours ago, Myles reluctantly turned down a dinner invitation from his siblings so he could hole up undisturbed at his pad and get his problems down on paper with adrenalin fueling the task. His only distraction was a phone call to Yvonne in Copenhagen to tell her what was happening and convincing her fears that he wasn't about to be going to prison or anything like that. She was missing him very much while keeping the understanding and patience of Mrs. Job, and he promised to keep her informed. It was the first time in his career that he could recall going to a gig with a case of writer's cramp, and he could only hope that Huey Persons would have mercy and not call too many up-tempo tunes. Myles dropped off pages of the complaint at Merle Williamson's office before remembering to count them, but he did leave room at the bottom for a couple of postscripts if necessary, and now he was headed to the gig in Golden Village.

His headlights were his gentle guide as he reached the dark and foreboding stretch of Highway 55 with an eye on the speedometer. There was enough traveling time for him to stay five miles per hour under the limit. His was the only car around besides an east bound vehicle on the other side of the median and as they passed each other, he caught a glimpse of the light reflecting police badge on the side. He could have predicted what he saw next — the brake lights coming on, and the police making a bumpy U-turn over the median and starting after him. With his free hand he straightened his tie and jacket lapels before sitting up straight, patting his afro down and licking his lips. He wanted to be presentable for the purveyors of flashing red lights which suddenly illuminated the night. Through practice, Myles had become adept at pulling over and stopping. If there was a pulling over and stopping event in the Olympics, he would win the gold.

The cop approached his car with his gun drawn and aimed. "Step out of the vehicle," he ordered.

"Do I get one final call to my family before I die?" Myles asked.

"Hands! Hands! Lemme see those hands," the office yelled.

Isabelle Andrews didn't raise any fool. Myles remained seated but exposed his palms to the flashlight mounted on the gun. "What's this all about?"

"Where are you headed?" the cop answered the question with a question.

"To my job at *The Point*."

"And you are . . . the dishwasher?"

"No," Myles said calmly. "I'm the musician."

"I see. Do you know you were exceeding the speed limit?"

Myles' hands were still in sight as he tweaked his chin, pondering the question. "What key?"

The cop was in no mood for games, again, gruffly ordering him out.

"Officer, I just want you to know that I'm in the process of filing a lawsuit against you guys and your police department, and you should be hearing from my attorney very soon," Myles declared.

The radio was already off, so all that could be heard was the chirping of crickets. "Lawsuit? You're filing a lawsuit? Har -har," the officer said with a dismissing tone. "You're just wastin' your time. Those municipal court cases against us never get off the ground and go anywhere. Outta the car, now!"

"This is going to *federal* court, officer," Myles corrected.

"You mean . . . *not* municipal c-court?"

"No, *federal* court."

The crickets again took a solo.

"Well . . .," the cop said cleared his throat and holstered his gun. "You'd better put your hands down and be on your way then, but here, lemme catch your windshield." He cleared his throat again, took out his handkerchief and started wiping, finishing the driver's side and then hurrying around to the passenger side and finishing the job off by volunteering the elbow of his shirt to rub off the dried guts of a splattered bug. "Have a nice evening," he said back at the driver's window. "Would you like a police escort?"

"I'd better not go for that," Myles said, "because it might look like a conflict of interest. You see, I've been trying to get *rid* of police escorts."

Like the placid eye of a hurricane, Myles drove off like a man who had thrown a big heavy book at the lawless law and hid his hand. All he knew for sure was that the time was right for the dirty gears and sprocket wheels of bad policing to get acquainted with a monkey wrench.

Myles completed the drive and made it into *The Point* too late to grab a quick sandwich from the fine dining kitchen, but just in time to disrobe his bass and pick up and couch some serious bottom, the first lyrics through the lips of Bertha Paradise. She captivated the room on the wings of her flighty voice while he kept telling himself to just ignore the aromas of sizzling, succulent entrees floating past the bandstand on the shoulders of bustling servers. His bass growled as he plucked the strings and his hungry, angry stomach seconded the motion, but he would simply man-up and perish the thought of easing close enough to the edge of the bandstand to snatch a passing chicken drumstick. Besides, the eyes of the leader were upon him, horn in mouth, bowing and swaying as he directed the tune to its conclusion, but the accolades, after all was played and done, belonged to Bertha Paradise.

Myles was learning that Huey Persons was a savvy veteran bandleader who knew the value of pacing a gig.

Between tunes, Huey turned to the players and threw stern looks at them over his bifocals. "We're not suppose to be out here in the suburbs," he said.

"Why not?" they all said.

"'Cuz we're the *Urban Jazz Quartet*," he said, the stern look held for a moment, then shattered into guffaw, because for him, stern looks were too hard to sell. He was just another one of those guys who liked to go to the zoo and take in the sounds of wild animals, and furthermore, he was a lover of the domestic of the feline species. Both were inspiration for his next tune, a fast thing that he claimed he wrote for his cat *Yord*. The name of the tune was *Kitten Yord Roars*. "C'mon guys, pick it up," he said, "you can't have bread and loaf. Lemme put it another way. You won't get the bread if you don't cook it, dig?" Huey kicked it off with his quick snapping fingers, and boom, they were into it with a tempo that could make or break the bassists of animals.

Myles could do the Ray Brown walk, but this was a sprint! He remembered the composition well from the rehearsals and ran with it in a dazzling display of pluck. It was an honor to play with cats who could exceed the speed limit with such balance and endurance. His strings were a blur which were flirting with the outer limits of mercilessness. Sweat was dripping from the tip of his nose and chin while he peppered the man's work with a relentless and accurate stream of deep, black cotton balls. Then it happened, his G-string popped under the strain, throwing the tuning of the other strings into flatted chaos. Myles couldn't sing bass on this one, so he winced and cheated a half position up the fingerboard to finish the tune, and eventually, the set. When they were done, he made a promise to himself that never in a million years would he ever buy another set of strings made in Afghanistan, because goat gut just doesn't measure up to cat gut. The clientele loved a great demonstration of what Jazz is all about, the art of improvising! All was well that ended well, and his forearm and writer's cramp would soon go away. Off stage, an elderly and appreciative diner was headed for the powder room with curiosity written all over her face, and Myles was her closest target.

"Your music is really nice," she said, "but what do you *really* do for a living?"

"Well, ma'am," he said quietly and politely, "I actually do have two jobs. One is playing music, and the other is trying to convince nice people like you that this really *is* my job. Maybe two jobs is too much, or maybe I'm just a workaholic. I don't know."

"Well, I'm so sorry you're so confused," she said as she redirected herself from almost walking into the men's room.

For Myles, it was enough said. His break was already planned out. He replaced the broken string and finished off a couple of big slices of cantaloupe from the kitchen just in time to go up for the next set. The melon's calcium was already starting to relieve his cramps.

Huey hooked his sax on the neck strap and waited until they were all ready. "What 'cha feel like?" he asked.

"*With Work Like This Who Needs A Job*?" Myles answered.

"Wow! It's been a long time since I did that one," Huey said scratching his temple, "but I'll give it a try." He was starting to count off a medium-slow swing by drawing a small infinity sign in air with his index finger. But before they played a note, he was blindsided by a question from below.

"Can you please play *Hava Nagila*?" It was a little old lady with a very light blue perm and very fine clothes.

"No," Huey said emphatically. "We can't possibly . . . do anything . . . until we play your tune." He couldn't possibly ignore the hundred-dollar bill that she pulled from her alligator purse and handed him. "How does it go?"

She did a little dance step of the hora as she sang it with her frail voice.

"Oh, *that* tune," Huey said picking up the melody from the pianist Noah Jameen and directing the others into it with abandon. Those of a certain kinship rose to the occasion and did the steps of the hora at their tables. The liquor was working just fine.

Myles played just fine while leaning precariously on his fiddle for a dear laugh. "Only in America," he said to himself.

The gig mellowed into the usual wonderful hell of a party. The music was great, but even greater was the cohesion of players, singer, listeners, and tastebuds. The golden age had a pulse. The gig got over its distractions and mellowed into its usually wonderful hell of a party. They played until the only thing being served was toothpicks as hotel-motel time rolled around and for sure, too soon for the enthralled guests of gastronomy. After the gig, Myles accepted his share of the tips only to decide tomorrow which charity to give it to. In the meantime, they would all pack it in and say their amicable good nights, only to suffer with the withdrawal of going home from an addictive gig. It was becoming quite the un-American *jones*.

Myles knew that somewhere along the way home he would see another jones, police car wheels that can't stop rolling. As flashing red lights approached from the distant rear, he could see that it was going to take a bit of work to make sure those rolling wheels aren't leaving tire marks all over the rights of people. How American is it to be getting pulled over once again? Between two fingers, he held his international driver's license out the open window and waited for the crunching footsteps. He knew the drill.

Three days later, reality was gripping his bones in a downtown Minneapolis courthouse conference room. With Merle Williamson seated beside him, Myles was up to the task of navigating the barrages of cross examination questions coming across the long, polished rosewood table from counsel for the police, Hompter Ryan. Off to the side, a court reporter relaxed at his stenotype machine with nimble fingers churning out neat attacks of narrow, pre-folded copy ribbon.

Myles was the man on the hot seat who *lived* the ordeal, and now he felt an obligation and responsibility to verbally recall it for the record. Merle Williamson gave him the briefing earlier that the other side has the right to badger him — that depositions can make or break the case, and that details are crucial for strengthening the complaint, so don't be shy. Merle had made it clear that he didn't want to leave any barn doors open for cross-examination to walk in without knocking as he spent the afternoon putting the nooks and crannies of a bass player's memory through a clothes wringer. For Myles, it became clear that the written statement wasn't enough, but those memories were fresh and naked. There was nothing to hide, and for the life of him, he couldn't make this stuff up. For seasoning, the long grueling session was peppered with angry admonishments about rules and guidelines exchanged by both lawyers until mid-afternoon when they arrived at a tentative satisfaction with dry mouths and simmering emotions. The deposition was a wrap, and the only thing it proved was that the battle lines were drawn, and this was a trial that was going to happen.

Myles waited as Merle Williamson reloaded all the notes into his briefcase and gave his opponent Hompter Ryan a note of courtesy. Myles and Mr. Williamson left a courtroom of bad vibrations and headed down a desolate hallway towards the building exit.

"There comes a time when the good, the bad, the pretty and ugly should allow fate to run its course," Merle said.

"I'm just glad you're here to give fate a little help," Myles said.

"Together, we . . ." Before Merle could finish his comment, he was distracted by a fellow approaching him carrying a travel bag and a briefcase in one hand and waving with the other.

"Well, well, look who's here," he said accepting the extended hand. "Myles Andrews, I'd like you to meet my partner from a lot of court cases that we've worked together over the years, Mr. Lee Malone."

"Pleased to meet you," Myles said. "I've heard about you."

"Good, I hope," Lee Malone smiled.

"Nothing but good," Merle admitted. "Lee just flew in from Des Moines to help us out with law archives research and obtaining subpoenas while I'm assembling our list of exhibits and preparing for jury selection. Together, we're all going to put our best foot forward to make the right impression on twenty-four eyes and twenty-four ears."

"I feel like I'm really in good hands," Myles said gleefully. "What do I do next?"

Merle put a hand on his shoulder, and they continued walking to the door. "I don't know how to break this to you, but justice is the front-runner, the king, the star. We're just pawns in a game of serious challenges."

"What do you suppose the biggest challenge is?" Myles asked.

"Institutional racism," Merle said, "those policies of biases that have been embedded in the fabric of our society for many decades. It's hard to prove because the powers that be, in government and business, have been sailing through time pretending that prejudice doesn't exist. Reasonable people like us know that nothing could be farther from the truth, and its our job to force-feed some truth into the courtroom. If we can sell the truth to the right jury, justice might have a chance to live and breathe again."

"Do you think this case has a chance?" Myles wondered with some skepticism.

"Nothing is guaranteed, and nothing is a slam-dunk," Merle said, "but this case has a lot of merit. We shall see. The next thing to do is to stay loose and be accessible because I'll be letting you know what's next."

"I hear you. You got it," Myles said as they parted ways for their own vehicles.

Hours later, Myles was at his mother's house having dinner with his siblings. The subject of conversation precipitated a long thoughtful silence accented by the sounds of munching and clinking of forks. Soon there was only sound of thinking. His sister Althea broke the silence with a sob. "They will *kill* you," she cried.

"C'mon guys, relax," Myles said. "Look, I have to do this. I should have done it a long time ago. Somebody else should have done it before now. It's time to go down in the swamp and see if there's any such thing as justice. Kinda feels right now like it remains to be seen, and I'm not afraid to be in on the search for that answer."

Althea got up and left the room with her quick step stocking feet thumping the floor and returned with a tablet and pencil which she slammed down on the table in front of him.

"What's this?" Myles asked.

"You need to write down right now what you want us to tell your girl in case something happens to you," Althea said wiping her eyes and standing over him with crossed arms. Al nodded in agreement.

Myles could only stare at a blank page for a few moments with visions of Yvonne, Copenhagen, and his pregnant overseas music calendar dancing in his head. "You know the address. She's an angel," he said, "just tell her I'll see her in heaven." He saw their eyes. "I really appreciate your concern, and I'll be just fine. All you guys have to do is help me by praying for this country to show us a little justice, okay?"

"That's what we've been praying for four hundred years," Al said, "but I don't know, maybe our prayers need loudspeakers."

"Well, what do you think I'm doing?" Myles said. "All I'm doing is trying to connect the wires to the loudspeaker. That's a *good* thing." Giving them another way to look at it seemed to settle them down and ease their fears. He glanced at his watch, and they understood that it was time for him to leave and go get ready for the gig.

After a whistle stop at his pad and loading up, Myles was making his westward drive, listening to the radio and wondering if the last two nights were just an anomaly. The cops were scarce. On a safe straightaway without intersections, he punched the gas pedal and reached fifty-five miles an hour — five miles over the limit. He couldn't help it, he needed to find out if the cops got the memo about the trial. His speed reached sixty in a fifty as he took it up the road and whizzed past a squad car idling on the median. Certainly, he thought, his car would be recognized as he passed through sudden blinding spotlight beams. He was watching carefully in his mirrors and saw the spotlight black out, but the squad car didn't take off after him. Just to make sure, he held his speed for nearly a mile before settling back below the limit. "They got the memo" he said with a sigh. Myles was confident that he could learn to live without flashing red lights behind him. Now all he needed was to find a way to make that happen. On the radio, *Chet Baker* was blowing his airy rendition of *The Lamp is Low,* but Myles' expectation was high because the legs for bad cops to stand on were *full* of termite tunnels.

In a few minutes the road led him back to *The Point*, which was feeling more and more like a sanctuary for the mind and a safe haven for the soul somewhere out in the village, the place where he could let down his hair and his nerves.

He was on stage with promptness and ready to go as he picked up the tuning G from Noah Jameen and was pleased that his strings held true from the last evening.

"Where's the singer/" Huey Persons asked the passing food and beverage manager.

"She's in her dressing room shadowboxing some ice cream," the manager said and continued on his way.

"That's why she's so healthy," Huey joked to the guys. "but seriously, she can do what she wants to do, because talent like that is as rare as a blue lobster."

"Wait a minute," Myles pitched in, "didn't I see a blue lobster on the menu?"

"The answer came in the form of Bertha Paradise bounding up on stage poured into a slick, shimmering blue dress and built like a city skyline. If only a city could sing like Bertha Paradise. Myles had done it before, the first chart on the music stand, a tune of hers that they were starting the intro for titled, *Don't be Rubbin" Your Sage On Me*. Myles locked in with the drummer and paved an upbeat tempo for Bertha's lyrics to ride on, oiled by the smooth and uplifting harmony of Huey's horn. The tune generated a kind of spirit that could make bartenders obsolete. Solid gold sets were the ones that nobody in the room wanted to end, but nobody had the power to stop the hands of the clock and so it was time to take a break in order to keep contractual obligations happy. Huey Persons was indeed looking at his watch and calling a chaser tune over his shoulder, the one and only and never forgotten *Green Dolphin Street*.

Myles was reignited, booming and skipping some bottom out of those strings. He cherished the treat of having the horn, drums, and piano riding his notes like world class skiers, up one slope and down another, complimenting, yielding and blending with color. Huey took the first solo and did a tenor sax proud before handing off to Noah Jameen who had just enough black and whites to feed his family of musicians a smorgasbord of chords before hushing respectfully for an inventive contribution from Myles, who closed his eyes and made his strings dance that *Dolphin* out of the water. Eyes still closed, Myles did a retroactive make good with an extra chorus of effort before finally handing it off for a drummer's turn. He opened his eyes. The drummer was gone! The piano player was gone! They were all at the bar ordering beverages. It was break time, and the joke was on him with that ancient jazz musicians trick rearing its funny head again. It was no problem. He closed it out by playing the *Green Dolphin Street* melody all by himself, including an exclamation tag of shave-and-a-haircut, two bits! He joined them at the bar with a smile and feeling like a properly christened immigrant. It was an honor bestowed, he thought, as he ordered a sparkling water, like going through a turnstile into the land of true acceptance, all in the absence of a sneaky bucket of Gatorade. But most importantly, jazz wouldn't be any fun without all the rituals, and neither would life. He was happy to join his esteemed colleagues in a toast to each other.

Three days later, Myles was out and about during business hours to attend a pre-trial meeting in the law offices of Merle Williamson, the big man on the phone wearing bifocals on his head, an open tie with a while shirt, and dark brown suit pants held up by red suspenders. With the assistance of his interns, a table of evidence for the case was gaining weight. Myles stood up from the plush couch when Merle got off the phone, and they shook hands. "Get Mr. Andrews a cup of coffee," Merle politely requested of his attentive secretary. "I wanted you to come by for a little briefing on the workings of a courtroom. Are you okay with that?"

"Absolutely," Myles said.

"Very good. When you're called to the stand, you'll just relax and be yourself and answer all questions to the best of your ability," Merle said. "I've known the cops' attorney for twenty years, and I know that his favorite tool in a trial is to try to rile or intimidate you. Just keep your cool at all times."

"You're in luck," Myles said. "I don't get hot under the collar very easily."

"That's good," Merle Williamson said with glad ears, "because juries don't like a plaintiff with too much heat under the collar."

"I just hope the jury can tell the difference between the color of a man's skin and the color of a man's neck," Myles said.

"Now, now, we're going to educate," Merle coached, "and we're going to give a jury that we helped to select a hell of a lot of credit for knowing how to read people and make the right decisions. The burden of proof is on our shoulders, and it won't be easy, but we're people with strong shoulders, right?"

"Let's fool everybody and pretend we are," Myles smiled.

That's the spirit," Merle laughed a second, but he was back to serious, lifting some papers from his desk and relocating his bifocals from his head to his nose. "Just so you know, we filed an affidavit of prejudice against the judge assigned to the case. He's a flip-flopper with a poor civil rights record, and we don't think he would be a good judge for this kind of case. Don't worry, we'll get a good judge."

"I knew I could count on you," Myles said.

"Well, you can count some more blessings," said Merle, turning the page, "because I was able to move the trial to a closer date. Don't ask, I was owed favors from the courthouse docket people," he winked.

"My girl overseas will be glad to hear *that*," said Myles.

"I was thinking of her," Merle said with an understanding heart.

"Bless you," Myles said.

Merle wasn't finished, turning another page and turning up his nose subconsciously, not because of a smell, but only to aim his bifocals at the text. "It's come to our attention that one of the defendant cops wasn't too pleased with the idea of going to court over this," Merle said, "so he quit the Golden Village police force and sneaked off to join the Minneapolis police."

"Can't you nail him for fleeing a lawyer?" Myles asked.

"My assistant, Lee Malone already did," Merle said. "He subpoenaed that cop and brought his shifty ass right back to the party, so when his time comes, he'll be sitting right up in court wearing a Minneapolis uniform."

"I'll drink to that," Myles said.

"There's no drinking allowed in these offices," said Merle, serious as a heart attack as he turned another page. Just then, his secretary returned with a tray of hot coffee cups, and Merle was the first to thank her and grab one from which he took a quick slurp. "We have to go in with a broader approach," he said after savoring a swallow.

"How do you mean?" Myles asked.

"I mean this case is being brought to trial not just against some police officers, but the village as a whole," Merle said, "from the mayor all the way down to the fire station dalmatian. As the old saying goes, '*somebody's got to answer for and be responsible for this kind of behavior out on the public highways*.'"

"I agree that no dogs should get off scot-free," Myles said, "but am I going to be tried by a jury of my peers?"

"You're not on trial. The police are," Merle said, "and their attorney, Hompter Ryan is with the law firm of Dick Tracy, Mike Hock, and Drew Waters. They have a pretty good batting average defending police in municipal cases, but they're really going to have their hands full with a federal civil rights case."

"Do you really think this has a snowball's chance in hell?" Myles asked.

"Nothing is for sure," Merle warned, "because the final decision is up to the jury, and that said, we're already scheduled to start jury selection tomorrow."

"Can my brother and sister be in on this jury?" Myles asked.

"I wish it were that easy," Merle chuckled, "but what we can hope for is that some people of color get drafted and pulled into the jury selection pool. Unfortunately, if your brother and sister get the call to serve on the jury, the other side would immediately use their authority to strike them for being lovingly biased, and of course, I can strike selections of theirs that I don't like. It's the way the game is played."

"Very well," said Myles. "I hope some Black folks get in."

"Let's send our hope to the gods of fate," Merle said, "and we'll just do the only thing we can do, which is to simply educate with the truth."

"That's fine, as long as the truth doesn't set a lot of bad cops free," Myles said.

"Look, I know you've already been formally deposed," Merle said returning his bifocals to the top of his head, "but refresh me again just so I'm perfectly clear. Why are you bringing this lawsuit? Be honest."

"Honestly? Because I'm a musician, and I'm part of a wonderful musical art form called jazz, and I believe jazz has rights that need to be tested in a court of law," Myles said.

"Don't make me laugh," Merle said. "I'm afraid this is not the right fight for the art of jazz, mainly because jazz never drove a car on Highway 55, and if jazz could drive and ran into the same problems you did, it wouldn't know the first thing about complaining."

"I guess that just leaves me," Myles conceded.

"It's all about you," Merle said. "There will be no hiding behind jazz."

"Okay, but just for the record, jazz is *always* complaining. Trust me," Myles said.

"I'll take that under advisement," Merle laughed, "but I will have to say that your case is timely. Kudos to you for having the courage to pursue this and own it."

"As a member of the civilized human species, I just had to," Myles said.

"As we've said, the well-publicized debate going on at city hall between a human rights commission and the city council has been kind of a stalemate," Merle said.

"What seems to be the problem?" Myles asked.

"Well, the city has concerns about crimewaves and public safety which they think calls for more aggressive policing. On the other hand, the human rights commission issued a manifesto stressing the immediate need to scale back racial profiling in order to ensure that law enforcement is applied fairly and constitutionally," Merle said. "So, you couldn't have come along at a better time, and speaking of timing," he went to the door with an extended hand when he saw who the smiling secretary let in. "Myles, I'd like you to meet Cicely Weston who is a reporter for the *Suburban Sun Newspaper*."

Myles rose and stepped over to greet her. She was a gorgeous Caucasian woman with a wiry blond afro. Under her bright, smiling eyes were circles of a hard worker. "Pleased to meet you," he said.

"Talk," Merle said to them both as he hurried to answer a ringing phone.

"The city council is my beat, and I've been covering some discussions about civil rights," Cicely Weston said, "and now I'm just hearing about your lawsuit from Mr. Williamson. It's great."

"Thanks," Myles said. "It would be even better if lessons could be learned which would bring about changes for the better, otherwise all we're doing is spinning our wheels and getting stopped by the police."

Cicely was nodding understandingly as they drifted to some nearby chairs and sat down. She took out a pad and pencil and licked her lips. "Tell me all about yourself," she said.

Myles cleared his throat but didn't know where to start, then was relieved that she kickstarted a dialogue with a series of snack sized questions, no doubt coming on like Wernher von Braun disguised as the Wright brothers. After an hour, she made him feel naked without even the mercy of a fig leaf, but he surmised that this would merely be duck soup compared to the nakedness he was about to be feeling on a courtroom witness stand, with not even so much as jazz to hide behind. He was J.O.D.; he was *jus'out dere.*

An hour after the law office, Myles got a call to hook up with cabbie buddy Lester Ride at *Le Zoo Jazz Club*, a well-run storefront joint which actually possessed a pulse and a wine license. A better-than-decent trio allowed people to converse softly without guilt. Their sarsaparilla glasses were half full as they bullshitted at the bar about the meaning of Thelonious Monk's titles. It was great sport.

"So how is Alberta Clipper treating you?" Myles meddled.

"Can't tell ya" Les said quietly.

"You mean you're sorry you called her one of your Z-list freaks?" Myles said and threw his head back, clapped his hands, and hunched his shoulders with a squelched laugh. "I understand," he said with a sudden deadpan. "It's the code of silence of cabbies."

'Somethin' like that," Les said sheepishly. "She's misunderstood. I try to listen to her problems."

"What's her main pain?" Myles asked.

"Guilt."

"Guilt? About what?"

"She told me her bosses at the newspaper want her to keep writing shitty negative articles about jazz places and musicians, and if she didn't, they would fire her," Les said.

"That's unbelievable," said Myles, "it's just hard to buy."

"I don't know it as truth," Les said. "I just know what she said."

"How long has she been following orders?"

"For five years," said Les. "That's what she's feelin' guilty about. She doesn't want to lose a pretty good paycheck, and so she feels like she's sold out."

"Sounds like she's made a lot of enemies," Myles said. "Do they all know about this?"

"I doubt it," Les said, "and if it's true or not true, it's not my place to go around telling everybody."

Myles was shaking his head with pity. "I think we better pray for her sanity or maybe all of us better start playin' so damn good that she won't dare to write anything bad about us," he said.

"Well, what about her job?" Les was having trouble hiding an affection for a secret friend.

"What about it?" Myles echoed. "Look, ask yourself who hasn't figured out where Alberta Clipper is coming from?"

"That's cold," Les said.

"Exactly," Myles said conclusively.

The subject seemed to change itself when a tune from the trio concluded with a flourish and drew a smattering of applause.

"So, you're going ahead with the lawsuit?" Les asked.

"Yeah," said Myles, "and God willing', I'll have a front row seat to see if the law of the land will stand up and be counted. I'm just real curious."

Les was concerned about a fellow musician and soul brother.

"You know what they say, '*curiosity killed the cat'*."

"This is one cat that has nine lives," Myles said as he poked his own thumb at his own chest, "and furthermore, somebody just might find out that this cat also has nine tails."

"Oh, oh," Les said, "sounds like you're about to make *Lash LaRue* look like a sissy."

"Well, Let's just say I'm not planning on having mercy on *Lash LaRue's* reputation," Myles said as the trio music resumed.

Before too much longer their glasses were empty and there was no desire for refills. They left on the middle of the tune, not out of disrespect or rudeness towards fellow musicians, but because they each had other things to do. Les gave a little salute, jumped in his hack and took off while Myles was headed for another volunteer shift at his brother's carwash. His job for the day was toweling windows dry and clean, a great workout, but he saved his best effort for his own car — his windows that needed to be spotless for drives along Highway 55 while looking for pictures that were worth a thousand words. After the workout he was headed over to his mother's flower shop to put in a little time repotting forget-me-nots. He could read his mother's influence on the neighborhood by the steadiness of the business traffic, and it was a great comfort to him to see that her legacy was intact. When the store hours expired at the end of the day, his batteries were already recharged with the knowledge that he would be going for another night on Huey Persons' gig, no matter how problematic the drive to and fro.

The next morning Myles got up, splashed water on his face, dressed, and fed his growling stomach before heading for a scheduled short meeting at Merle Williamson's law office. The secretary greeted him and opened the door to Merle's chamber.

"Come in, come in," he said and offered a seat. "I must tell you that we got lucky with the judge selected for this case. He's known as *the state fair* because he's very fair," Merle said very seriously.

"You mean he's light-skinned?" Myles asked innocently.

Merle Williamson chuckled just a little. "Sorry, I was already overdrawn at the bank of favors," he said, "and besides, I couldn't have asked for an African American judge because it would have been viewed as unethical."

"I trust you to do the right thing," Myles said.

"Good, and that's exactly what we are going to be doing starting at eight o'clock Monday morning," Merle said, "but only if you care to proceed," Mr. Williamson said.

"I care to proceed," Myles said without hesitation.

"I knew you would, but I wanted to be absolutely sure," said Merle, "but having said all that, I must also tell you that we're going to have to live with the jury finalists."

"Is something wrong?"

"Well, I tried to construct at least a partial jury of your peers by picking a few people of color, but the other side struck down each and every one of them, so it looks like the jury for this case is going to be all-White," Merle said with a neutral tone.

"Ouch! Where are the purple and polka dot people when you need 'em?" Myles said half joking. "All-White sounds like bad news for justice."

"Not necessarily," Merle cautioned, "give them a chance."

“Right,” Myles agreed. “Everyone deserves a chance.”

They stood and shook hands firmly and finally before going to battle. “My secretary will have some information for you with directions and parking,” Merle said. “I want you to just relax over the weekend, play your music, get a good rest, and come out refreshed and ready Monday morning, okay?”

“I wouldn’t miss it for the world,” Myles said before leaving. Armed with a folder of court documents, he was out the door and in front of the building. “America has a chance,” he said to himself.

Monday morning was like the end of an eternity, and a steady rain did not deter him from a scamper out of a nearby parking ramp to a front row seat in a court of law. His army raincoat protected his dress-up-with-suit-and-tie routine, Merle’s orders. The gloomy wet day brought back vivid memories of his first day in kindergarten, and now here he was all these years later, arriving at the sacred doors of blind justice and bright lights, full of a kindergartner’s attitude of show-me, a big desire to be taught, and an even bigger desire to learn. It just incidentally occurred to him that he didn’t have to be from Missouri to get a little taste of *show me*. Merle Williamson had been waiting for him and ambushed him by the elevators with an extended hand.

“You’re on time,” he said, “so far, so good.”

“Well, it was such a nice day, I thought I’d stop by for a spot of tea,” Myles joked.

“That’s fine,” Merle smirked, “but you won’t get a lemon until I call the first witness. Let’s go up,” he said when a green elevator light pinged and the doors parted open. Merle pushed button five as others entered the lift behind them, so they pleaded the fifth until they reached their floor and the doors opened. It was a short walk to the courtroom where they paused just outside the mahogany doors and took simultaneous deep breaths.

Merle was wearing a midnight blue pin-striped suit which was well tailored for his rotund frame, a fat briefcase in one hand, and a London Fog raincoat over the other arm. Myles removed his army wrap and shook it out all over the carpet.

"Ready?" Merle asked.

"Let's do it," Myles said and pulled the door open. Up front, assistant attorney Lee Malone was already hovering over the plaintiff's table as he positioned a substantial spread of exhibits. The courtroom was far from full, with only a few die-hard trial watchers waiting with the patiently seated jury. Those lucky decision makers in the box, some with pillow wrinkles still impressed on their faces, were a group made up of seven white men and five white women. Myles did a quick study of their faces as he tried to read what all these strangers were thinking, and how much experience they had judging people of color. There was plenty of time to ponder the question. Lee Malone greeted them at the table and took their coats. They were still standing when the courtroom deputy commanded everyone's attention with, *"All Rise, The Honorable Judge NaVell Phillips Presiding."* The white-haired man of the robes emerged from his chamber and climbed up behind the bench where he settled into a black leather easy chair with a taller-than-man backrest and put on his wirerimmed glasses.

"Please be seated," the judge said and then glanced at the readiness of the court reporter. "Mr. Williamson, please proceed with your opening remarks."

Merle stood again and thanked the judge who was sitting in front of the fine mahogany wall adorned with a relief carved figure of blindfolded *lady justice*, flanked by a bright, fresh-looking American flag. "Good morning ladies and gentlemen of the jury, nice to see you," he said. "I just want to make one thing perfectly clear. We're not here today to show our disrespect for officers of the law, and we all know the importance of good police work." Merle said with emphasis walking slowly along the jury box. "We wouldn't be here if the police had no power. But we acknowledge that we're here because police indeed do have power, and also, we're here about abuse of that power, which is outside of our Constitution. We're here because Myles Andrews is here, asking the court why he can't drive his car to and from his job in Golden Village without being stopped constantly by the police for no apparent reason. The good news is that there is an answer to the question floating around out there. We are challenged to find that answer, and we will. Make no mistake, there is nothing wrong with hunting for due process whenever it gets lost. We need to remember that it was laid out very clearly in the great charter of English political and civil liberties, the Magna Carta, granted by King John at Runnymede on June 15, 1215, which states that a person's rights, life or property may not be taken away unjustly or without . . . due . . . process," Merle said, pausing to look them over. "that was over eight hundred years ago," he continued his slow walk, "and thousands of miles away. But King John's Magna Carta was one of the fundamental building blocks of our belated civil rights movement, but better late than never for the people. Well, the 1964 Civil Rights Act was late, but it was finally approved by Congress and signed by President Johnson. It clearly embraced that eight-hundred-year-old way of thinking, due process for all. I have no double that we are a society which embraces high standards of human rights. We do make mistakes," Merle said, "but the wonderful thing about making a human mistake is the chance to correct that mistake. Are we asking ourselves if the playing field is level? Is a white driver just as likely to be pulled over as a person of color? Witnesses and records tend to cast doubt on this."

"Objection, Your Honor." It was Hompter Ryan again. "Records of this nature have varying degrees of accuracy. How . . ."

The judge banged his gavel. "You're out of order, Mr. Ryan. You'll have your turn to address the jury. Please continue Mr. Williamson."

"All we need is open minds, ladies and gentlemen," said Merle as he stood facing the jury with his hands clasped behind his back. "Look, *The Constitution* and *The Civil Rights Act,* which is the basis for this suit, say that when you act for the State, you treat everyone equally. We'll show violations of the law and trust the judgement of others," he said and sat down.

Judge NaVell Phillips took a moment to finish writing a note. "Mr. Ryan, if you please," he said.

"Thank you, your honor," Hompter Ryan said as he rose to his feet in his reddish-brown suit and opened the jacket of his three-piece suit to show off the buttons on his matching vest. He hooked his thumbs in the dual watch pockets, and he was ready after he cleared his already clear throat. "good people of the jury," Hompter began, "it must be understood up front that the city puts millions of dollars into the training of our fine officers. These are people who chose law enforcement as a profession. They are well-trained and dedicated to their jobs. And they stick together as a team. They have each other's back no matter what," Hompter Ryan said and paused for effect. "We count on our fine officers to keep us safe," he resumed, "and these officers know what that entails. Golden Village is a peaceful place, and we know how dedicated our police are about keeping it that way. Every day we read in the paper about hot spots for crime, and it's no secret that nearby North Minneapolis has a lot of police calls, and that some of those calls end up with pursuits of suspects fleeing westbound into Golden Village. It's been a well-known fact through many generations of policing that this is a job where you can't be too careful. What did these well-trained and well-disciplined police officers know about a driver when a car is pulled over? The burden of proof lies squarely on the shoulders of council," he said with a sweeping hand in the direction of Merle Williamson, "and his client, to prove ill-intent doesn't exist, as we will prove. Furthermore, records will show that not one single Black person has come into the police station to complain about alleged wrongdoing by any police officer. Personnel at the police station are not mind readers sitting in front of crystal balls. They need Black people to bring their complaints to them because they have plenty of pencils and plenty of paper to write them down. But to date, nobody ever has, and all they're left with is he-said-she-said rumors that can't be substantiated. Believe me, evidence will show that Golden Village police officers did absolutely nothing wrong. So, ladies and gentlemen, as you observe these proceedings, think of these officers and their families, think of them returning home safely at night because they did the job with skill and correctness. What more can we ask of them?" Hompter said, content to stretch his time like a long red rubber binder, taunting the borderlines of boredom before he realized it was time to put a pin it, thank the jury, and sit down while the judge was still awake.

The courtroom was quiet until Judge Phillips was ready, "I just want to caution everyone in here that tolerance for any outbursts or disruptions of these proceedings is very low," he said, "so please do not give me a reason to have anyone removed. Thank you. Mr. Williamson, call your first witness."

Merle Williamson stood and quickly scanned the neatly laid out table with an extensive chronology of exhibits. "Thank you, your honor," he said. "At this time, I call to the stand Myles Andrews."

Myles stood and stepped smartly towards the man holding out the Bible which he was asked to swear on, a hand raised, to tell the truth, the whole truth and nothing but the truth so help him God. He agreed wholeheartedly and sat down doing a little mental musing about coming all the way back to America only to get sent to the chair where he will gladly fry for social justice, and later he should fly back *over easy* across the ocean without bacon, he thought, but he would simply call it one personal final blue book exam for America, because the *blues* book has already spoken, don't you know. There was a little benign introductory small talk to settle nerves.

"Tell the court, Myles Andrews, isn't it true that you have traveled to many countries where you have played your music?"

"Yes, I have," Myles said.

"Do you play music kind of as a hobby?"

"Well, as it turned out, it's both my hobby and my occupation. It's my livelihood."

"I see, and how long have you been playing music?"

"Almost all my live, over forty years."

"I see. Isn't it true that you're a bass player?"

"Yes, I play bass, but nobody knows the treble I've seen."

The judge tapped his gavel once, "I'm not up to snuff on my musicals," he said, "so I'll just trust that the court reporter knows how to spell. Carry on."

"Thank you, Your Honor," Merle said. "Tell the court if you would, Myles, did you drive a car in other countries?"

"Objection, Your Honor," Hompter Ryan chirped, "irrelevant!"

"Overruled, he may answer," the judge said.

"Yes, I drive in other countries," Myles admitted.

"How many times have you been stopped while driving in other countries?"

"Just once in thirty-five years," Myles said.

"What happened *that* time?"

"I ran out of gas," Myles deadpanned.

"Cars in other countries do have rearview mirrors, don't they?" Merle was fishing for lunker.

"Objection, Your Honor . . ."

"Mr. Williamson, where is this going?" the judge demanded.

"It's going around the world, Your Honor, just to show what kind of driving conditions a human being could become accustomed to and expect."

"sustained, move on," Judge Phillips ruled.

"Very well, Your Honor," Merle said. "Tell the court, Myles how long have you worked a job in Golden Village?"

Myles pondered the question not because he couldn't remember, but because he was momentarily distracted by an entrance into the courtroom. Dressed in *Sunday-Go-Meetin'* clothes and tipping to their seats wearing smiles was his brother Al and his sister Althea. It was the kind of support that could make a grown man feel at home in a courtroom, with great appreciation for a forgiving family behind him.

"Shall I repeat the question?" Merle asked patiently.

"No sir, not long," he stammered, "about six weeks."

"Very good," Merle said with his nose pointed up snobbishly, but only to see his notes through his bifocals," and how many times have you been pulled over by the golden Village police?"

"Fifteen times."

"What time of day did these stops happen?"

Myles rolled his eyes to his brain just to make sure. "All of the stops were at night," he said.

"Did the police officers who stopped you ever give you a reason for being stopped?"

"Yes, they gave me reasons."

"What *were* those reasons?"

“Oh, once they said they were stopping me for my own good,” Myles recalled, “but they wouldn’t tell me what my good was. Another time, they said they were looking for a burglar. Still another time, they wanted to see my bass, so, right out on the highway, they made me unzip it and pull it out. It was humiliating.”

“Were you able to see the faces of those cops who were stopping you?”

“Not at all,” Myles said, shaking his head.

“Why not?”

“Because they either shined a bright flashlight in my eyes or their caps visor were pulled down to their noses,” Myles said.

“Did it look like they were attempting to hide their identities?”

“Objection, Your Honor,” Hompter Ryan stood and pointed, “that’s leading the witness to speculate.”

“Sustained, next question.”

“If you heard them individually, would you recognize any of the voices of the policemen who have been stopping you?”

“Objection, Your Honor,” Hompter interrupted, “that’s speculation, and ah, besides, the crickets along the highway are too loud to hear anything clearly.”

“Overruled, he may answer,” the judge said.

“I have a pretty good ear as a musician,” Myles said, “so I probably could recognize them by voices, especially the one I heard the most.”

“I see. Tell the court, Myles, about the night of several weeks ago when you were pulled over on Highway 55 and when you were subsequently arrested and taken downtown Minneapolis to the county jail. What happened that night?” Merle asked.

“Well, I was driving very carefully as usual, and I pulled over because a cop car came from out of nowhere with the flashing reds and spotlights.”

"I see, and *then* what happened?"

"It took a while, but the officer finally came to the back of my driver's side window with his gun drawn and asked to see my driver's license."

"I see," said Merle, "and did you show him your license?"

"I told him I would show my license if he would please tell me why I was being pulled over."

"What happened then?"

"Well, the officer asked me to step out of the vehicle with my hands up, and said I was under arrest. I asked him what for, and he said for speeding, failure to show my license, and insubordination towards an officer of the law. When I got out peacefully, he grabbed me and spun me around slammed me face down across the trunk of my car with the barrel of his gun against my skull."

"How did that make you feel?"

"It was kind of surreal. At that time, I could only think that if I breathed wrong, I could die. I was just a guy on my way to the job, but now I'm in handcuffs and on my way to jail."

"I see, and tell the court, Myles Andrews, did the arresting officer read you your rights?"

"No, he did not," Myles said.

Merle deliberately stalled for a moment before asking his next question. "Have you ever been in jail before?"

"Never," Myles said with pride.

"How long were you locked up?"

"It was more than two hours," Myles said, "and I missed two sets and finally go to the gig in the middle of the third set."

"I see, and how did you manage to get out of jail?"

"I was allowed to make one phone call," Myles said, "and I called the restaurant and told them what happened, and the manager sent two guys downtown to bail me out."

"Isn't it true that you were pulled over some more times after the jail incident?"

"Yes, I was," Myles said, "many more times."

"Were you caught speeding on any of those occasions?"

"No sir. I keep thinking if I don't exceed the speed limit I won't get stopped, but apparently driving under the speed limit isn't good enough."

"Tell us about these stops," Merle probed. "Where did they occur, I mean, in what area along the highway?"

"They all happen all along the highway from the "Minneapolis border to about two blocks from *The Point*," said Myles.

"I see, and were you ever followed inside of *The Point*?"

"I saw them come in a couple of times while we were playing, but they soon turned around and left, probably because the music was too hip for them," Myles said.

"Objection, Your Honor. These officers are family men with children, so they certainly wouldn't be intimidated by hips," Hompter said with the theatrical flair.

"Overruled," said Judge Philips, "and the witness will please leave off the editorials when answering questions."

Myles nodded in agreement.

"Are there other ways to get to The Point?" Merle continued.

"Yes."

"Did you try those other ways to get to work?"

"I did once."

"And, what happened?" Why not again?"

"I got stopped," Myles said, "so I decided that using extra gas to drive way out of my way didn't make any difference or any sense."

"No further questions at this time, Your Honor," Merle said the wheels in his head already turning for readdress as he took a seat.

Hompter Ryan stood and tugged at his vest as he casually walked around to the front of the defendant's table and reached into a briefcase. He pulled out an item shrink-wrapped into a clear, square plastic sheath and brought it to the witness stand. "Do you recognize this, Mr. Andrews?" he said with raised eyebrows. "the fine print on it says, *'made in Stockholm'*."

"Objection, Your Honor," Merle said rising to his feet, "isn't this a surprise bit of evidence? Who knew about this?"

"Mr. Ryan," the judge said patiently. "What does this have to do with the price of beans?"

"I'm just returning a belonging that was taken from Mr. Andrews by county jail deputies, Your Honor," Hompter said and handed the clear package to Myles. "Somehow it got separated from his other belongings, but they returned it to me just today."

"You?" Merle scoffed. "Why not me?"

The judge tapped his gavel once. "This is highly irregular, Mr. Ryan. Again, what's the item have to do with these proceedings?"

"Hold it up if you will, Mr. Andrews," Hompter Ryan invited.

"Myles held up the transparent shrink-wrapped item too small to see.

"It's a tiny figure of a nude White woman with a key ring right through the feet," Hompter Ryan said, folding his arms authoritatively and rocking up and down on the balls of his feet.

"They gave me back the keys without the key ring," Myles explained.

"Oh, but isn't this more than just a key ring, Mr. Andrews? Doesn't this show a blatant disrespect for women? Be honest."

"Objection, Your Honor, that's way out in left field irrelevant," Merle protested.

"Sustained. Mr. Ryan, you are flirting with a contempt citation," Judge Phillips warned. "Put that thing away, and I promise you I won't tell your wife you've been studying the fine print on a nude toy. Move it along please."

"Yes, Your Honor."

"The court reporter will please delete the exchanges about the key ring," Judge Phillips said and waited until it was done before nodding for Hompter to continue.

"Mr. Andrews, do you believe people have a right to feel safe on our highways?"

"Yes, I do."

"These fine police officers of Golden Village are providing great protection for citizens," Hompter said, "what more do you want?"

"If I want to see *Dennis the Menace*, all I have to do is read the funny papers. I don't need to see him on the highway every night or in a courtroom," Myles said.

The judge kept a poker face as he tapped his gavel at tittering in the courtroom while half of the jury members cleared their throats and the other half shifted in their seats instead of laughing. Lawyers for the plaintiff and the defense thrusted and parried back and forth until Judge Phillips banged his gavel and ordered a well-deserved recess.

Merle was rounding up and briefcasing his notes as he slowly shook his head with a knowing smile. "A courtroom lawyer never knows what the other side will do," he said. "With our legal language, we have the colors of pheasants, but the smart lawyer has to be the pheasant flying with a shotgun."

"I have a feeling you're a good shot," Myles said.

"I don't like to brag," Merle laughed.

Suddenly Myles was in the arms of his proud family members who he introduced to the departing lawyers. That wind in his sails was blowing in from family support, a breeze that would make the next session so much easier, he thought.

Myles survived the afternoon session, the third and final of the day where the defense cross-examined him nearly to the shores of badgering, only to be rescued by a Saint Bernard named Merle Williamson. Now he was driving westward into Golden Village, but with the feeling of being behind the wheel of a dirigible. It was like the arrival at Dr. King's *mountain top*, a vantage point which made an eastbound police car look like an ant, although a little too high to hear the police cry *"Uncle, dog, Uncle already, will ya?"* Yet he was still on the ground, but with very little interest in his rearview mirror. He was perfectly comfortable with letting the owls give the hoots for him. In a short time, he drove up to the triangle of a block where *The Point Supper Club* stood. Street parking was usually scarce, but a spot across the street opened up when a car departed. Myles did a quick U-turn to get it. Before he could parallel park, he was blinded by flashing red lights and harsh spotlights. He tensed up with disbelief and reacquainted himself with his rearview mirrors. A door slammed, and a cop approached his car on foot, backed by more light than a B-movie filming set, but it wasn't enough. The cop still needed the help of his raised flashlight to see the blackness behind the wheel.

"See yer driver's license, bub?"

Myles gave him the international, and the officer returned to his squad car and stayed there for some long, serious, crucial minutes. The officer finally returned with a freshly written ticket which he presented through the window, holding it across his forearm like a maître d' suggesting a fine wine label.

"I'm citing you for failure to signal a U-turn," he said.

"That's silly," Myles said. "There was nobody to signal to."

"Well, there was me," the cop said, "but if you got any complaints, buddy, better take it up with the judge, and I wouldn't hold my breath if I were you. Have yourself a good evening," he said before tossing the license in the window and walking away.

"Guess I'll see you in court," Myles said with a cautionary tone.

"I'll be there," the cop said over his shoulder.

"Yes, I suspect you will," Myles muttered to himself. He was left feeling like Santa Claus with a highly questionable traffic ticket as a perfect present for Merle Williamson. "Ho-ho-ho," he said as he finished his parking and hurried inside. He was finished gritting his teeth by the time he reached the stage and got set up, just in time for Huey Persons to kick off the first tune, a ballad oddly enough called *Hot Peppers Lay Out*. Myles smiled because the last time he played that tune was at a Heidelberg University jazz festival on the banks of Neckar. Back then, he helped make it a booming, crying success. This time he was offering a foundation of smooth helium cinder blocks for Bertha paradise which were meant to stand the test of time while supporting a great instrument of vocal cords. Landil Hakes was a renaissance painter with his wire brushes, providing exquisite shades of swish on the canvas of a drumhead, along with the ballad's chord mastery of pianist Noah Jameen. Huey Persons took the solo and guided the group and his mellow tenor sax through an evening of highly appreciated standards as Myles once again nodded repeatedly like a *bobblehead*, savoring the music and the luck of being on *the* gig which was a perfect hiding place from worries.

For the past few days of court, subpoenaed Golden Village police officers reluctantly took their turns to be called to the stand dragging their heels like school children told by the teacher to go stand in the corner for misbehaving. They were braced for the crafty and corrosive techniques of Merle Williamson against the infamous *code of silence* of a badge. As expected, head counsel for the cops Hompter Ryan came to the battle with a glut of objections, challenging every single attempt to get at that damned, detested truth.

Nevertheless, time moved along, transitioning into the second week of a bitterly contentious trial which was punctuated by numerous gavel raps and threats of contempt from the bench.

Myles hadn't done it for many days, but he finally placed a procrastinated international call. Yvonne in Copenhagen was in utter disbelief about the highway trouble with the police back home, and she was further shocked that a trial was lasting so long. Lunch time in Minneapolis was dinner time in Copenhagen, and she let him know, the great cook that she is, that she was imagining him sitting across the table from her as she ate, deliciously and devilishly smacking the food in her mouth just to tease him. She was definitely making him regret that he didn't have a fork long enough to steal something off her plate. She missed him dearly and wanted him back. Myles let her know that the feeling was mutual and promised that after the gig and the trial, they would reconnect. But for now, the short recess was over, and Myles returned to the courthouse and seated himself at the plaintiff's table for the restart of the afternoon session. He watched attentively as Merle Williamson thumbed through his yellow page note pad with the expression of a hungry man salivating over a Las Vegas casino buffet. It didn't take Merle long to find something to chew on.

"If it please the court, Your Honor," he said after clearing his throat, "I'll now call to the stand . . . ". He had a sudden change of mind and searched for another hand-scrawled page. The room was at capacity with cops sticking together to form a complete line of wallflowers, waiting with anticipation. "Yes, Your Honor," Merle said when he found it. "I'll now call to the stand Officer Cecil Hills."

As if on cue, two nearby officers stepped up with precision and pushed open both of the tall mahogany doors. In walked a tall and broad cop dressed in the police department's most formal snow-white uniform complete with white gloves, white watchband, white shirt, white tie, white shoes, and white socks and *White Air* after shave, which reeked of a notion that how could anybody dressed like that possibly be *wrong*? The entire look was contrasted by a Viking Purple strip of cloth threaded from his right hip across his chest and under the epaulet on his left shoulder, down his back to the right hip. The two policemen walked ahead of him to hold open the short mahogany swing gates leading to the stand. The spectacle dropped lots of jaws, but the ceremonial trumpets were just a figment of everyone's imagination. The court deputy swore him in with the help of a white leather-covered Bible, and he took a seat. The judge had served on the bench enough years to know when to pull out a big handkerchief and turn a laugh into a sneeze.

Merle Williamson was almost finished looking the cop over, both with and without his bifocals. He leaned an elbow on the box around the stand. "What is this, corn on the cop?" he said with a wry smile, "Where's your golden sword?"

"Objection, Your Honor, counsel is attempting to denigrate the uniform of a sworn police officer of Golden Village," Hompter Ryan protested.

"Sustained," Judge NaVell Phillips said. "Let's show some respect for a legitimate uniform sometimes worn by police officers. Move it along."

"Very Well, Your Honor," Merle said with a promissory tone of voice. "Officer Cecil Hills, do you like Black people?"

"Objection, Your Honor," Hompter shouted. "Irrelevant!"

"Overruled. He may answer," the judge said.

"I've known a few of 'em in my life," Officer Hills said.

"That's not what I asked you," said Merle. "I asked you if you *like* Black people or people of color."

"Objection, Your Honor. Counsel is badgering the witness."

"Overruled. The question is still allowed."

"Do you understand the question?" Merle Williamson asked with the gentleness of a cattle prod.

"Some ya like and some ya don't like. What can I tell ya?"

"I see. Well would you let your daughter date one of . . .'em?"

"I don't have a daughter."

"Perhaps not," said Merle, "but the question is the same whether you have one or not."

"Absolutely not."

"Why not?"

"Because I think the colored, ah, you know, the Black people should be with their own kind. What can I tell ya," said the cop in white.

"You've told us a lot Officer Hills," Merle said as he approached the table for another exhibit. "You've told us a lot. So if it please the court, I'd like to enter this exhibit already numbered, a St. Louis newspaper article which covers some interesting policing by Officer Hills while working in that city."

"Objection, Your Honor, this is highly irregular," Hompter stood and shouted, "that exhibit has already been struck because it is too old."

"I'm old too," said the judge, "but that doesn't mean I can't get caught up on my newspaper reading from other cities. Overruled. And now Mister Williamson, we'd all like to know what is your point with this newspaper business?"

Myles was still watching intently from the edge of his seat, and still regretting that he didn't have a box of popcorn or a handful of *Milk Duds*.

"Your Honor," Merle said clearing his throat. "If I may use an analogy, a skyscraper is built on a foundation of integrity which is what keeps it standing. Just as true is that a career is built on some kind of foundation, and if that foundation is suspect, I think it is reasonable to question the integrity of a career. We're doing no worse than structural engineers in San Francisco whose job it is to examine buildings for soundness after an earthquake."

"The point, Mr. Williamson," said the judge in a monotone of boredom, "we're all starving for the point."

"Officer Hills, you are a rather large and strong officer on the police force. How much do you weigh?"

"Officer Hills proudly sat up in his chair and tucked in his chin. "Three hundred and fifty-eight pounds," he said.

"Isn't it true that during a protest against police brutality in St. Louis you dropped all of your weight with your knee on the side of a Black man's head while he was lying on the ground being handcuffed, fracturing his skull and breaking his eye socket?"

"He was resisting arrest," Officer Hill calmly said.

Merle turned up his nose again, but only to scan some high-lighted newspaper points through his bifocals. "The newspapers and community leaders, as well as cops in your precinct knew you as *Beat 'Em — Cecil Beat 'Em Hills*," he read. "Why do people call you *Beat 'Em*?" Merle was trying his best to ask as innocently as he could.

"Objection, Your Honor," Hompter Ryan said. "This calls for speculation of the part of the witness."

"Overruled," the judge said. "In the interest of public record and public perception, he may answer."

"I got the name because I like scrambled eggs, and everybody knows it," said Officer Hills.

"I see," said Merle, "and just how do you know everyone knows it?"

"Because I make great scrambled eggs, and the only way to make great scrambled eggs is to beat 'em. Everyone in the station break room has seen me do it, slaving over a hot mini grill with two dozen eggs and a beatin' fork so fast that it disappears during the beatin'."

"Let me remind you," Merle said, "you do realize that you're under oath, right?"

"Cecil *Beat 'em* Hills cast his eyes to the floor and shook his head. "Well, I cannot tell a lie," he said. "Maybe it was just one dozen eggs."

The judge rapped his gavel at the tittering in the room.

Merle read on from a line that suddenly appeared on the ceiling of his mind. "They also say you're so strong that your suits are made of linoleum."

"Objection, Your Honor," Hompter Ryan protested. "Linoleum suits can't be proven."

"Sustained," the judge said shaking his head.

Merle Williamson strode back to the plaintiff's table and glanced at his client Myles Andrews to see that he was still wide awake. They exchanged nods. The table was a neatly laid out chronology of exhibits and Merle carefully selected another one before slowly returning to the witness stand with his nose turned up as he read through his bifocals.

"Officer Hills, the record shows that you have a number of proficiency awards and honors for your use of the nightstick. Kinda makes you feel useful, doesn't it?"

"Objection, Your Honor. Leading the witness," Hompter said.

"He may answer," the judge granted. "Overruled."

"The police department is glad to have the use of my services," said Officer Hills, "because I spend a lot of hours a week polishing that big black nightstick."

Merle raised his bifocals to rest on top of his head. "I see. How many hours a week are we talking?"

"About a hunnert."

Merle accurately pointed at Myles without looking at him. "Isn't it true that you once or twice struck Myles Andrews with that well-polished, big black nightstick?"

Officer Hills scratched the side of his head without making eye contact with the plaintiff. "When we had to arrest him for not showing a driver's license, he was a little slow putting that other leg in the car, so I just used my stick to speed up that leg. I didn't have all night to monkey with it. What can I tell ya."

"Tell us if you have ever killed anyone?" Merle asked formerly floating like a butterfly, now stinging like a bee.

Hompter Ryan launched out of his chair. "Objection, Your Honor, irrelevant."

"Overruled. He may answer," said the judge.

"Yes, I killed two people," Officer Hills admitted, "but it was in the line of duty."

"Did you know those people were Black before you drew and fired your weapon at them?"

"Objection. Please, Your Honor," Hompter almost begged.

"Mister Williamson," roared the judge. "What is your point?"

"Your Honor, I am only trying to show a pattern of prejudice from a policeman, a sworn officer of the law who has unlawfully harassed, assaulted, and incarcerated people of color for five years while never once arresting anyone who is White," Merle Williamson said as he held up and waved the documents to prove it. "It's all right here."

"Strike those comments from the record," the judge said to the court reporter, "and I'm also instructing the jury to ignore the comments pertaining to other cases. Mister Williamson, you are beginning to try my ability to hold you in contempt. This is the only case we're trying in this courtroom, not every other case under the sun. Move it along in an orderly fashion or so help me God, I'll hurt your wallet."

Merle faced the judge, brought his heels together with a pop and bowed slightly. "Very well, Your Honor," he said softly and walked back to the table for more ammunition.

Meanwhile, Myles had been trying with a fixed stare and finally caught the eye of the assistant attorney Lee Malone who rose from his seat and tiptoed to him in a crouch. "I'm a little worried that the jury might be starting to believe the court reporter," he whispered. "Can we do anything about it?"

While Merle Williamson continued the questioning, the court reporter continued playing the keys of her machine like a superstar of a Rachmaninoff concerto on a nine-foot Steinway, head swaying with every spoken work, eyes rolling to the ceiling, an act which was starting to command the attention of an impressionable jury.

"I see what you mean," Malone whispered and tipped back to his seat where he scribbled out a note which was discreetly relayed to a court deputy and then to the waiting hand of the judge. A momentary interruption of the proceedings was called for.

"Even though this is a Cecil *Beat 'em* Hills production," the judge instructed, "would the court reporter kindly refrain from over-acting? Thank you."

Having the sense to know that every production needs light, Merle relinquished the floor to permit Hompter Ryan to return with his lantern of hope for his current client, officer Cecil Hills. Hompter Ryan showed his skill at building a good character picture by asking elementary questions without the appearance of leading the witness. Officer Hills was lured into telling the court under oath that he was a law-abiding family man. His two sons looked up to him. They had to; he was very tall. His wife, who he praised for being a sweet person, made and delivered sugar doughnuts to his precinct station. But most importantly, Officer Cecil Hills loved his job of using all the tools he had to arrest bad guys and throw them all in jail in order to protect society from criminals. Hompter Ryan was hoping this was enough to send a weary jury home for the day with some good thoughts about a fine police officer. He had no further questions at this time and took his seat. The judge offered Merle Williamson a follow-up turn, which he declined, and the witness was excused.

Myles watched as the cop assistants sprang up to open the little front gates and the back doors as Officer Cecil *Beat 'em* Hills rose up as the great white hope and strode majestically out the courtroom. The judge dismissed the jury and rapped his gavel for a recess.

"What chance do I have up against all that?" Myles asked of his smiling lawyers.

"Our worry is not with a cop dressed in all white," Merle Williamson said, "our worry is about what's going on in the heads of an all-White jury."

"You're right," Myles said, "it's hard to tell. They look like a bunch of poker players hiding their hands."

After the layout of notes on the table were gathered up with care, they professionally and respectfully ignored their opponents and headed out the door.

"I'm keeping an eye on you because I want you to feel comfortable at all times," Merle said. "What were you thinking while this was going on?"

"It was enough to give me calypso fits," Myles smiled, "but I forced myself to stick with jazz. I was cool."

"You've got it bad, don't you," Merle laughed.

"Yeah."

"Well, keep your chin up," Merle said seriously, "we will get through this."

"If you had to guess, what do you think is going to happen?"

Merle studied the passing sidewalk as they strolled, shifting his fat briefcase to the other hand. "There's a systematic tendency that's going to be leaning towards denying you the right to protest by civil disobedience, but there is usually a reason for actions. In this case, the reason is either going to be the star or the villain of the show," Merle said, "and this is about tolerance in the mind. How much tolerance does the collective mind of the jury have for cops who exercise abuse of power? That's what we're here to find out."

"We have high hopes for reason to prevail," assistant counsel Lee Malone chimed in, "because you're a good witness."

"I appreciate your confidence in me," Myles said, "but does your firm have time to represent every Black man in the country? I think every Black man in America is a good witness."

"We're patient. We'll take them one at a time on their own merits," Merle said.

"Thank you for that," said Myles.

"Are you still driving that rattletrap, or can we give you a lift?" Merle offered, glancing at his own aging vehicle in a reserved lot.

"I'm in the ramp, but thanks anyway," Myles said.

"One o'clock tomorrow," Merle said, and they parted ways with salutes.

Myles only drank sparkling water for three sets last night, but he had a hangover from the exhilaration of the gig. The best thing for a sweet hangover was that tune *Black*

Coffee, playing over and over in his head, the theme coming from the brass bell of a sassy trumpet's wah-wah mute. He had given up on hoping that head music would take five as he seated himself at the plaintiff's table for the start of the afternoon session. The judge had been seated, the table was set with Merle's exhibits and a fresh new court reporter who couldn't act was in place. A few courtroom spectators and curiosity seekers were trickling in looking mostly like law school students. They were the unleashed watchdogs for civil rights.

After a few minutes of studying notes, the judge finally invited Merle Williamson to recall his witness for a point of clarification.

"Thank you, Your Honor," Merle said. "I'd like to bring back Myles Andrews." He took out a handkerchief and blew his nose while Myles took the stand. "Mr. Andrews, you're telling us that there was a police car following you on the night of July twenty-seventh, is that correct?"

"Yes,", Myles said.

"And you're telling us that the car following you did not turn on any flashing red lights or sirens, is that true?"

"That is true," said Myles.

"So, Mr. Andrews, earlier in this trial you also told us that the car following you stayed back and at one point, as you kept an eye on your rearview mirror, you saw the headlights turn off, is that true?"

"Yes, it is."

"Tell the court, after you saw the lights go off, what else did you see in your rearview mirror?"

"It was kind of strange," Myles said. "I noticed that the car didn't pull over or stop. There were no other headlights back there at the time, but that dark blob of a car was still coming, and I was keeping a sharp eye on my speed."

"To the best of your memory," Merle Williamson said as he walked a couple of steps closer to the stand, "how far do you think this blob of a car followed you?"

"That car followed me without lights into the highway darkness from a little west of Theodore's Parkway to almost where my gig is, then it disappeared."

"I see. Well, just to be honest," Merle said, "you've seen it in your lifetime, and I've seen it in my lifetime, there are some nutty people out there who love to do night driving without headlights. In the dark, what could make you so sure it was a police car that you saw?"

"Because when it passed by a couple of dim streetlights along the way, I saw one of those Fu Manchu grills, those bumpers, I guess," Myles said, "and the only cars that have those are police cars."

"Okay, let's move to another question," Merle directed, "on the night of your arrest and incarceration, tell the court what happened to your car."

"It was towed away," Myles said.

"Where was it towed to?"

"It was towed way out of the county to the JKL Junk Yard where they take cars apart and sell the pieces."

"Like an alleged chop shop," Merle said flatly.

"I believe so," Myles agreed.

"How did you know where to find your car?"

"I called the Golden Village police, and they told me."

"Tell us, Mr. Andrews, how did you get to your car?"

"I had to take a Greyhound bus, then I had to walk about a mile off the road where the bus dropped me off."

"Did you say a Greyhound bus? Why a Greyhound bus?"

"Because everybody, and I mean everybody was busy, and because I checked it out and found out that no city buses run out there, and because no cab company wanted to drive that far, claiming that they wouldn't be able to pick up a fare on the way back to make it worthwhile."

"I see," Merle said as he leaned on the rail with one elbow and removed his bifocals. "What did you do on the Greyhound bus all that time, did you cry, or what?"

"Objection, Your Honor. Leading the witness," Hompter Ryan asserted loudly.

"He may answer," the judge said quietly.

"No sir, I didn't cry," Myles said. "I just finished reading *Gone with the Wind.*"

"No further questions, Your Honor," said Merle. They both took their seats when Hompter Ryan didn't seem to want to touch that book with a ten-foot pole. At the table, Merle was jotting some notes as he leaned close to the plaintiff's ear. "Did you ride out of the county in the *vistadome*?" he whispered.

"No-no," Myles whispered back. "I was stuck downstairs by the funky bathroom."

"Good," Merle said continuing the whisper, "that's excellent. Bring that up if Ryan has second thoughts and recalls you. Tell 'em that you were stuck downstairs by the funky bathroom, comprender?"

"You got it," Myles smiled.

The judge was studying notes for a few moments and finally looked up. "Mr. Ryan, call your character witness for the Village police."

"Very well, Your Honor," Hompter Ryan said as he stood and fastened the top button of his suitcoat which didn't quite cover his impressive robin red vest. "I'd like to call to the stand Sergeant Oaklew."

When the policeman arrived, the court deputy was Johnny-on-the-spot with the Bible and the perfunctory questions about telling the truth, the whole truth, and nothing but the truth to which the cop agreed. He was the epitome of a show of force and a readiness to fight. He wore his service belt fully equipped with a semi-automatic gun, handcuffs, nightstick, taser gun, tear gas, brass knuckles, boxing gloves, and a uniform shirt which covered the boxy look of a bullet-proof vest. He rattled like a junkyard when he accepted the invitation to have a seat and listed slightly to the right to accommodate all the protrusions.

"Give the court your name and rank for the record," Hompter requested.

"I'm Sergeant Cotton Oaklew," the officer of the law said proudly.

Myles and Merle exchanged glances which could only convey hope.

"Sergeant Oaklew, are you a family man?"

"yes, I have a wife and two sons."

"Tell the court," Hompter asked, "what do your sons want to be when they grow up?"

"They've both told me they want to be police officers," the sergeant said.

"Do you approve of their wishes to be police officers?"

"Absolutely! My wife and I can hardly wait to have two more cops in the family," Sergeant Oaklew said.

"What advice will you give them when their time comes to wear a badge?" Hompter was rolling the dice with an eye on the jury.

"I would tell them to just do their jobs without being afraid of making mistakes, because the department will always have their backs, no matter what they do."

"How long have you been in law enforcement, Sergeant?"

"I've been on the force for fifteen years," Oaklew said.

"In your view," Hompter said, "what's the best thing about being on the job?"

"I love going out every day and trying my best to keep the bad guys off the highways and sidewalks. We keep everybody safe."

Hompter Ryan opened a button to dazzle the jury with his red vest. "Your witness," he said to Merle Williamson and took his seat.

Myles watched as Merle sauntered to the stand and just happened to stop at a spot where the American flag is the backdrop. In his mind, Merle was starting to awaken an American system of justice that had been in a decades-long slumber, distant, ignorant about civil rights, and stubborn about accepting history changes and now, this guy who has the guts to get out there and rattle the cage of the *1964 Civil Rights Act*. But Merle Williamson, he thought, wasn't *acting*. He was for *real*.

"Sergeant Cotton Oaklew, please tell us," Merle asked, "do you have any other duties besides being a policeman out on the street?"

"Yeah, I'm the head of the police union."

"I see, interesting," Merle said. "You . . . you mean you're not on some police boxing team?"

The judge tapped his gavel at a little tittering in the back row.

"Oh, you mean these ol' things?" Cotton Oaklew was pointing to those twin weapons from *Everlast* tied to his belt. "That's just a reminder to the guys to keep those union dues paid up, that's all that is."

"Sergeant Cotton, have you ever had to use the gloves?"

"Not yet. Nobody has ever dared to miss a dues payment."

Myles swallowed nervously hoping that musicians were exempt from a beating at the hands of the blushing gloves of a cop collecting union dues.

"Sergeant Cotton Oaklew," Merle was playing the big cat in the weeds. "On an average summer night, how many frogs hop across Highway 55?"

"I dunno, but I never skidded on one in my life," said Cotton.

"Objection," Hompter Ryan pleaded. "This calls for speculation."

"Sustained. The point, Mr. Williamson, the point?" said the judge.

"The point, Your Honor, is that on some summer nights in the fog, frogs are known to cross the road in the park area, going from lake to swamp or swamp to lake in big numbers, and if enough of them get under the wheels, they can cause a car to skid sideways."

"That will be enough, Mr. Williamson," said the judge. "Carry on."

"Sergeant Cotton Oaklew," Merle continued, "how many tickets have you given out for skidding cars?

"None as far as I know of," said Cotton.

"Have you ever seen a car skidding in the park area because of frogs?"

"Dozens of times," said Cotton Oaklew.

Merle was already walking to the table to fetch a document which he carried to the bench for the judge's mandatory look-see. From the judge's hand, he offered it to Cotton Oaklew as a memory-jogger.

"Would you tell the court what you are holding, Sergeant Cotton Oaklew?"

"Well, it's the copy of a ticket of course," Cotton snapped. "I'm not stupid."

"I didn't call you stupid," Merle insisted, "because I'm very sure you can read. So please, Sergeant Cotton Oaklew, do you recognize the *badge number* written on that ticket?"

"It's mine."

"Where was the ticket issued?"

"On the stretch of highway which runs through the park."

"Tell the court," Merle said nodding his head nicely at the last answer, "what is the offense written on that ticket?"

Cotton Oaklew held the paper close to his face and squinted. "Looks like reckless driving," he said.

"Sergeant Cotton Oaklew," Merle said courteously, "is that a good enough copy for you to make out the name of the offender?"

"It says Myles Andrews."

"Isn't it true that you're looking at your own handwriting?"

"It is."

"Sergeant Cotton Oaklew," Merle said as he stiffly swung his arm around and pointed to the plaintiff at the table. "Is *that* the Myles Andrews who you gave that ticket to?"

With the boxing gloves starting to work on his kidneys, Sergeant Oaklew winced and shifted in his seat. "Sometimes some people all look alike, but I believe that's him," he said.

"Did Mister Andrews mention frogs as the reason for what you thought was reckless driving?"

"Nope, didn't say a word," Cotton Oaklew said, his glance falling to the floor.

"Myles refrained from shaking his head negatively as he knew he would certainly beg to differ if he had a chance. But as the theatre of due process proceeded, he was feeling the tough luck of no popcorn, no *Milk Duds*, and no cotton candy.

"Sergeant Cotton Oaklew," Merle was pointing to the table again. "This musician who uses his hands on his job showed up to play music after he was released from jail with his wrists black and blue. Is this normal in the procedures of making an arrest?"

"Well, if you don't resist, you don't get hurt."

"I'd like to remind you," Merle said after clearing his throat, "that you are under oath. Did Myles Andrews show any resistance whatsoever the night he was arrested and jailed?"

“If he was black ‘n blue, he must have resisted,” said Cotton.

“Which comes first,” Merle said with a straight face, “the chicken or the egghead?”

“Objection, Your Honor. Counsel is continuing to malign the intelligence of a good all-American policeman,” Hompter Ryan shouted.

“Take it easy, Mr. Ryan,” said the judge. “I’m going to allow the witness to finish the answer to the question regarding *resistance*.” He then requested and got the court reporter to read back the resistance question. The spotlight was on Sergeant Cotton Oaklew.

“All I can say is that I’ve put cuffs on hundreds of ‘em but nobody ever complained. It’s just a known fact in the police department that some of the smaller wrists require a few more clicks on the irons, otherwise they might get away, and for sure, everybody knows they all run pretty darn fast.”

Under the table Myles Andrews was rubbing his calloused fingertips with his sweaty palms. American justice was showing a pulse that was foreign to his memory. Eye contact with the jury was out of the question because sympathy-seeking glances would only serve to stifle what little pulse justice has. Their collective twenty-four eyes and twenty-four ears, he thought, would do just fine with making up twelve minds.

“I’ll ask you again, Sergeant Cotton Oaklew, because I don’t think the court reporter quite heard you,” Merle said. “Take your time and answer to the best of your memory. Did Myles Andrews resist arrest on the night he was taken to the county lockup?”

“He’s known as a type who refuses to show a driver’s license. That’s resisting,” said Cotton Oaklew with a sarcastic palms-up shrug.

“Merle Williamson dropped his arms limply to his sides and turned to the judge, but the judge held up his hand to block the comment mid-throat. The judge again looked at the court reporter and ordered the last remark stricken from the record. "And Sergeant Oaklew," he scolded, "please confine your answers to the questions asked. Move this along."

"Was Myles Andrews resisting arrest on the night he was jailed?" Merle was holding with his patient determination.

"Yes, he was," Cotton insisted.

Merle picked up the ticket copy and stared closely at it with the help of his bifocals. "For the life of me, I don't see a single word about resisting arrest. Was he charged with an awful crime against society? I mean, where's the record?"

"Sometimes when resistance is de-escalated quickly, we don't write it down. That's probably what happened that night," said Cotton.

"I see," Merle said, his voice trying but failing to project belief. "Did you read Mr. Andrews his rights on the night of the arrest?"

"I don't know" said Sergeant Cotton Oaklew. "I may have, but I just don't remember."

"Sergeant Cotton Oaklew," Merle was again licking his thumb and flipping yellow pages in his memory, "Let's move on. Explain for the court if you will the mechanics of the radar system in your squad car."

"Objection, Your Honor. That's classified information," said Hompter Ryan.

"I believe he can answer," said the judge.

"The radar sends out a beam, see, and if that beam don't bounce back to me on time, you're speed'n," said Sergeant Cotton Oaklew.

Merle was looking at everybody by looking at nobody. "Would you care to repeat that in layman's understanding?"

"Objection, Your Honor," Hompter Ryan protested. "You can't get any more *layman* than that!"

"Sustained," the judge said. "Get to the point, Mr. Williamson."

"Yes, Your Honor. My client has already stated that he uses cruise control while driving through the Golden Village, and swears by its accuracy in keeping him under the speed limit, so, Sergeant Cotton Oaklew, could your radar be out of kilter enough to make you write six speeding tickets that were, each one of them, fifteen miles per hour over the limit?"

"No chance," said Cotton. "It must be a bad cruise control."

Myles watched attentively as Merle spent almost the rest of the session deflecting the *jack-in-the-box* objections from Hompter Ryan. Merle Williamson was taking Cotton Oaklew to task in and out of a series of legal rabbit holes. Cotton was starting to clinch his boxing gloves, but it wasn't going to help. Merle Williamson could *float like a butterfly, sting like a bee* as he tried his best to stimulate the thought processes of the jury, a group of pokerfaced and polka hearted lovers of gourmet sauerkraut. With Copenhagen just around the corner, he could afford to view the lot of them as harmless, because the principle of it all was a worthy pursuit, and because their decisions would be nothing more than something they'd have to live with.

It was half past seven in the evening and the relaxing dinner and talk with his siblings at his mother's house was just the ticket after a grind of a day in court. The night was clear and beautiful as the bright lights of the city faded behind him. As Myles drove into the darkness and fog around Wirth Lake in Golden Village, he was transmitting a telepathic dare to the demons of intolerance. Those demons were lurking out there in the dark with eyes of evil, waiting to unjustly ensnare the freedom of a man of Blackness. Myles was seeing this drive on this night through a new pair of eyes. It was just a matter of time for him to find out if those demons got the memo about the legal proceedings going on in a certain downtown federal courtroom. Across the grassy divider, a lone pair of headlights got closer and brighter, speeding past in the east-bound lanes. Before he left for the gig, Myles put a lot of elbow grease into the cleaning and clearing of all his windows and rearview mirrors. His cleanliness enabled him to better see that the passing vehicle was a police car that was suddenly showing brake lights as it maneuvered for a bumpy U-turn across the divider. His heart pounded as those same headlights were now coming after him. His speed was below the limit, no problem with that. Tonight, there were no frogs on the road to keep him from driving in a straight line. The music on the radio wasn't too loud for the wilderness, but in his next glance at the rearview mirror, he saw those all-too familiar flashing red lights approaching rapidly. The wailing siren and *blaring Klaxon was the wrong music to his ears*. Myles pulled over in anticipation of the inevitable, but the police car sped past him with the kiss of a bright spotlight in his face and the smell of an abused engine muffler in his nostrils. The flashing reds were turned off, and they sped ahead in a cloud of dust and out of sight. Myles could only conclude that they indeed got the memo and now they're just showing off the sourness of their grapes. All Myles Andrews could see when he rolled his eyes was the moon. What a place to be!

Much to his relief, the rest of the drive to The Point was uneventful as he pulled into an open spot in front of the restaurant, locked up and walked briskly inside. The serving staff hustled to keep up with a healthy capacity of weekday diners. By now he was getting pretty good at dodging shouldered dinner trays as he made his way to the stage while fighting the temptation to swipe a passing lamb chop.

He forced himself to just be satisfied with the magnificent aroma. Myles climbed onstage where his fellow musicians were setting up and quietly tuning. He picked up a handshake or fist bump from everybody. Noah Jameen on piano, hornman Huey Persons on his leader's perch, Landil Hakes on drums, and the fetching singer Bertha Paradise standing by the piano in her shimmering green gown as she arranged the chronology of her tunes. She was nice to see, but the only disrobing Myles was going to do was to take the cover off his shapely bass. The clock struck starting time and professionally, they were stoked and ready to take care of business.

"We're playing a request," Huey Persons said over his shoulder as he kicked off the tune with his stomping heel, "*Luna Tune*."

There was no need for interpretation, Myles picked up the intro with the rest of them. It was *Fly me to the Moon*. He knew all too well that musician talk is not only an international reality, it is also a universal staple. The tune's lyrics from the honey-kissed throat of Bertha Paradise took off above the accompaniment of a truly fine-dining combo.

As Myles pulled a few strings to get to the bottom of it all, his eye caught a glimpse of a television screen on the wall in the nearby cocktail lounge. If he had a free hand, He would've pinched himself. The screen was showing a newsclip of a tall rocket lifting off from the pad with a fiery blast. The words on the bottom of the screen were large enough for him to read Moon Shot. Myles could only think that nobody could make this up, the night was just starting but getting high was already in the process of stealing the show! But there wasn't a distraction anywhere in the heaven that could cause him to miss a beat as Bertha Paradise made it through her opening choruses beautifully and handed off to the wonderful tenor Sax improvisation of Huey Persons. As Myles played with pluck, he savored the room's warm ambiance and thought of the foolish management notions far in his American past, those numbskull know-it-alls who preached that fine dining and jazz just *didn't* go together. His nostrils were failing to detect the scent of chopped liver, so this whole scene must be some kind of a quietly kept anomaly. Many times, Myles preached to the choir of his mind that Europe embraced American jazz decades ago and made this kind of scene normal and prolific. It was the kind of systematic pandering that appealed to him like a fine wine and lured him away from drinking a cheap American punch. The American gift of jazz to the world has long since been known as coming from the land where there were so many good players and so few gigs. Myles took his turn to fly solo to the moon, navigating beautifully through the craters of changes before Bertha paradise took over the flight and brought it all back to Earth amid a warm and welcoming round of applause. With a landing like that, Myles could naturally see it as the only way to fly around *God's Green Earth.* There was room for country, there was room for rock, there was room for rap and hip-hop, there was room for bluegrass, there was room for classical, and by golly, he thought, give it up America, there sure as hell is room for *jazz* too!

Huey Persons turned his grinning face back towards the group and nodded his proud approval. He then telegraphed a ballad with his half-raised, slowly swinging hand. Everyone was on the same page in carrying Bertha Paradise into the wonderful lyrics of *Star Eyes*. Her voice beckoned some of the diners away from their gourmet meals and onto the irresistible lure of the dance floor. Myles felt the honor of being a co-conspirator in causing this phenomenon.

Towards the end of the set, Myles saw Huey Persons invite a pianist friend up to sit in for a couple of numbers. Noah Jameen agreed graciously and stepped down. Huey awarded the keyboard man a chance to call the first tune, and his thrashing fingers whipped the piano keys into a long, rambling trembling intro. It was a gospel camp meeting, a dazzling display of sanctified cliches which had some of the diners crossing themselves and looking left and right for the passing of the silver offering tray. The players were poised to hit the first notes of the tune, but the manager approached the stage repeatedly slicing his index finger across his throat, the universal signal for *stop*. The pianist paused with a surprised expression.

"What's the problem?" Huey said softly, but loud enough for the players to hear.

"In case you haven't noticed, Mr. Persons," said the manager with a forced smile, "there are no stain glass windows in this restaurant and bar lounge."

"Well, I . . ."

"We have a definite policy of separation of church and steak," the manager interjected with a wink before walking away.

Huey Persons gave the pianist a moneyed handshake and excused him apologetically as Noah Jameen reappeared to finish the set atheistically.

Myles could only guess if it was a saving grace for the appetites for the diners. After all was said and done, he thought, it was just another night to remember.

The next morning, Myles left his pad with a good night's sleep, a large Danish roll and a hot cup of tea in his belly. The drive to the courthouse was paved with the good fortune of green lights all the way to his destination.

Inside the building, he navigated the halls while straightening his tie and tugging the bottom of his jacket. He arrived at the designated conference room and entered without knocking.

Merle Williamson lighted up and rose from his table of busy papers to shake hands and give his usual upbeat greeting. It wouldn't be long, a ten-minute pep talk before rounding up the ammunition and leading the charge to the courtroom.

Merle Williamson had the experience to sling notes around like a cook slinging hash. No sooner did he get his chronology of exhibits set up when the judge's chamber door opened, and the man in the unbiased black robe walked in with a deputy's order for all to rise. The judge was anxious to get started so he invited Merle to call his next witness.

"Thank you, Your Honor, calling to the stand Officer Webster Gatelock," Merle turned and said to a cadre of blue uniforms who were stationed for the duration on the back pew of the courtroom.

The witness rose and approached the stand with a swagger, wearing a three-piece, pin-striped, blue suit.

"Officer Webster Gatelock," Merle Williamson said with a near reprimanding tone, "You're out of uniform."

"I had this option, sir," said Gatelock as Hompter Ryan rose to object but changed his mind and sat down.

"I see," Merle said lightly. "So, tell the court, Officer Gatelock, on your third time of pulling over my client Myles Andrews, what option was he given?"

Myles' mind was three thousand miles away but quickly came back to shore when his name was called.

"Same options as I would give anyone else," Officer Gatelock said, "show me your license or I'll give you a free ride downtown."

"And, what happened?"

"He refused to show his license," Office Gatelock said without looking at the plaintiff, "so I thought he could've been a terrorist infiltrator, and I took him straight down to county jail."

Merle Williamson paused long enough for the statement to sink in with the jury. "Were you wearing a three-piece pin-striped business suit at the time of the arrest?"

"No sir," Officer Gatelock said, "but I meant business."

"Did Myles Andrews ask you for a reason for being stopped?"

"We are the law, sir," Gatelock said, "we don't need a reason to stop him. When we turn on those flashing reds and blues, you'd better pull over because if you make us turn on that siren, you're really asking for it."

"Myles was nodding with every last word because mentally, he was already writing the tune, a blues thing called *Reds and Blues*.

Merle opened his suitcoat, hooked his thumbs in his vest pockets and turned to Hompter Ryan with a subtle grin. Hompter was sitting there with the outlines of his eyeballs visibly rolling behind closed eyelids. "No further questions of this witness, Your Honor," Merle said, "but if it please the court, I'd like to call the next witness."

The judge offered Hompter a chance for rebuttal which he declined, and Officer Webster Gatelock was excused.

"Proceed," said the judge.

"Thank you, Your Honor," said Merle. "Calling to the stand Officer Yanzup, Office Butchie Yanzup. Please come forward," Merle invited.

An officer from officer's row sprang to his feet and made his way to the front in a regular police uniform of jingling bells and whistles.

"Officer, I notice your nametag reads *Turner Hound*," the judge said. "Where is Butchie Yanzup?"

"He had to run to the men's room, Your Honor," said Officer Hound. "You see, he's had a loose stomach and vomiting since eating a whole box of tainted doughnuts late last night."

"That is most unfortunate," said Judge NeVell Phillips, "but since you're Butchie Yanzup's partner, you can go ahead and sit on the stand." Hound was sworn in, ready and willing to uphold the *almighty* jewel of police integrity, the code of silence.

"How do you like being a cop, Officer Hound?" Merle started right in before the witness seat was re-warmed.

"Objection, Your Honor. Irrelevant," said Hompter Ryan.

"He may answer," said the judge.

"I'm an equal opportunity police officer," said Turner Hound. "Whether you're black or brown or yellow or pink polka-dot, you're going to get a fair shot at going to jail if you break the law, and I like that."

"That's very honest of you," Merle said. "And I gotta tell ya, you sure know your colors. Have you always been this color conscious?"

"Not since I put on the blue uniform," Officer Hound said.

"Interesting," Merle said.

Just then Officer Butchie Yanzup returned to the courtroom. He looked woozy with a greenish-yellow face.

"Your partner is back and both of you officers are excused for the day, the judge said. "And off the record, you might want to lay off the gas station doughnuts. Carry on Mr. Williamson."

"Thank you, Your Honor," Merle said, turning up his nose again to peer at his notes through bifocals. "I'll now call to the stand Officer Sawfulhot."

The subpoenaed officer came forward to be sworn in by the deputy and then obediently took a seat.

"Officer, state your name for the court, please," Merle asked.

"John Sawfulhot."

"Thank you, Jack. May I call you Jack?"

"Objection, Your Honor . . ."

"I believe, the officer clearly said that his name is John, Mr. Williamson," said the judge.

"No disrespect intended, Your Honor," Merle said, "but we did have a very famous president named John who everyone affectionately called Jack."

"Yes, but his last name was Kennedy, *not* Sawfulhot," said the judge.

"Very well, Your Honor," Merle agreed. "If the officer and counsel prefers John Sawfulhot to Jack Sawfulhot, I will certainly respect that preference."

"Objection, Your Honor," Hompter Ryan said with a red face. "Counsel is playing a childish game which is beneath the dignity of this courtroom."

"Proceed," said the judge with Valvoline in his voice.

"Officer Sawfulot," Merle continued. "Who is your squad car partner?"

"Patrolman Rosey Palm," John Sawfulhot answered.

"Touché," Merle Williamson surrendered like a gentleman. "So, officer Sawfulhot, tell the court, have you ever seen the plaintiff before?"

"Nope, I don't believe I have," the cop in him said.

"Well, let me ask you another way. How many times have you stopped the car of the plaintiff?"

"I have no idea."

Merle Williamson turned up his nose in order to verify the facts on paper through bifocals. "The record shows that you stopped Mr. Andrews nine consecutive times without giving him a citation."

"I must've been in a good mood," Officer Sawfulhot shrugged.

"Well at this time we won't attempt to entertain the notion that we're all here today because of your good mood," said Merle, "but isn't it true that when you pull a car over, the license plate verification is recorded?"

"You apparently found that to be true," said Office Sawfulhot.

The judge moderately rapped his gavel a few times for order in the tittering courtroom. "A simple yes or no will suffice," the judge said to the policeman before swinging his glance back to Merle Williamson. "Continue."

"Okay," Merle said. "Let's move on shall we? Officer Sawfulhot, on a Saturday spring night, you pulled Myles Andrews over and ordered him to remove his instrument, his bass fiddle, from the car. Do you recall this incident?"

"Objection," Hompter Ryan said, thinking hard to come up with the appropriate explanation.

"He may answer," said the judge, taking Ryan off the hook.

"Yes, I recall that," Sawfulhot reluctantly admitted.

"Then what did you do?"

"I told him I needed to look under the cover."

"Why did you need to look under the cover of a bass fiddle?

"We had reports of lewd activity going on in a moving vehicle, so it needed to be stopped in case there were some innocent kids in the area."

"At night? Kids can accidently cast their young, innocent eyes on a . . .a bass fiddle?"

"We had to check it out. Just doin' our job," Officer John Sawfulhot said with a shrug.

Merle Williamson removed his bifocals and held them in the fist on his hip. "And what did you find?"

Officer John Sawfulhot had the look of a man who had better things to do. "Well, the reported shapely female rolling around horizontally in a moving vehicle turned out to be a musical instrument, that fiddle box."

"I see, and then what did you do?" Merle pressed.

"We called off the alert and dismissed the driver with a warning," Sawfulhhot said. "I was in a good mood."

"No further questions at this time, Your Honor," Merle made the lawyerly *your witness* hand sweep towards Ryan, and then walked back to his seat.

Myles had a notion but decided to send the fist bump a restraining order until another time.

"Ha-rum!" Hompter Ryan cleared his throat and approached the stand with his arms folded and a half smile on his face. "Officer Sawfulhot, when was the last time before this that you inspected a musical instrument out on the highway?"

Thinking, Sawfulhot tweaked his chin and fixed his baggy eyes on the ceiling. "About two years ago," he said.

"What happened?"

"Well, I pulled over a car for a broken taillight. I smelled marijuana and saw a black case in the back seat," Sawfulhot said. "I asked politely for a look inside the case."

The wheels were turning inside the head of Hompter Ryan. He had a reputation for finding the smallest pebble to trip up Goliath. Feeling close to something, he began wringing his hands like one who would squeeze a turnip for blood.

"What did you find?"

"It was an accordion," Officer Sawfulhot said. "So, I had him take it out of the case and spread it open."

"What did you do next?"

"I didn't see any marijuana cigarettes falling out of the bellows, just a nice polka."

This was it! Hompter Ryan held up an index finger. "So, tell the court, Officer Sawfulhot, you *do* believe in equal treatment for instruments, don't you?"

"Objection, Your Honor," Merle said casually while writing a margin note. "Leading the witness."

"Sustained," the judge said while writing his own note.

"No further questions," Hompter said and walked back to his seat at the *drawing board*.

The judge finished writing some notes. "Do you wish to call any more witnesses, Mr. Williamson?"

Merle heard the question but looked to the right at his assistant. Lee Malone, who shook his head. Then he looked to his left at Myles Andrews who was already leaning toward him to say something. "They all have those uncle looks on their faces," Myles said under his breath through twisted mouth.

Merle smiles and half-stood facing the judge while bracing himself with fingertips. "No, Your Honor. At this time, we rest," he said and sat back down.

Hompter Ryan got the same question from the judge, and after thumbing through his own notes just to make sure, he declined the offer. The sigh of relief from the rear police pew was audible.

The judge finally and mercifully tapped his gavel. "This court is in recess," he said, "and after lunch, we will commence with the closing arguments."

Merle was helping to clear the table as trial watchers exited the courtroom. He took a look at Myles who was remaining seated. "How are you holding up?"

"Me? For me it's like getting a peek under the hood of the justice system," Myles said. "It's got a lot of moving parts, so every now and then, it needs a little oiling."

"I couldn't have put it any better," Merle said.

With the great outdoors bathed in sunlight, Myles took a deep breath as they walked briskly to the parking lot and Merle's car. Fast, but without squealing tires, they were headed to a working lunch at the Monte Carlo restaurant. Meanwhile, the blindfolded *Lady Justice* would remain as steadfastly patient as Yvonne in Copenhagen until court was in session.

Myles was the only one who returned to the courtroom with a full stomach. His lawyers were too busy discussing strategy and ate very little of what they ordered, as fine as it was. He saw a significant difference in the room from the morning session. There weren't enough seats to accommodate the people standing around the walls, many with press passes around their necks. It was obvious to him that civil rights trials must have a grapevine which rivals the famous jazz musician's grapevine. Sitting at the table with his lawyers, Myles panned the courtroom and was delighted to spot his siblings, giving him subtle waves and smiles and thumbs up when he caught their eyes. Nearby was his buddy, cabbie and drummer Lester Ride with all the presence of a rim shot. Myles then did a double take when he spotted the newspaper's antagonist jazz columnist, Alberta Clipper. Someday, he prayed, she may find it in her heart to shed better light on a neglected American Black art form. He regretted that he wouldn't have time to thaw out an iceberg with the blazing heat from a mean 'ol angry German bass fiddle serenade.

The attention of everyone in the room was captured with the court deputy's call for all to rise, which they did. The shiny mahogany door behind the bench opened and out walked the honorable and robed judge NaVell Phillips. He sat down in his black leather chair and swiveled it forward. After pausing for moment to look over his display of notes, he peered over his bifocals in the direction of the plaintiff's table.

"Mr. Williamson, you may proceed with your closing arguments," he said politely.

"Thank you, Your Honor," Merle said as he rose to his feet and took a few relaxed steps. "I appreciate the compliments of counsel when he said I was eloquent and adept. I don't really *feel* eloquent, and I don't feel adept. I don't really want to be eloquent. I couldn't anyhow. I just want to talk with you about this case.

This is the time for me to do that, and particularly, please understand, and I'm sure you do, that while I appreciate counsel's compliments, please don't be confused by this. It is not I who am on trial.

The *Civil Rights Act of 1964* is currently, literally being road tested in Golden village, and guess what? The *Civil Rights Act* is already a success. This success has nothing to do with whatever your decision is going to be. It is successful because this case made it into a Federal courtroom."

Merle took a few slow steps in silence near the jury box to let it sink in.

"What we have on trial, really, is our system of government, the Constitution of the United States, the Federal laws, the ability of persons in the community to get along, and this is what is on trial . . . and, yes, Myles Andrews sitting here is on trial. . . and every one of these defendants is on trial, and ladies and gentlemen, you as the jury are going to be the final deciders in this case as to who has come through this trial. It will not be we lawyers. We lawyers are officers of the court, and we have the responsibility to our clients and to the court and to our judicial system to uphold the Constitution.

You see, like police officers, we take an oath to uphold the law and to work within the law. The truth is that no one is above the law.

In the orderly process of things, we come now to my summation. I promise you that I could go into more detail. I trust that I will not impinge or trespass on the prerogatives of the court. It's the function of the court to state the law. I can comment about it, but what he says about it is what is final, and it is your prerogative to recall the facts and to decide the case on the facts, with the law as the judge gives it to you. If I seem to impinge or trespass upon this, please forgive me. I have no such intent.

I think the word 'arrogant' has been used about me in this trial. I don't *feel* arrogant. I don't think that any lawyer can feel arrogant with the terrible responsibility I have on my shoulders. I am humbled with history, with the prospect of pointing out to you that we are dealing with the Constitution of the United States. I said it to you in my opening statement, and I want to repeat it. I am not against police. We are not attacking police as such. I believe with all my heart that we must have law and order if we are to survive, and to have law and order, we must have police. I like good policing. Everybody wants good officers on the job. But nobody needs a few rogue booger cops running amok out on our streets and highways, making the good cops look bad."

Hompter Ryan rose to his feet to object, but the judge finger-waved him to sit down and wait his turn.

"Putting a badge on," Merle continued, "does not give a man the power or the right to abuse that authority, that power that is given to him. Anyone who attempts to abuse power is a tyrant.

Ladies and gentlemen, that is what we are really here about, period.

You will forgive me if I do talk a little history again. Let's go back to the year 1215 in England when they had a king named John, and his subjects rose up against him and said, 'We will not submit to this tyranny, and you will change your ways,' and he did.

And he signed what is known as the Magna Carta. As I recall, there were some 15, 16 provisions, and it is written in an old kind of English. Everyone should read it. Everyone concerned with liberty should read it. Among other things, there was an agreement that the king would no longer take carts and horses from his subjects on the highway, and there was an agreement that the king would not any longer detain or imprison people except by law and in the regular course of law or due process.

There was an agreement in the Magna Carta in the year 1215 that the king would no longer take property without due process of law, and that's why we are here.

When our forefathers . . . and for some of us our forefathers don't go very far back and with some of us, our forefathers go all the way back, but in every case, our forefathers came here to make a life in a country that offered the opportunity of a decent living with freedom and justice.

Do you remember from school, as I do, the Declaration of Independence, 'We hold these truths to be self-evident, that all men are created equal, that they have an inalienable right to life, liberty, and the pursuit of happiness.' Do you recall from school, as I do, the Constitution of the United States, the preamble? 'We, the people of the United States, in order to form a more perfect union, establish justice,' or the old song, '*My Country 'Tis of Thee, Sweet Land of Liberty*.' If I seem to be a flag waver, let it be. Don't judge me.

One more step in history, if we may. The civil War and the soldiers and the first regiment from Minnesota. Do you know the history of the first regiment from Minnesota? I will tell you about that a little later in the summation, and a victory for freedom, for liberty, and the slaves were freed. The Congress and the states adopted the 14th Amendment. The judge will tell you about that, the 14th Amendment, but essentially, it says that no man, no citizen in the United States may be deprived of life, liberty, of property, without due process of law, and Congress passed the Civil Rights Act with which we are going to be dealing here.

One statute says that you may not deprive a person of his rights under the Constitution. Another one says that you may not conspire so that others may deprive him of his rights, and that is why we are here. Another one says that you may not conspire to deprive a citizen of the privileges and immunities due him under the Constitution of the United States. Another one says that if you are a government official and if you know of such a conspiracy to deprive a person of privileges and immunities, if you know of it, and if you then do nothing, although you *could* do something to prevent it or help prevent it, that that is wrong. That is what we are here about, the right to equality of treatment under the law and pursuant to the rules of law, not to the arbitrary actions of men. That is why we are here.

We are going to be dealing with a conspiracy, and the judge will instruct you about what that means. Let me tell you something that you don't get in the proof of a conspiracy. You don't get people on the stand saying, 'I did conspire.' They don't admit it. A conspiracy will never live in the light of day. It needs darkness. It needs quiet. It needs confidentiality, and you don't find written agreements, 'We agree to deprive Black people of their rights.' You don't get agreements like that. You get the subtle pattern of prejudice that I told you about in my opening statement.

Ladies and gentlemen, this is about a conspiracy and once this kind of conspiracy to deprive a person of his rights, once it comes to the light of day, it cannot exist, and Sergeant Cecil '*Beat 'em'* Hills said he wasn't going to have his officers go into *The Point Supper Club* and take this man off the bandstand because it would be bad public relations. Bad public relations for whom? Was it bad public relations or good public relations when they seized him in his car, slammed him face down on the hot hood of his car to put handcuffs on him, putting him in the squad car, taking him to jail?" Merle walked a few silent steps. "That wasn't good public relations for Myles Andrews, missing work. For whom would it have been bad public relations to go into *The Point* to seize this man on a traffic warrant which was, in fact, a warrant for not putting enough quarters in the parking meter? Bad public relations for the conspirators, for the police, that is who it was bad public relations for, because a conspiracy will not stand the light of day, so they didn't do it.

A conspiracy is proved by circumstantial evidence, evidence which shows that on any reasonable basis it could have only resulted from a conspiracy, and that is what this case is about, and if the result shows a participation in a conspiracy and the objectives of it, then the conspiracy is proven.

Let's discuss a little bit more of the law involved. I do not intend to nit-pick. I hope I don't fall into that pit. I think words have some meaning. When you talk about investigate, you talk about inquiring into something, looking into something to try to make a determination of what actually happened. I don't think that word is difficult to thinking people, and I know you are thinking people, but words like 'arrest,' the word 'arrest' has a technical meaning, and I believe the judge is going to read you a statue about that in Minnesota, and that statue will say when you stop somebody and detain him, that is an arrest, when you stop and detain him.

I don't mean that you can't ever stop anybody without an arrest, but if you put them in the squad car, that has to be an arrest.

I think the court is going to tell you that this case has to be decided as if all of these persons were equal, no one on a higher standing than the other, because the law is no respecter of persons. Every person stands equal before the law, and every person is to be dealt with as an equal in a court of justice. Certainly, chief of the Golden Village police department, Olaf Hart, *must* have had some knowledge of the daily activities of his subordinates. *The chief of police sees all.* At least that's what it always looks like in the movies. We are conditioned to the lawful concept of accountability.

Another phrase that you will be concerned with is color of law. Well, an act is done under color of law, even if it is contrary to law, if the person who does the act is pretending that he is following the law when he knows that he isn't.

Let's talk about an example, the towing of that car. Ladies and gentlemen, I'm not too concerned about a lousy car towing bill of, shall we say, $13.50. I would be ashamed if I were here before you for two weeks as we have been, to argue about a towing bill of $13.50. That is not what we are here about, and we are not here about *any minor traffic cases*, either. We are talking about something that goes back to the Magna Carta where King John promised that he wouldn't take carts and horses form the street except in accordance with the law.

Counsel has not produced one single bit of law that permitted him to move that car. Not one. That village has ordinances. That village has ordinances guiding the conduct of the police, and there was a contract, obviously, some kind of an agreement between the towing company, which is no longer a party, and the village about towing. But not scrap of evidence in the way of an ordinance has been shown, has been produced in evidence to show any authority on the part of the police to move or touch that car. They justify it on the basis that it was done for the benefit of Myles Andrews, and that's the heart and substance of despotism. When you need a dictator, some arbitrary person to tell you what is good and bad for you, you are on the way to losing your freedom, make no mistake about it. That car belongs to Myles Andrews, and he didn't need these police officers to protect him in that way."

Myles was already sitting straight up in his chair before he heard his name. From his ringside seat, he watched attentively as a determined warrior lawyer fought hard to pry open the stubborn doors of denial to let in some fresh justice.

"You will take that map up there in with you to the jury room," Merle continued. "I am simply not going to get involved in insignificant details as to whether the car was parked east or west of the intersection. That doesn't matter.

There were so many places that the car could have been parked on Rhode Island Avenue.

Let's stop there. This brings up the next subject about what these police officers were like. You saw them on the stand. You are going to judge them based on how they acted, how they reacted, what they said, did they change their testimony, did they turn *color*, and in this respect, let's talk about Rhode Island . . . one other thing.

I believe the judge is going to instruct you, and we didn't go over these instructions fully, so I have to say *I believe*, I can't say for sure, the judge is going to instruct you that if you find that any witness on the stand was deliberately lying about any material fact, you are entitled to disregard all of his testimony except insofar as it may be corroborated by other proper testimony.

Chief Olaf Hart sat on that stand and told you that the car could not have been parked on Rhode Island without the lights on. Every other police officer refuted that and said nothing like that, and if there was an ordinance that required lights on at night for parking in Golden Village, they would have produced that ordinance, and they did not, and the only possible assumption is that there is no such ordinance.

Another officer sat on that stand and said, 'Well, it might snow, so you can't park the car there.' It might snow. I think we all may take notice that it does sometimes snow in Minnesota in the wintertime, as the song says, '*Let it snow, Let it snow, Let it snow,*' but we all park cars on the streets and when it snows we move the cars as need be, or if the car isn't moved, then it is towed. You don't tow the car in expectation of the snow, months away.

One officer said that sometimes the manager of the shopping center asks them to move cars, and they do. Then tried to use that an as excuse for not letting him park it in the parking lot, but he admitted, one of the officers, admitted that any signs restricting the parking were off on the other side and not near the hardware store, which is closer to the location where the car was stopped.

You, ladies and gentlemen, are entitled as thinking people to consider your own general actions, what you do when you go to a shopping center about parking. And do you have to get permission? Leaving a car for a couple hours or overnight is not leaving it for two weeks. But the final thing about the towing was that it's such a short distance, and please look at the map, ladies and gentlemen, please look at the map when you go in. It's such a short distance to *The Point Supper Club* parking lot where the car could have been parked. I know I didn't even bring it out in the testimony, but on the map, even the village property, the Civic Center has a parking lot. If there are any rules about it, I don't know, but *The Point Supper Club* is right there, and he parked the car there every night, and, in fact, his testimony came in, uncontradicted, that he sometimes parked on Golden Village Road right across from the Police Department, and he never got a ticket for that.

A towing bill, no, that is not what we are talking about. We are talking about the right of an American citizen to be secure in what is his, and if they can take your car without due process of law, they can take your house without due process of law and your money and your tools, and what next? That is what we are talking about, the right to be secure in your property. What is yours is yours. That's what we are here about. Not the taking of a car and getting a towing charge, but taking the substance of Liberty, the right to own property. Ladies and gentlemen, that is worth more than *any* towing charge.

Let's talk about these patterns of prejudice, and let's see how this shines through as if it were luminescent fluorescent, that shines in the darkness. In every case that we presented as examples, there is one pertinent feature that must not be ignored . . . I beg your pardon, not in one case, but in every other, there are accusations of equipment violations, defects, mufflers, taillights, some headlights — all of these. Remember Taylor Franklin, they said he had a bad muffler, Myles Andrews had a bad taillight. But in spite of all this stopping, all of these accusations, we have not one single piece of written evidence of any charge being made for an equipment defect. Not one. Not of Myles Andrews and not of anyone else. Not a warning ticket, not a citation not one, and if there had been, they would have produced it. So, you know that there wasn't.

Ladies and gentlemen, we look for our police officers to be impeccable because it is in the best interest of the law abiding public, and when there is wrongdoing, our public officials, supervisors, and an obligation to identify and weed out problem employees while paying better attention to hiring standards. Due process is what I do. We're here because something about due process is broken and needs fixing. Due process is just fairness, and it goes hand-in-hand with respect. Calling a grown man a boy when he asks why he is being stopped is not showing respect or professional behavior.

Sergeant Cecil *'beat 'em'* Hills was not just a police officer. Sergeant Cecil, as they call him, '*beat 'em'*, was a Sergeant in charge of other things including the Traffic Division. Qualities of leadership can be for good and they can be for evil, and Sergeant Hills' qualities for leadership were extremely important in this conspiracy to deprive Black persons.

Ladies and gentlemen, there is a lot of confusion. We are not really talking about any conspiracy to deprive Black people of their rights, and he is Black, so the conspiracy hit him. The pattern of prejudice, the abuse of power, that is what we are talking about, not only with this case, but with other cases.

Ladies and gentlemen, I am not hardhearted. If I was a police officer, I would take every precaution I could. I believe in this, and if you have any apprehension, any fear of danger and you want to come out with a gun in your hand, come out with a gun in your hand, that is what it is given to you for, but don't deny it later, don't deny it later. And the same reason that they shined the spotlight in the rearview mirror to blind him was the reason they came out with the gun. That is why they did it.

And what were they afraid of with this Black musician? A bass fiddle? You saw their demeanor on the stand. They're upset because a person of color brings a suit. To them, it's about questioning their integrity. That's why they're upset. Is it wrong, ladies and gentlemen, to bring a suit? My God, we lawyers would be out of business. Do we lawyers have a function? I have heard some people say no, but I don't believe that. I believe we do have a function. I believe in the Bible, but I don't want to go to the Old Testament where it says, *'an eye for an eye and a tooth for a tooth'* and every time somebody does what I think is wrong, you go out and fight. I don't own a gun. I haven't had one since way back when I was in the service. I don't believe in an eye for an eye. I believe one should settle it here in court, and if a man brings a suit, he is not only doing something for himself, but for society as a whole. That is why, and we taxpayers pay for this courtroom so that we can settle disputes, so we can settle laws, so we can have precedents to go by, and if that is wrong, God help us all. God help us all.

We are not asking for damages for Myles Andrews for what happened to anyone else. But we want to show you the characters of the people that are defendants in this case and the pattern of prejudice, the abuse of power that was going on until an attention bell was rung by Myles Andrews. That is why we are here.

You recall the stop where Myles didn't tell his occupation, said he refused to answer without a reason for being stopped. But Sergeant Cecil *Beat 'em* Hills knew his occupation, knew he worked at *The Point* by his own admission on cross-examination. But what really puts it all together is this word on the arrest sheet, 'nationality, Negro,' and you remember, I asked three officers about filling out a ticket, 'Is this his nationality?' Color is not a nationality. A Black man in the United States can serve in the armed forces, and this man did. He served in the United States Armed Forces, and he is an American citizen, and he was born in Memphis, Tennessee, which is part of the United States, and his nationality is American. Look at that, ladies and gentlemen, because it puts it all together.

I want to comment briefly about the events with Myles Andrews. One of the facts of life is that when you go out on the highway and you are charged with a traffic offense, it's either that officer's word against yours or those officers' words against yours, and ladies and gentlemen, that is what you have got in this case. Either you believe him, or you believe them.

But let's look at some facts, because if you look at the surrounding facts, maybe it will help you to determine the truth as it really was.

The testimony is not really contradicted that for a period of six weeks, Myles Andrews was stopped ten times by my count, nine times by Mr. Ryan's count. Let's say nine. He was stopped several times. There was never any charge, no warning, ticket, but admittedly, they stopped him. They admit once.

Now, there is a man who is Black, who knows it, and he is stopped several times in Golden Village along this same route he takes every night. Ladies and gentlemen, does it fit with any concept of common sense that that man would come through that village speeding, knowing that the police were recognizing his car and watching him on their theory that if you follow a Black man long enough, he's bound to break the law? Say what? Does it make any sense? Not to me.

Details are important. I don't want to nitpick. Details are important as to truthfulness and as to ability to recall, and you remember I asked Sergeant Cecil *Beat 'em* Hills if he stopped suddenly or if he stopped slowly. He said that he knew that in the deposition he said suddenly but after thinking about it for the trial, he stopped slowly or vice versa, I don't remember which. In the deposition, he said, 'I read it and I know it said that when we turned on the siren he stopped, but I testified on direct examination that I had to shine the spotlight on him to make him stop, and after thinking about it for trial, that is my recollection.'

Ladies and gentlemen, I don't want to nitpick, but the ability to recall to some extent can be measured by whether the statement is true, because if we once fabricate there is no firm foundation, no basis for recollection. It is not like the event itself. Time is growing short already, and I have to move along."

Myles nodded in agreement when Merle glanced at him.

"You told me that you would accept one person's word as well as another's. That is what you promised me, and you promised me that because a man was Black and the other one was a White policeman, that that wouldn't make any difference. Ladies and gentlemen, I don't want anything but what is fair. I don't want any privileges, not for me, not for Myles Andrews, but I want fairness."

The folded ribbon of paper oozed from the court reporter's machine, like lava from an unrelenting volcano. Myles could only hope to not get burned.

"I ask you to look at what went on, on that stand. Consider how many inconsistencies there were in the testimony of those individuals as compared to the depositions. Think about their behavior, how they reacted on the stand and think about how he reacted on the stand, and you come to the truth of this, and the truth is that there were no real violations.

Now, again, we are not here to try a traffic case. I mean, for goodness sakes, not this much time, not this much effort, and if he was guilty of speeding, which he denies and which all the facts indicate was not true, but if he was guilty of it, so be it, but again, we are not trying a traffic case. We are trying to question why he was stopped nine or ten times, why repeatedly, why he was told there were all kinds of equipment violations and no charge. That is what we are here to resolve, not a traffic violation. Whether he is guilty or not of a traffic violation is beside the point.

This is a situation where some, not all, but some police officers are fighting a systematic urge to pull over persons of color, even when no violations are apparent. It's an inherited urge. Their great grandfathers who were policemen did it, so they think, why shouldn't they do it too without impunity. Those are the police officers paid from our taxes who can't resist those tendencies, and we're here to learn why the department's upstairs brass and white collars don't know about a police department problem that needs fixing.

Myles Andrews refused to show his driver's license until he was told why he was being stopped. Cecil *Beat' em* Hills became angry and put him under arrest without justification. It was like, 'How dare this Black man ask for a reason for being stopped?' Officer Hills considered himself the law of the land and certainly didn't think he needed a reason to justify stopping this Black man. Myles Andrews went to jail having committed a civil disobedience. This is why we are here. Sergeant Hills said it was bad public relations to arrest him in *The Point Supper Club*, so he didn't do it. He said he called the sheriff's office. You remember that deputy sheriff' was here from the warrant office. There was nothing on record there and he said it would have been if they had called the warrant office, and you will recall that we had the man from the dispatcher's office with the log. He said that the log records would show it, that they would be found, but counsel didn't produce it. We have the bare statement by Hills that a call was made, but nothing to verify it from the sheriff's office and nothing to verify it from the Golden Village police department records, and nothing done pursuant to it.

But, ladies and gentlemen, we have further the statement by the deputy sheriff called by the defendants, who said that in a warrant of this kind for not putting a nickel in the meter in time, that they customarily call the defendant and tell him that there is a warrant out for his arrest and give him a chance to come in and straighten it out, because, you see, the testimony shows that this is not the kind of a ticket that is given to a person. It's the kind of a ticket that is put on a car. That is what the evidence is. I asked him if this was a true of police, also, and he said that it depends on the municipality if they notify, and these police officers in Golden Village said they had a policy not to notify.

Sergeant Hills said, 'I told the men not to go into *The Point.* Wait until you might stop him for something else and then serve the warrant.' That is what I told you in my opening statement, that this is a part of the pattern of prejudice, the abuse of power, to have a warrant like this, not to notify, keep it in the dark and quiet, and then at the right time come and use it to emasculate the human being.

Remember the officer who kept referring to the male. That is part of the prejudice, not to call a man but call him a male because that dehumanizes him. Because as long as he is a human being, you can't treat him that way, but to make an animal out of him and you can kick him around. Talk about the male passenger, not the man, talk about the female passenger, not the woman. Don't talk about the man or woman or girl.

And yet, ask him why he came here, where his is coming from, where he is going, as if it were any of their business, and after he answers these questions, politely, he gets called a smart ass. My esteemed colleague and opponent in this case Mr. Ryan is trying to get this court to believe that it's pure paradise for the African American to drive on the highway through Golden Village," Merle said walking slowly in front of the jury, "and you know what? He's right! For an African American it is paradise, but unfortunately, *that pair o' dice for a person of color tends to come up snake eyes all too often.*"

The judge picked up his gavel but decided not to tap it, setting it back down with a barely noticeable nod.

"Again," Merle continued, "Village Councilman Stockton said he tried to get them to do something about complaints against these officers, but they wanted to send people to school for retraining. I believe in school. I am an educated person. I have a Doctor's Degree in Law, and I am sure my opponents and the judge do as well. I believe in it, believe me. It's wonderful, but it's not always enough. It doesn't always change your heart, and it doesn't always change your actions if you don't have some discipline to go with it, and there has been no discipline. There has been no real investigation about the problem.

We must own up to the reality that a pattern of prejudice exits in the Golden Village police department, a pattern involving the corruption of power also known as abuse of power. Call it harassment, call it racial profiling, call it whatever you want, but in bringing this suit against the Village as a whole and not just a few implicated police officers or for one Black man is because we believe it is the decision makers who are accountable for setting policy and seeing that the laws of the land are carried out.

Cops are people. You have good people, and you have bad people, but it's the bad people who are always thinking it's a good thing angels can't see in the dark. Well you, ladies and gentlemen of the jury, are the angels for justice, and I can see nary a blind one among you. There are no white canes and no seeing-eye dogs resting at the side of your chairs. So, I am humbly confident that you won't believe what some people think about angels' night sight."

A couple of the jurors took off their eyeglasses and wiped them with handkerchiefs.

"I've said it before, and I'll say it again," Merle reminded them, "that the worst enemy of police departments here and across the country is the so-called *code of silence.* This is true because it encourages a high tolerance for wrongdoing by police officers. If a cop sees a fellow cop acting outside of the law, dire consequences awaits that one who squeals or rats to superiors about seeing some bad conduct in the field, and generally, the public would like to support and embrace the difficult job of police work. But the people's confidence in the integrity of a police department is shaken and set back when we see policemen with crisp uniforms and shiny badges continually getting away with misconduct. Make no mistake, ladies and gentlemen, there are plenty of good police officers on the force who know what's right when they see wrongdoing, but they have been *silenced* by *the code* for a hundred years. We wouldn't be here today if the *code of silence* wasn't here. But we *are* here, collaborating on the search for justice."

Myles sat up higher in his seat, awestruck by a Merle Williamson home run, yet uncertain if it would be enough to win the game. If he were a betting man, he would bet his G string that twelve Caucasian minds wouldn't stray from the tradition of exonerating bad cops, but if push comes to shove, he could always buy another G string.

"We don't want to fight," Merle said with his hands on the edge of the jury box. "Myles Andrews isn't the kind of person who gives away his rights, but he is not a fighting man. You can tell. Sergeant Hills said he got a little bit angry when Myles Andrews refused to answer questions without justification, and you will remember that I asked him toward the end, right at the end, 'Did you give the Miranda warning?' which is a warning required by the county attorney's office which we discussed earlier, required by the county attorney because of a lawsuit involving a defendant named Miranda before the United States Supreme Court which said that when you interrogate someone with apprehension in mind, you must give them the Miranda warning. He admitted he was supposed to and admitted he forgot or didn't. He said he didn't. Okay, so he forgot. They just arrested him and hauled him off to jail, but what was the Miranda warning? Number one, you do not have to answer questions, and that is what these police officers couldn't stand. They could not stand this Black man. Let's call him what they called him, this male. They couldn't stand this male, this sub-human male, as they saw it, defending his rights as a citizen of this great country, and this is what made him a little bit angry. It's the very defense of those rights which are precious, those rights which are beyond value that we seek redress for. Not just the $250 that has to pay me for defending him in traffic court sometime in the future. Not the money for the tow charge, and he should be paid for that, too. Not just the fifty dollars he lost from work. Not just the bail money. He must be paid the value of the rights that were taken from him, rights given by the Constitution of the United States. That is what we are going to put the value on.

Ladies and gentlemen, we bring this suit for money. We don't know how else to get redress. We don't believe in war and fighting for this kind of thing, so we ask you for money. We ask you to determine what those rights are worth, and the rights to due process of law, the right to the equal protection of the law, the right to all the privileges and immunities of other citizens under the Constitution of the United Sates, and we ask you to value those rights without regard to the fact that he is Black or White or green.

As we have discussed before, Myles Andrews has traveled over many hills and valleys in his life, but he had to come all the way back home to get shocked by the reality that he traveled a valley too far. We ask you to pay him for the humiliation of handcuffs and arrest and nine stoppings on the way to work, including twice going home, of being taken down to the county jail and booked and having his fingerprints taken, the humiliation, the emasculation, because this is a matter of so much importance, because it's difficult to put a price on, and I made a pact with you. I made a pact that I would present the proof that I said I would present, and we presented it, and you made a pact with me, each one. You made a pact with me and with the court that you would be fair and treat him like a man, not like a Black man, like a man, Black or White, it makes no difference, and I ask you to hold me to my pact, and I ask to hold you to your pact to be fair and award this man damages of $25,000. Thank you," Merle said, seeking and getting contact with all twenty-four eyes before smiling and heading back to the table.

Myles greeted him with a handshake and maintained order in the court by simply studying the faces of the jury and weathering the ominous cloud of predictability hanging over the proceedings. They were all White and selected for the purpose of judging White policemen. He was positive that it would be a super-easy decision for them. They were a slice of the White American fabric. At the end of the day, it would just come down to a reaffirmation of his long-ago reason for wanting to live someplace else, but at least this is a memory he could take back with him. Seeing Merle Williamson close up and first-hand, stirring up the civil rights pot like this had him thinking that Merle might as well be wearing one of those good ol' Cajun cooking aprons, splattered with mustard and hot sauce. But unfortunately, Merle's fabulous specialty would be getting a chance to cool off because the judge finally finished writing some notes and looked up in the direction of the defense table.

"Mr. Ryan, your summation," the judge said invitingly. Hompter Ryan stood up, thanked the judge, and did his own promenade in front of the jury, arms folded across his chest while making eye contact with each face in the box. They were the jury of his peers. Somebody forgot to tell him that a price tag on a string was dangling from the tail of his new suitcoat. $39.95 was hard to miss, so, polyester came to the right place to get busted.

"Ladies and gentlemen," Hompter said as he held up an index finger. "I am urging you not to get caught up in all the media hype about conspiracy theories. There is no conspiracy. The incidents in question were separate and handled properly by the officers involved. These officers are trained to do the right thing when facing defiance and threats. They're only human, you know. The entire police department is built with the most talented officers in the history of policing. Even the police dogs are beyond reproach. They have *never,* and I repeat, they have *never* bitten a person of color, and mind you, these dogs *do* bite. Why, it was just last year that an uncooperative Polish fellow was bitten in northeast Minneapolis. The issue was the conduct of these police officers towards *Mr. Andrews*, not towards minorities in general. Ladies and gentlemen, put yourselves in the policeman's situation. In the critical seconds, when he observed the violation, what was apparent to the officer? He didn't know if the driver was Black when he turned on his reds and stopped the car. But the evidence shows that some of the Blacks who testified about being pulled over had spit at officers or kicked them or called them *motherfuckers*. Nobody wants their mother talked about like that, I mean, c'mon."

The judge loudly hammered his gavel three times. "Mr. Ryan, that kind of heresy language is beneath the dignity of this family court. Let us please be respectful of the women in this courtroom."

"Very well, Your Honor," Hompter Ryan said shamelessly. "I was only standing up for the dignity and honor of the mothers of America. As I was saying, ladies and gentlemen, police are human too, so to impose a greater standard of patience and forbearance on them goes beyond the ambit of law and order or equal justice. In fact, there was no mutuality of purpose to deprive Mr. Andrews of his rights. To ask a police officer to have more forbearance when it comes to making a routine stop is to compromise the very act of law enforcement. Just consider, good people, would one ask one's self if a person of color should be treated different from everybody else just because he is a person of color?"

The court reporter frowned and faltered, but quickly recovered.

"Don't let anybody fool you," Hompter resumed with a raised index finger, "this is not a case about race. No, this is a case about righteousness. At what point does a policeman go from being a passive observer to being a trained keeper of law and order? I think we can all agree that taxpayers have very strong preference for knowing that our streets are safe from those who would continue to refuse to abide by the law. What does this have to do with race? It's just about people, human beings, even though we know there are devils among us. But the important thing to know is that Golden Village police aren't out there looking for devils. It's just that devils are so good at letting the police know where they can be found. All these police officers are doing is trying their best to keep the entire area safe. It's just an honest way to make a living, the dangers of the job notwithstanding.

Ladies and gentlemen of the jury, it would be totally fitting and proper for you to exonerate these fine officers of all of these bogus charges against them. Thank you."

Myles could wait no longer to shake the hand of his trusted mouthpiece, Merle Williamson. "Thanks for standing up for justice," he said quietly.

"I'm afraid I can't take the credit for that," Merle said under his breath. "You're the one. Without you, I wouldn't be here. I only tried my best to convince a blasé jury that the insidious problem that you flagged courageously is real. It's not something that most people would have done. You should be proud of yourself, no matter what the jury decides."

The judge cleared his throat after writing a few more notes. "We will take a brief ten-minute recess. After that, the court will instruct the jury, and then I'm going to give you your option, after you have retired and elected a foreman or forelady, you may if you care to, return tomorrow, which is Saturday, although we would want to know that so the building would be available, or you may return Monday. You can be thinking about those three alternatives," he said before one light tap of his gavel.

With the nearly full courtroom of trial watchers standing and stretching their legs, Myles looked around and *saw* the smiles and thumbs up of his siblings, which reminded him of his mother's voice from the distant past, telling him with passion that one day, justice will be more of a friend to Black folks than a fugitive. From the other side of the courtroom, he could at least send his blood a smile and the shrug of a proud plaintiff, and no jury in the world could take that away from him.

One day turned to two and then three as the un-sequestered jury rehashed the mountain of evidence enroute to their decision. On the afternoon of that third day, Myles got a short notice call from a secretary at the law office requesting him to return to the courtroom for the impending choice of the jury. When he arrived at the courtroom door, he took his folded airline ticket out of his coat pocket and kissed it before putting it back. Then he steeled his backbone, pulled the door open and walked in. His eyes were immediately fixed straight ahead at the iconic carving of the blindfolded Lady Justice above the judge's seat. With all of her reputation and dignity, he wanted so much to believe that she just had a long talk with his mother. His eyes then fell upon Merle Williamson and his assistant, Lee Malone who were waiting at the plaintiff's table with poker faces.

"Well, this is it," Merle said, "we'll just think positive."

The court deputy called for all to rise as Judge NaVell Phillips emerged from his chambers wiping his glasses and putting them on as he sat down. He requested the room to be seated. Law students and media people were among the near capacity gathering, hungry for something historic to fill their note pads with.

"Please call in the jury," said the judge.

Another door near the bench opened, and they filed in and quickly filled up twelve seats.

"Will the jury foreman please rise," Judge Phillips directed. A middle-aged White gentleman wearing wire rim glasses and a tan tweed jacket over a blue denim shirt stood up.

"Have you reached a verdict?"

"We have, Your Honor," the foreman said, clearing his throat and twitching his mustache, "we the jury, duly empaneled and sworn, in case number 4-69 civil 306, Myles Andrews vs. the suburb of Golden Village and the police department, find the defendants guilty of rights violations against Myles Andrews under the Civil Rights Act of 1964. The guilty defendants are Chief Olaf Hart, Sergeant Cecil Hills, patrolman Osh Hottum and Sergeant Barnwood Tinks. Exonerated were officers Butchie Yanzup and Turner Hound."

"Very well," the judge said as he took the relayed written decision from the deputy. "Court is adjourned, and the jury will use my chambers to decide a monetary award. You have one hour," he said.

Myles could only watch as Hompter Ryan approached the plaintiff's table with his hands on his hips and his mouth agape. Words were not coming out of his mouth right away, but visions of a re-trial danced in his head like a jar of fireflies.

"It will not stand," Hompter said to Merle Williamson with a tone of vengeance. "The Supreme Court will hear about this."

"Good luck," Merle said and extended a hand to his defeated opponent, who took his time but reluctantly shook it with his fingertips.

Myles was the only one at the table with a smile coming out of his ears. His mother must have had that little chat with Lady Justice after all, giving him the feeling that it was all worthwhile.

The allotted hour gave Myles a chance to go back to the back row and do some preliminary celebrating with family, but time was up, and the jury was re-entering the courtroom, so he returned to the table. The room fell quiet while the judge made some notes and then took a sip of water.

"The jury has come to a collective monetary decision, against the defendants, and for the plaintiff, Myles Andrews, in the amount of twenty-five thousand dollars. Are there any question? No questions? These proceedings are concluded," he said with a light gavel tap.

"Only in America is what I never thought," said Myles.

"Congratulations again," Merle said, "a check will be prepared and ready for you tomorrow."

"I'm counting the hours," said Myles.

One of the reporters wearing an I.D. badge walked over and shook hands with them.

"This is Bob Lundy of the Tribune," Merle said. "He called me a few times pertaining to a story he's doing about this case. I guess the time is right for you two to talk this thing over and remember to put your best foot forward. I don't want to be rude, but I've got to rush back to the office to meet another client. So long until tomorrow." They shook hands profusely, and he was gone.

"I'd like to drive you to *The Point* for a little background as a place where you worked, if you can spare a minute," Lundy said.

Myles looked around and saw that his siblings indeed had to get back to work, and he would see them later. "Sure, I'd be happy to," Myles said, "just for the sake of finishing touches."

They started for the exit. "There is some good news out this," said Lundy.

"For real? What?"

"I found out golden Village is establishing an annual human rights award."

"Very nice," Myles said. "Looks like things are changing right before my eyes."

"And you helped," Lundy said with admiration.

As they were leaving the building, Myles was so full of it that he twirled through the revolving door and danced down the front steps of the Federal Courthouse like Bojangles Robinson without Shirley Temple. Lundy was impressed but he didn't write it down. They were across the street and into Lundy's Mercedes which whisked them westward across the city limits and into Golden Village. They soon spotted the black and white of a squad car parked on the median of Highway 55 and facing them.

"Don't duck down," Lundy said. "We'll just play it straight."

"Relax," Myles said with a chuckle. "They're looking for the car that I'm not driving right now. Besides, the weather report says that the wind is out of their sails at the moment."

Following his GPS map, Lundy navigated the smooth ride to Golden Village Road, which runs through the middle of the Golden Country Club gold course and leads to *The Point Supper Club* ahead.

Lundy turned on his wipers with the wash fluid. The view was clear without a smear. "Nope, that wasn't a monarch butterfly stuck on the windshield," he said, his voice trailing off in anticipation of something else.

"I know this has been kind of a cloudy day," said Myles as he stared down the road at the foliage clearing less than a mile away, "but isn't it a little early for an orange sunset?"

"Quite a bit early," Lundy agreed.

They traveled the remaining distance with growing concern, and when they arrived at the clearing, their widening eyes popped at the sight before them. *The Point Supper Club* was engulfed in flames and nobody was around. Trees no longer hid the black smoke rising and being windswept southward, away from the bright fire.

"I-I can't believe we're the first ones here," Myles said with great astonishment. "This is weird."

"Especially with the fire department right across the street," Lundy said, pointing.

They came to a stop and frantically got out of the car only to become helpless bystanders with their mouths agape as the timbers in The Point popped and crackled with a radiant burn. They exchanged looks and trotted to the door of the Golden Village Fire Department. Inside, three shiny red fire engines sat idle and apparently ready for some other fire. In the corner, the older uniformed fireman was leaning his folding chair back to the wall while reading the newspaper and smoking his pipe. He proudly wore the gold-plated badge on his chest that he was sworn to uphold. The station Dalmatian lay calmly at his feet, spot-on with obedience.

"Excuse me, sir," Lundy said firmly. "I hate to break this to you, but there's a fire right across the street!"

The fireman finished reading a paragraph and blowing out a puff of smoke before he looked up. "Probably just a little kitchen fire," he said, turning to the sports page while blowing another puff from the pipe. "They'll take care of it."

"No-no, you're not hearing me," Lundy insisted, "the restaurant is burning badly. Aren't you going to at least try to put it out?"

The fireman removed his pipe to speak more clearly. "Be patient, it'll burn itself out," he said with conviction.

"Where are the other firemen?" Myles had to ask.

"They're upstairs sleeping and can't be disturbed," the fireman said, getting back to his reading and pipe smoking.

Myles was trying his best to keep his own smoke from coming out of his ears. "I see," he said. "Well, where's the alarm button? I'd be more than happy to push it."

"It's resting, sorry."

"Well, where are the police?" Lundy pleaded.

"Them? Oh, they wouldn't have any hoses. They've got their own job to do, and they're good at it." He leaned his head back for a better bifocal view of the page and puffed.

Myles and Lundy exchanged exasperated looks about the station stonewall who was determined to keep those engines cool. They walked their frustration back outside where it was at least warmer.

"This thing stinks," Lundy said. "It smells like a conspiracy."

"All I smell is the fire that's burning up my bass fiddle," Myles said.

"My Lord, is your bass in a case?"

"Yeah, it's in a case."

"Well, maybe it will survive this."

"It's no use," Myles said sadly. "I've played the bass for many years, and by now I know the smell of burning cat gut, but I never played any tune *that* hot."

"I'm sorry," Lundy said with empathy, "what kind of a bass was it?"

Myles listened for a moment to hear the crackles and pops of a blazing inferno. "It was like a friend of the family," he said. "The jazz family."

"How does this make you feel?"

"The inaction of this fire department makes this fire feel like a burning Black church in the south," Myles said as he thought of the tragic scene back in the day. "But all I can go on is what I know," he said while the light from the flames licked his face, "and I know we're looking at the end of a fine establishment which featured great food and tasty jazz, and I know this kind of an ending only happens in America, and that's all I know."

"Well, ya don't need to be a rocket scientist to figure out that somebody higher than us wanted the fire department to leave this fire alone," said Lundy. The pencil led on his writing pad was just a blur getting duller by the second. "What do you think? Do you think there's some kind of a message in this fire?"

"Out here in Golden Village, I would doubt if the message has anything to do with the *golden rule*," Myles said as the flames were reaching the apex of fury, "but I gotta tell you, I just wouldn't have the heart to burn down anybody else's bass."

Lundy stepped aside to make a quick call on his work phone. When someone at the office picked up, he calmly requested to have his photographer, Larry Lenz, sent to the location that he dictated.

"If you can wait just a little bit, I'll get you back to your car," said Lundy. "Photo documentation is on the way."

"The gig is toast," Myles said, "so I guess I'm free to take more than five."

"What will you do after all of this?" Lundy probed.

"I'm going back home where I belong," Myles said assuredly.

"What would you have to say to anyone who cares about your case, or even to those who don't care?" Lundy asked.

"You never know," Myles said, his eyes spellbound by what used to be. "There's always the chance for a good remedy for a bad situation, so if bad things happen in the dark of night, people have to remember that *the night has a thousand eyes*, even when *night is only a frame of mind*, and when that remedy comes, we can all say on a *clear day*, we can see forever."

After a long, deep interview with pictures, Lundy kept his promise and dropped Myles back at his car downtown. Myles was already in a bubbly mood before he drove a little detour on the way back to his pad, going in any old liquor store and coming out with a babe-in-arms double-bagged purchase of a few bottles of chilled champagne. When he drove up in front of his place, he didn't have to guess how all those jazz musicians even knew where he was staying! It was the good ol' reliable jazz grapevine that kept everybody ahead of him about celebrating. They were there, ready to do it with him. The neighbors needed a little mercy from the outside pow-wow of congratulatory high-fives, hoots, and loud verbal accolades, so he unlocked the joint and had them in, electrified with gratitude. Amid the din of happiness, Myles turned on a light and spotted a big cockroach standing still on the wall. He set his bag down and carefully, keeping his eye riveted to that roach, and took off his shoe. Coiled like a spring to give it a super-fast hard slap, he held off when he noticed the body language of the disgusting bug. It was giving him the victory sign with the antenna. That made all the difference. Suddenly he didn't have the heart to turn it into an instant piece of splatter art from the nineteen-sixties, because this is a day of celebrating rights, and even a cockroach deserves the right to celebrate before dying. He put his shoe back on and joined the party, popping open some bottles and passing out the plastic flutes.

"Thanks for making some folks think," someone behind him said. He looked around and saw the smiling drummer-cabbie extraordinaire Lester Ride.

"Thanks anyway, Les, I appreciate it, but I'm more than happy to pass that honor to Merle Williamson who won the case for all of us," Myles said, raising his glass, "and I'll toast to that."

They all did.

Myles weathered a burst of fizzing carbonation in his eyes and sinuses. "Because there is not better right time for rights than the present," he said with *Extra Dry* tears.

"Right!" they all agreed in unison.

Myles embraced the comradery with the bittersweet thought of soon being airborne across the Atlantic, but he dreaded the thought of goodbye talks that he will surely have with Huey Persons and the group about the loss of the great venue that doesn't grow on trees. But those cats in that group played their axes like the final seasoning on a gourmet dinner, and they will be missed as much as singer Bertha paradise. He was thankful for the valuable time that he was given to learn that they were the type of players who could get burnt in one place and land on their feet in another place with no quit in their souls. Very soon, other chefs would be benefiting from their cooking.

Myles worked the room and felt the mutual respect from the more familiar, and some musicians he didn't know, but he exchanged cards anyway, as a courtesy. He was happy that they had gigs to go and start getting ready for, but too soon, his crib was empty enough for him to come to grips with not having a job. The only living things left was a cockroach and the certain sweetness of being officially on-the-clock for his impending departure.

The next mid-morning, Myles was out of bed and on his phone battling busy signals before finally getting a connection with Huey Persons and wearing his phone battery down with a long conversation about events of the past months, and then yesterday's devastating fire. Luckily, the phone didn't go dead before Huey assured him that the fire wasn't his fault and joking that the place burned down because the cook didn't know how to make gourmet chitlins. Huey Persons sent him best wishes for safe travels and made him promise to come back before another thirty years, then Huey cursed him for forcing him to find another bass player. That was enough of a compliment to sustain him until he could recharge the phone.

Myles hurried up his preparations for rejoining the human race and made it to the offices of Merle Williamson and Associates, P.A., downtown. Myles wasn't three steps inside the door when the well-groomed and stylish secretary leaped to her feet with smiling congratulations and a business envelope. He accepted the gracious spoils of the verdict, thanked her, and tucked it in a jacket pocket, knowing it was as good as new strings to pluck. She also had a message for him, that Merle wanted to see him, so she led him to the suite and opened the door, and then announced his arrival.

Merle was sitting on the edges of his desk watching a TV screen with his arms folded across his chest, sleeves of his blinding white shirt rolled, tie loosened, and a smile on his face. When Merle waved him in without taking his eyes off the picture, the door was quietly closed.

"It's the news," he said, tapping up the volume a little, "watch this."

"We are here with the chief of police of Golden Village, Olaf Hart," said the reporter with the microphone. "Chief Hart, what is your reaction to this surprising outcome of a lawsuit leveled at your department because of the plaintiff's claim of civil rights violations?"

"Amazement and utter disbelief. I never heard of him," said Chief Hart, using a handkerchief to wipe Nixonian sweat from his upper lip. "We should've used police dogs. I thought I did all I could to prevent this kind of thing from happening." A banner appeared at the bottom of the screen with his name on it.

"Well, Olaf Hart, you didn't do enough," Merle said with a laugh as he pushed the button to turn the thing off, "but you did," he said, turning to Myles shaking his hand again. "You're the one who did it."

"I had just a little help from you, sir," Myles said, facetiously minimizing his counsel's role.

"Our paths coincided at an opportune time," Merle Williamson said, shoving his hands in his pockets, "because this case was needed for a little clarification of human rights. We got some of that and we can be thankful for what we got, but the verdict was a vindication of faith, faith that a man can just be a good law-abiding human being on his own initiative without always having to prove it to every single cop in the land."

"That's why they call you guys *mouthpieces*," Myles said, "because there is no way I could have said it any better."

"But having said that, we're not done yet," Merle warned. "We've got a long way to go."

"You're right," said Myles, "all the way until nobody thinks we've gone *a valley too far*."

There was a knock at the door. It was the secretary with the message that the client for his next appointment had arrived, so they wrapped up their chat to clear the way.

"God's speed," Merle said with sincere eye contact.

"Thanks for everything," Myles said with one more handshake before he was out the door with the roar of jet engines in his head and the yearning for some ear-popping altitude.

The light of the next day was upon him, and in spite of a night of wishful sleeping, Myles rolled out of the sack with the energy of a three-year-old hopeful coming out of the gates of Churchill Downs. There was so much ground to cover and so little time. Reviving the roundtrip airline ticket was first, and sweet talk wasn't necessary to get it approved in record time. At nine o'clock, he was left with only eight hours to tie up loose ends before catching the 5:00 non-stop jet to Amsterdam where he would make a surprise call to Yvonne in Copenhagen. Myles could only guess that there was enough time to close out his pad and turn in the key, take a nice bouquet of flowers from the shop to his mother's grave at the sad but wonderful Laced Hill Cemetery, drive his car to the family house and turn the keys over to his brother, Al, then sit down for a nice rib and chicken dinner that his sister Althea cooked up, and for the life of him, he guessed right, he *did* have enough time to do all those things, and on top of it, make it to the airport on time.

The four of them including cabbie buddy Lester Ride were hurrying at a break-neck clip through the parking lot and into the terminal lobby, then on to the yellow concourse. Their afros were blowing in their own wind and their shoes were gathering no moss as Myles led the way, just ahead of Lester.

"But what the hell," Lester said, puffing from the pace and picking a fine time to start agitating. "You gotta admit it, this is great stuff. An all-white United States District Court jury awards a Black man in a civil rights case, and America elects a Black man to be President of this country, pinch me."

"It is unbelievable, isn't it?" Myles said over his shoulder without missing a quickening step.

"If you think this place is trash," Lester said, keeping up but wheezing from years of cigarette smoking, "just remember that the phoenix rose up from the ashes and started something new and beautiful, and this place has plenty of ashes to build on," he said and then shut up to concentrate on keeping up.

Myles walked in silence but kept his lead with the long strides, looking to his left through the floor-to-ceiling windows and seeing a line of colorful planes slowly taxiing to the takeoff runway to freedom. From the other direction, he spotted a lucky plane on a smooth liftoff trajectory. He walked and watched until the wheels retracted and until it was out of sight. Suddenly, his legs found another gear and slowed down a bit, enough for the others to close the gap in the marathon. Then he was walking slower by the yard until coming to a stop a hundred feet from the security doors. Now they were all together, but they were intuitively reserving comment for a moment while the man thinks. Again, Myles still quiet, found himself leaning on the window with his elbows. He was like that same lead hopeful at Churchill Downs, pulling up lame on the home stretch as the crowds of travelers caught up and passed them by.

The pleasant and orderly lady's voice on the loudspeaker gave the numbers of boarding gates opening in ten minutes.

"That's me," Myles said, but he stayed on his elbows, looking out the window. He saw another plane lifting off routinely, and that, he thought, may as well have been his plane.

"So . . .," Al hesitated, "is there something I can do? I *know* you don't need money."

"No-no, I don't need money," Myles said as he continued to watch the plane activity.

"Did you forget something? I've got your bags right here in case you want to have a look, but we'd better hurry, Bro."

"Thanks, Al, my brother. I appreciate it that my bags are right here," Myles said, standing up from the rail. "They might as well be here because this is where I'm at. I'm staying."

"What?!!" They all said in unison.

"Aren't you feeling well?" his sister Althea asked and used the back of her hand to check his forehead for a fever.

"I feel just fine," Myles said. "It's just that I'm not only staying, but I'm also not going."

It took a few moments for the shock to wear off before the four of them imploded into a long group hug that temporarily made Lester a member of the family.

"But . . .but," Lester said, breaking loose and gesturing with his hands like he was conducting *The 1812 Overture*, "what about your lady over across the pond?"

"I'm sending her an airline ticket," Myles said, "and ya know what? I'll bet they'll let her in the country, no problem."

His sister Althea was looking at him sideways. "Are you messing with international relations?"

"Yeah, and as President, I promise to never mess with international relations again," Myles said with a straight face.

They laughed and collectively, the body language of family and friend was starting to favor the direction back towards the parking ramp. With the urgency bubble popped and the decision all but carved in stone, they were walking back to Lester's *free* cab at the more civilized pace.

"You can take the boy out of the country, but you can't take the country out of the boy," Lester said with his crazy ass laugh.

"Yeah, I'd better stick around just in case Merle Williamson needs me," Myles said jokingly, "but for real. I'm on a mission."

"What's that?" Les asked.

"It's called preservation of our gigs," Myles said, setting the bait with a devilish and determined twinkle.

"Okay, I'll bite," Les said. "How do you think you're gonna do that?"

"Simple. I'm gonna give it my best shot to make life absolutely miserable for that disgusting Octavius Killjoy character. Gig-wise, he is scary alright, but we can't start calling him *The Boogieman*, because he couldn't boogie if his life depended on it. But if he messes with me, I'm gonna teach him the toughest lesson he's ever had. I'm gonna teach him how to pat his foot without patting his feet! No sir, this town ain't big enough for me *and* Octavius Killjoy. Nope, it just won't work, I tell ya. It just won't work. There's no room *in the inn* for a gig thief. Besides, who the hell needs a player piano when ya can have a piano player?"

Now they were all walking a little faster toward the parking ramp, and Lester Ride was already well into his crazy laugh before the end of Myles' promissory spiel. "Go get 'em tiger," he whooped.

"Do me a favor, Dog," Myles said calmly, "never call a buzz saw tiger. It's not polite."

THE NEW BEGINNING

Made in the USA
Monee, IL
07 November 2021

81604359R00155